60 Ways to Die in South America

Tracy Ashworth

Copyright

Cover design by Mino Design Studio
Formatting by Polgarus Studio

Dedication

This book is dedicated to anyone who has ever thought there was something wrong with them.

And to my parents who seem to love me no matter what weird shit I write.

Chapter 1

The first time I found myself under my desk was almost by accident. That day I'd slouched down in my chair until my bum hung off my seat and my chin rested on my chest. From that position it'd felt like the distance to the floor was too far, so I'd ducked my head and crawled under, quickly, before anyone saw.

Safely hidden I'd shuffled up against the inside of my desk, hugged my knees to my chest and let the loud hum of the computer drown out all the questions that usually clamoured for space in my brain. You know, like did I have something in my teeth? Would I survive a zombie apocalypse? Would swearing off cheese shrink the size of my ass? Would I ever get out of debt? Was Margot over in Marketing an alien?

My small grey cubicle was on the far side of the floor, away from the elevators and the coffee machine, so foot traffic was minimal. The paper shredder was the only thing that brought my colleagues anywhere near my work space, so I think I must have stayed like that for at least half an hour—before my bum fell asleep and I had to get up.

There were worse things in the world than my job in the Classifieds section of a regional newspaper, i.e. leprosy and those guys who insist on strumming their guitars but never actually play anything (strum, strum, fiddle, strum). Writing ads about hairless Egyptian cats that cost more than I earned in a year wasn't particularly stressful or revolting. It didn't make me want to lie down in front of oncoming traffic. It was just the elevator muzak soundtrack to my already beige-coloured life.

That first game of "Office Hide and Seek" had been several months ago and I'd found many opportunities to seek refuge under my desk since. Today was looking like one of those days when hiding from life was preferable to facing it. My credit card statement announced I was one tube of Pringles away from being maxed out, I'd been alerted by my Internet dating account that I'd been "winked" at by a fifty-three-year old man who wanted to "brush my hair", and a homeless woman spat on my feet on my way to work.

"Lucy, what are you doing under your desk?" asked Sam from Sport, appearing out of nowhere. Crapsticks.

"I was just looking for my ~~dignity~~ paperclip," I said, scrambling to get up, bumping my head as I did. "Can I help with anything?" I asked, yanking at my dress that had bunched up around my generous hips.

"I just wanted to make sure you were coming to the workshop," he said. "They're taking attendance and I know you're usually a no-show to these things."

Sam was the unofficial office know-it-all. I was sure he'd bugged the office because he knew everything. Just that morning in the kitchen, while I'd been making a cup of coffee, he'd told me that Linda from Real Estate used to be a man. Apparently her name used to be Lionel. Before the afternoon was up Sam would probably have told everyone he'd found me hiding under my desk.

"I'm right behind you. I just have to finish this *very* important email," I said, before spinning my chair around to knock out a quick email to my best friend Jules.

Email:

To: j.henry@gbk.com.au
From: l.hart@standard.com

Jules,

Just in case you were just sitting at your desk thinking 'I wonder what Lucy is doing right this very second?', you should know I'm heading to a 'Communicating in the Workplace' workshop. I know. It's very exciting being me.

Please may we meet for a drink after work before my date tonight?

Thanks. Bye.

Lucy X

* * *

I signed my name on the register at the entrance to the conference room and found a seat towards the back. I'd brought my notebook and pen and was looking forward to scribbling away the time under the guise of taking notes. I opened to a blank page and clicked my pen a few times. Writing in my notebook made me happy. I loved nothing more than jotting down random thoughts, snippets of conversations I'd overheard and ideas for stories. Words just made my world go round.

I looked around the huge room. The entire newspaper staff had to be here, including Linda-who-used-to-be-Lionel. She waved, and I waved back, admiring her beautiful auburn hair and artfully applied make up. She always looked so lovely and I made a mental note to ask her for some beauty tips. My shoulder-length, mousy brown hair was pulled into a messy bun on the top of my head. Somehow, as much as I tried it was always less 'sexy secretary', more 'sexy scarecrow'. The rest of my routine involved jabbing a mascara wand at my hazel eyes and smudging concealer across the scattering of stubborn freckles on my nose and forehead.

I was dressed in my usual black shift dress and black cardigan. This ensemble served to play down the curves I'd developed at fourteen, the ones I'd been attempting to ignore ever since. Said curves had arrived almost overnight, so suddenly in fact, it was almost like a scene from a cartoon. One minute I was Olive Oil, the next I was Jessica Rabbit. I pulled my dress down over my knees and yanked my unbuttoned cardigan across my chest.

A bald man on the stage held up his hands and the loud buzz of the crowd dropped to a whisper. "Hello, folks, I'm Bob," he yelled, holding his arms out wide.

I jumped in my chair, surprised at how loud he was. I doubted whether he even needed a microphone.

"I'm going to be running your 'Communicating in the Workplace' workshop today and I've got to tell you I'm *pumped* to be here!"

I got the sense that Bob was the kind of guy who winked at his reflection while telling himself he was 'The Man'. On a particularly good day he would definitely shoot off a few rounds of finger guns. Hell, I bet he'd even throw in a quick pelvic thrust for good measure.

"Do you know why I'm so pumped?" he asked.

Because you snorted cocaine out of your lunch box in your car on the way over here?

A few people in the audience shook their heads.

"Because this workshop is going to change your lives!" he said, holding his arms out, channelling his inner Oprah.

After that little warm-up Bob brought up his presentation on the projector and started strutting up and down the stage like a TV evangelist. *The Gospel of Workplace Communication according to Bob.*

"Communication is key. Without effective Co-mmu-ni-ca-tion

our lives would be chaos," said Bob, after which I half-expected him to punctuate this with "Can I get a hallelujah?"

Instead of paying any attention to what Bob was saying, I spent the next half an hour trying to picture him in his everyday life. I decided he'd probably start the day with a morning step class. He would wear a headband and be one of those enthusiastic people who clapped and 'woo-woo'ed at the instructor. Breakfast would be some form of complex carbohydrate to ensure he had sufficient energy for whatever life decided to throw at him. Then he'd shine his beautiful bald head and go dry hump the shit out of his day.

On stage Bob had broken out into a fierce sweat. His head was shining like a disco ball, and large sweat patches had bloomed underneath his armpits. As he marched up and down, I was so busy thinking about what he would be like in bed (I'm going to CHANGE YOUR LIFE BABY!) that I almost missed him utter two words that made my heart trip and stumble:

First word: Role

Second word: Play

I squeaked then slouched in my chair, dropping my eyes to my lap in a desperate attempt to avoid accidental eye contact with Bob. I even tried to stop breathing so I wouldn't draw attention to my heaving bosom.

"I'm going to pick two people to join me on stage to play out a common workplace scene. We have the 'supplier' and the 'customer'," said Bob, adding air quotes around the respective roles.

"Now these are just generic terms. To relate them to what you guys do at the newspaper, I'm going to say that the supplier had to write an article for the customer and it's overdue. Let's pretend the customer is an editor and is angry because the supplier has missed their deadline. I'm not going to pretend to know how you guys do your thing around here."

The audience laughed. Bob had them eating out of his hand. Why was no one else freaked out? I looked around in amazement. Did they not know what role-play was?

"Okay, so the supplier needs to explain why the piece is overdue. And I'm just going to pick some names from the register at random because for some reason voluntary participation tends to be low during the role-play part of the workshop." Someone like Bob couldn't fathom why people didn't jump at the chance to get on stage in front of a crowd of 150.

"The customer will be—drumroll please—Donald Jones! Come on up, Donald!"

I could see Donald jump up from the front row and bound up the steps onto the stage like an excited puppy. I groaned and sunk even lower into my chair. That dickhead loved confrontation. Bob couldn't have picked a worse person to play the 'customer'.

Slumped down out of Bob's direct line of sight, I calculated I had less than a one percent chance of getting picked, which made me breath a little easier, since I was more likely to get run over by a rogue rollerblader. I did feel sorry for the poor sucker who got chosen to face off against Donald though.

"And the supplier will be … Lucy Hart!" announced Bob.

No-no-no-no-no-no-no!

I wondered if I could get away with leopard crawling for the exit through people's legs, on my elbows, with my notebook clenched between my teeth. Someone next to me poked me in the side, but I ignored them. The seconds limped along and still I didn't move.

"Where's Lucyyyyyy Haaaaart?" sang out Bob. By now he had jumped down from the stage and was prowling up and down the aisle, his hands on his hips. A few hands went up and pointed at me. I scowled. Arseholes.

"There you are!" said Bob, standing next to the row where I was seated, his hands on his hips, flashing me a set of bright white veneers.

"Can you guys give me some help with this one?" he asked the people seated on either side of me, his head cocked.

Two guys I didn't even recognise stood up and pulled at my arms to get me to my feet. Bob pushed me firmly down the aisle towards the front like I was a cripple being helped to the stage. Except, I wasn't getting a TV miracle. I was getting a bollocking from Donald Jones, who was no doubt dying to demonstrate what a man he was. (Why Donald what a ~~small~~ large penis you have?)

Bob gave me a final push up the steps onto the stage, thrust a microphone into my hand and wheeled me around by my shoulders to face my "customer." A customer who looked like a boxer ready to spring from his corner and knock me out. Donald worked in the finance department and was a rotund, red-faced man who owned an alarming number of pink shirts. Today he had chosen an angry shade of salmon, which really brought out his double chin.

"Okay, so Donald, you're not happy. You need this piece so that you can edit it and send it to print. Lucy, you've been experiencing technical issues with your computer. The article has disappeared from the network and IT is working on restoring it. You need to explain why you're late while placating Donald. I want you both to use some of the tools I've presented so far. You think you can handle that?" asked Bob.

Donald pumped his head up and down. I felt sick, but took a deep breath and gave the tiniest of nods. I couldn't remember any of the 'tools' he'd mentioned but I wanted to get it all over with as soon as possible.

"Also, full disclosure, I'll be filming this for the educational video I'm putting together. I hope you don't mind? No? OK, cool," Bob said, not waiting to hear our response. "And, action!"

"I needed that piece yesterday! How the fuck am I supposed to do my job when you can't do your job. What are we paying you for, you idiot?" Donald shouted.

I stepped backwards, but he just moved closer. So close that I could see the veins bulging in his fat forehead. I wanted to turn and run but my feet were stuck.

Bob calmly held up his hand. "Okay. So, Donald I'm going to stop you there," he said, before turning to the audience.

"Can anyone tell me why I'm stopping Donald at this point? What do you think happened?" he asked.

"Donald called Lucy an idiot?" offered someone in the front row.

Another helpful hand went up in the air. "He said 'fuck'?"

Bob nodded thoughtfully, with his eyes closed, putting his hands to his mouth as if in prayer.

"That's right," he said, opening his eyes and lowering his hands. "Donald, let's try that again. This time without any cursing or emotive language," said Bob, still the picture of calm, probably because Donald wasn't yelling at *him*. "You think you can do that?"

Donald nodded. He shut his eyes and took a breath to get back into character. I probably would have found this hilarious had I not been about to hyperventilate. The 'role' seemed as though it was made for Donald: Dickhead on Power Trip in Office #1.

"Great. Okay," said Bob, raising the camera again. "And action!" he yelled, pointing at us.

Donald took another step towards me. He ignored Bob's direction and picked up his angry tirade where he'd left off. "Did you hear me?" he yelled, even louder this time. "I said I need that PIECE. You told me you'd have it ready yesterday. You lied!"

Angry projectiles of spit flew out of Donald's mouth into my eyes. I blinked furiously and took a step back. But Donald just kept coming.

"I, I …" I stuttered, stopping when my microphone emitted a high-pitched squeal. I looked at the sea of blank faces in front of me and took a deep breath. I looked at Bob. "I'm …" I tried again.

I looked back at the audience. I looked at Donald. I looked at Bob.

"Well? What do you have to say for yourself?" yelled Donald. He wasn't going to give an inch even though he could see I was struggling.

A wave of nausea rose up from the pit of my stomach and I clamped my mouth shut, hoping to stem the tide. But it was all too much. Someone in the audience coughed. Donald snorted, probably thinking that this meant he'd 'won'. My eyes darted between him, the audience, Bob and the stage. I couldn't vomit. I thought about brown paper packages and whiskers on kittens, anything to keep my mind off the rising panic. My shoulders shuddered in a dry heave. My eyes widened. I searched for a bin, pressing my lips even tighter. My shoulders heaved even more violently and Donald and Bob took a step away as the room buzzed all around me.

I dropped the mic with a thud and hurried off, cupping my hands over my mouth. I managed to make it a third of the way down the aisle when I just couldn't hold it down any longer. One minute I was scuttling towards the door, the next minute I was hunched over with warm vomit in my hands as my colleagues gasped in horror.

Chapter 2

In the bathroom I washed my hands and used paper towels to dab at the vomit on my dress. I needed to get out of there. I didn't want to have to deal with someone running in after me. How would that conversation even go? I quickly finished cleaning myself so I could scuttle back to my box.

I had a few more ads to do, but after returning to my desk I just stared at the cursor blinking accusingly at me while I waited for my shame to simmer down. Usually, I managed to fly under the radar at work, a familiar face, but no one of note. I wasn't the office flirt or the clown or the know-it-all or the bully. I was nobody and I was happy to keep it that way. When I heard my colleagues filter back onto the floor I slunk further into my seat and tapped at my keyboard, hoping to appear as though I hadn't just chundered on myself in a fit of panic. As people passed by my cubicle their voices lowered to a whisper, and I fought the urge to dive under my desk.

I heard a cough behind me. "Knock, knock."

"Who's there?" I called, sniffing my dress for any missed spots before swivelling my chair around. One of the Sarahs from Human Resources was standing at the entrance to my cubicle.

"Just me," she replied, a wide, tight smile stretched across her face.

"Hi, Sarah." I looked down at her feet and picked at the hem of my dress.

"Mint?" she asked, holding out a tin of mints while craning her neck away from me. I nodded and she popped five mints into my hand. Sarah waited for the crunch before she deemed it safe enough to come closer.

"I just wanted to touch base to see how you were holding up?" she whispered, leaning in, her hands on her knees.

"Why are you whispering?" I asked, pretending I hadn't just made a fool of myself in front of the whole office. She screwed up her face and looked embarrassed for me.

"I didn't want to draw attention to the fact that I was in here talking to you about what happened."

My face burned. People slowed past my cubicle to get a good look at what was going on. Sarah's stage whispers weren't helping my cause. I was still feeling a bit queasy and didn't want another excuse to vomit.

"I'm fine thank you. I just want to forget that it happened and get on with my work," I said, hoping she'd get the hint and leave immediately. Someone turned on the paper shredder. It was old and loud and made conversation near impossible.

"Did you know that the company offers a free counselling service?" she shouted—just as the shredder stopped. Her voice carried across the floor and I shrank down further. She dropped back to a whisper, an apologetic grimace on her face. "Anyway, all the details are on the intranet. I just want to make sure you know there is always someone available if you need to talk."

"Thank you, Sarah. I'll keep that in mind." I was desperate for her to leave and never come back.

"Okay then. I'll leave you to it," she said, throwing me one last *I feel so bad for you* face, before she flounced off, her stupid mints rattling in their tin.

I sighed and turned back to my desk to find the following treat in my inbox.

Email:

To: <u>All Standard Staff</u>
From: <u>Office of the CEO</u>

Subject: Important Announcement (PLEASE READ)

Dear Staff,

As you are well aware the current economic environment has been unkind to The Standard. Over the past year we have been implementing budgetary cuts throughout the business in a bid to keep the newspaper profitable. Unfortunately the cuts haven't had the desired effect and we, as management, have been forced to take a more heavy-handed approach.

We will be looking to leverage the revenue-generating parts of the organisation like the Online Division and cut back spending on areas that are not pulling their respective weights when it comes to our bottom line.

Over the next few days we will be announcing the first phase of forced redundancies.

I would like to take this opportunity to reiterate how important everyone is to the newspaper during this difficult time.

Please don't hesitate to contact your immediate manager with any questions or concerns you may have.

Warm Regards,
Arnold Shneider
Chief Executive Officer
The Standard

Oh God. I couldn't be without a job. And Classifieds definitely wasn't pulling its weight in the revenue department. The demand for adverts had been in a steady decline over the last few years. There was still that part of the population who liked to kick it old school, mostly escorts and stamp collectors, but the rest of the world had moved on. There were only the two of us in Classifieds: Smelly Simon and me. Poor Simon suffered from breath that smelled like a mouldy pigeon soup that had been lightly seasoned with three-year-old sauerkraut. He'd been at the newspaper for over ten years and had a family. I'd worked there for only 18 months and was single and childless. If anyone was going to get the boot it was going to be me. My boss, Rob, managed both Classifieds and Online, so theoretically we could be counted as the same area, but I doubted management would see it like that.

Another email pinged in my inbox, distracting me from the bad news.

Email:

To: l.hart@standard.com
From: j.henry@gbk.com.au

Luce,

How did the workshop go? I think I can swing a quick drink at the pub if you're still keen? X

Email:

To: j.henry@gbk.com.au
From: l.hart@standard.com

THE WORKSHOP WAS HORRENDOUS. I WANT TO ELECROCUTE MYSELF.

I need a drink ASAP! Meet you at the Bearded Lady in 15?

Without waiting for a response, I grabbed my bag and tiptoed towards the elevators, head down, eager to forget today had ever happened. When I reached the elevators I could see the doors of the furthest one just starting to close and I ran to catch it, jamming my arm in the door just in time.

A familiar voice wafted out the doors as they opened. "I can't believe she did that. I would have died of embarrassment. I wish I could have seen the look on her face." I locked eyes with Donald through the now-open doors as everyone in the elevator laughed— until I stepped inside.

Chapter 3

"Shut up! You didn't?" Jules' pretty blue eyes widened with horror, almost falling off her bar stool.

"Into my *hands*, Jules!" I cupped my hands in front of me for emphasis.

She wrinkled her nose and reached for her wine glass.

"You're not just exaggerating for dramatic effect?"

"I wish." Even though I was prone to hyperbole the scene was horrific enough without having to exaggerate.

"Well on the bright side, your day couldn't possibly have gotten any worse." Jules was a bit of a Pollyanna, always looking on the bright side of life. Wine bottle half full and all that.

"I don't know. The whole day was kind of a shit show." I tore off little bits of the cardboard coaster in my hands and told her about the impending retrenchments, the knot in my stomach growing a little bigger and a little tighter as I said the words out loud.

"Oh God, Luce. But doesn't your boss think you're the bee's knees? Can't he move you around or something?"

Rob *did* seem to have an interest in my career, although I wasn't sure why. I'd actually ended up at The Standard through Jules' husband, Martin as him and Rob were squash buddies. I'd been so thrilled to have found work but I'd always assumed my getting hired had been more of a favour than being related to any skills I had as a writer.

I sighed. "That's what I'm hoping for, but I can't really count on him to make something happen. It wouldn't be fair to pressure him like that." There was only so much he could do for me given the situation.

"No wonder you were so eager to get a drink." Jules made a face, took my hand in hers and finished off the last of her wine. She'd been my best friend since kindergarten and she knew when to comfort me. She also knew when not to say a word and sympathy-drink with me instead.

"Do you want to come over for dinner after this? Martin would love to see you." Jules and Martin had been together for one hundred blissfully happy years, married for about fifty of those years. If I didn't adore them they would have annoyed the shit out of me.

"I can't," I said, screwing up my face. "I have to go on a date with that guy I met on DateMeStupid.com, remember?"

"That's right! Which one is this? I know you've been talking to a few. The oboe-playing accountant whose profile was written in the third person or the stamp-collecting teacher who likes hiking?"

"Neither. It's the fly-fishing engineer."

"Let me know how it goes. You're due for an amazing date after all the bad ones you've had lately. Especially after the last guy texted you a picture of his willy. While you were across the table from him …"

"… eating chorizo. Yes, well I can only hope."

Jules loved discussing my disastrous love life. Since she'd only ever been with Martin she thought being single was fun and that Internet dating was exciting.

"Honey," said Jules, glancing at her watch, "I have to head off."

I nodded and grabbed my bag. The bar was starting to fill with the after work crowd and I wished that I could stay with Jules and polish off a few bottles of red.

When we'd paid for our drinks I followed her out the bar, dragging my feet like a kid going to the dentist.

"I almost forgot," she said, rummaging around in her handbag before pulling out an envelope and waving it in the air. "A little memento. I found it when I was cleaning the garage. I know things have been tough for you for a while and I just thought you might need a little reminder of what a badass you are."

She handed me the envelope and gave me a big hug before heading off down the street to her car.

Things *had* been tough for a while—for the last two years to be exact. Before that I'd had a "dream job" as a features writer at a woman's magazine and was engaged to a "dream guy" who I lived with in a "dream apartment". You can therefore imagine how upsetting it was to walk in on my fiancé shagging my boss on her desk at four o'clock one afternoon. My life imploded and I lost everything—the man, the job, the apartment—just like that. Eventually I'd picked up the pieces of my life, and had kind of shoved them into my handbag, hoping at some point they'd just reassemble themselves … but I was still waiting.

I took a deep breath and opened the envelope, praying I wouldn't find some variation of a motivational poster.

You have to look through the rain to see the rainbow! Dance like no one is watching! Dream as if you'll live forever but run as if you're being chased by the Terminator!

Thankfully, it was just a photo of me. One that looked like it had been taken when I was about four or five, probably not long after I'd first met Jules.

In the photo I was standing on the top of the climbing gym that stood in the middle of a playground, my arms raised in some kind of victorious salute. My head was tilted back and my mouth was open wide in a gleeful shout, my hair was ruffled and my feet were bare. I looked as though I literally had the world at my feet. We'd called that particular jungle gym 'Big Yellow' because it was so big and so yellow. (We must have spent all day coming up with that one.) Many a kid got stuck halfway up its metal body and would cry, clinging to the yellow bars while waiting for a teacher to rescue them. But not me. On top of 'Big Yellow' I was invincible.

I stared at that version of myself and attempted to remember what it was like to feel like that—like I could do anything. I knew that Jules was trying to make me feel better, but somehow she'd just succeeded in making it worse. Because, tucking the photo safely back into its envelope, I realised that if bravery was a muscle, mine had withered from lack of use a long time ago.

* * *

I stared at my phone for the ninth time. My date was half an hour late and I hadn't heard from him. Approximately 70% of me was hopeful that he wouldn't show so I could go home and face-plant into a plate of leftover lasagne, but the rest of me wasn't sure I could deal with being stood up after the day I'd had. Jules had forced me to set up an Internet dating profile several months ago when I'd announced I was considering taking up crochet. One night over dinner, she and Martin had staged an intervention and fed me bullshit stories about people they knew who'd met their wives/husbands/life partners online and were all so madly in love with each other they wanted to stab themselves in the eyeballs.

So far I'd been on a date with a sheep farmer named Nigel, a violinist with a foot fetish, and Bevin, who suffered from a mild case of Tourette's. And let's not forget Willy Guy. None of them had gone to a second date. The sheep farmer confessed he preferred blondes. The violinist had taken one look at my bunions and fled screaming. And Bevin called me "dick sucker" twenty-three times and repeatedly stuck his fingers in my gin and tonic.

After being cheated on by my fiancé just weeks before our wedding I had understandably low expectations when it came to the opposite sex. Somehow though, all potentials still managed to limbo right on under the low bar I'd set, even though it currently hovered about seven centimetres from the ground. I wasn't asking for a trilingual water-skiing neurosurgeon. All DangerousDave5000 had to do was *not* show me a photo of his junk, and like the look of my feet, and he'd be in there with a chance. That's if he ever showed up.

After another 15 minutes of waiting, a woman who was sitting on the other side of the bar walked over to me and rubbed my arm. "I'm sure he's just stuck in traffic or is running late," she said, with her head tilted sympathetically to the side. I smiled awkwardly and pretended I was from Slovenia. When she'd returned to her seat and had her back to me, I stood up to leave, feeling mortified. Random people were so embarrassed for me they felt the need to walk across a bar and tell me. Jesus.

"Lucy?"

I turned to see a man who was attached to a mustard-coloured shirt.

"Dangerous Dave 5000?" The man in front of me, a smidge taller than my 5'6", had accessorised his ugly shirt with a tentative smile.

"I wasn't sure you were going to show," he said. "My last date actually stood me up."

That's debatable.

"Uh. Are you sure she stood you up? Were you also 45 minutes late for her?" I asked, in the super patient, super calm voice I usually reserved for small children and stupid people.

"Et tu?" he said, nodding like he knew something I didn't. "My ex was always having a go at me about my time management."

Houston, we have a big fucking problem and his name is Dave.

Instead of Tom Cruise-running out of the bar like I should have,

I gestured to Dave to sit down on the stool next to me. Everyone was nervous at the beginning of dates so I decided to give him the benefit of the doubt. His profile was inoffensive and normal so I hoped the mention of his ex was a once-off. Everyone was allowed to say at least one stupid thing on a date, weren't they? I often allowed myself up to twelve.

"I hope you like the bar I chose? It just opened and looked cool on the website," I said. I preferred to arrange dates that weren't at the usual bars Jules and I frequented so that none of our favourite places would be tainted with shitty date memories.

Dave shrugged. "It's a bit pretentious. Exactly the kind of place my ex would have chosen." He looked around the bar. "But don't worry, I'm giving you the benefit of the doubt."

I dug my nails into the sticky bar counter.

"Great," I said, pretending he'd answered my question with something like: "I think you made an excellent choice. The ambience is cozy, the décor is cool and I particularly like the barman's face tattoo."

I wondered if I could get away with knocking back a shot, thanking Dave for the lovely three minutes we'd spent in each other's company and leaving. As far as I knew there wasn't any time limit on what constituted a date. I *had* been there for 45 minutes after all.

Dave ordered the most expensive whisky on the menu, while I ordered the cheapest. I liked to pay my way at least on first dates and I'd only budgeted for one drink. When we had our drinks I took a deep breath and, flashing Dave my brightest smile, tried again.

"I seem to remember you saying in your profile that you like fly fishing? How did you get into that?"

"I started fishing so that I could get some quiet time away from my nagging girlfriend, now my ex-girlfriend."

Donkey balls! I vowed not to take the bait. If I did I'd never hear the end of it. And so for a while I continued to dodge all mentions of his ex, which was no easy feat.

When I asked why he'd gone into engineering, he responded that his ex liked shopping so he needed to make good money.

When I talked about the newspaper, he mentioned that his ex lived just down the road from our building.

He even managed to get one in when I told him about my cousin's recent wedding, which he thought was the perfect time to tell me that I actually looked like his ex's cousin's mother.

If I was playing a drinking game, taking a swig every time Dave mentioned his ex, I could have gotten absolutely trolleyed. But instead, I nursed my sad little whisky and waited a polite amount of time so I could leave.

When I couldn't take it any longer I escaped to the bathroom, put the seat down, then sat on the loo and counted to ten.

One Mississippi. Two Mississippi. Three Mississippi …

Ten Mississippis later, I returned to the bar, looking forward to wrapping up the date, but Dave plonked another drink in front of me.

"I ordered you another one. Wasn't that thoughtful of me?" When I didn't respond he continued. "I think the date is going really well." He looked at me expectantly.

"I agree," I lied.

"You're so much nicer than my ex," he said, reaching along the bar to clasp my hand.

"When did you break up with your ex, Dave?" Damn. The words had slipped out because I'd been so focused on getting my hand back.

His bottom lip wobbled violently. "Last week."

Oh God.

And so it came to pass that he sobbed like a teenage girl then spent the next hour telling me all about his ex. I sipped my second watered down drink as Dave ordered whisky after whisky until he was very drunk. I heard all about the break up. How she'd told him that she needed to find herself, and how Dave had responded by burning all her clothes and stealing her mail. Several people around us were listening and shaking their heads and clucking sympathetically. I wanted to leave but I couldn't, not while the poor guy was pouring out his heart. I knew what it felt like to have your heart ripped out while it was still beating. Dave must have seen this kinship in my eyes because he suddenly leaned over and rubbed my leg.

"I want to sex you, Lesley."

Gah! Who the hell was Lesley?

Thinking quickly, I picked up my mobile and stuck it to my ear. "Sorry, I've just got to get this." I could have put a hamster to the side of my face and Dave wouldn't have known the difference.

"Hi, Charlotte. What's wrong?" I said to no one. "What? You've locked yourself out the flat and need me to open up for you? Okay, fine, I'll see you soon." While the call was a fake, my flatmate was real. And locking herself out was something she would have done.

I peeled Dave's hand off my leg, one sweaty finger at a time, and broke the news to him. "I'm sorry, Dave. My flat mate, Charlotte, locked herself out of our flat and I need to go let her in."

Dave nodded gravely. "My ex-shhh did that all the time."

When the barman bought over the bill I pulled out some cash to cover my two drinks and pushed it towards Dave, who made a big show of patting his chest and pockets for his wallet.

"I left my wallet at home. Would you? I'll get the next one," he slurred and winked at me aggressively.

Which next one? I wanted to scream. The only way I'd go on another date with him was if my brain was replaced with a stapler. I calmly pulled out the last of the money in my wallet, which I was supposed to be spending on food for the rest of the month until payday.

"Goodbye, Dave." With teeth gritted I excused myself and stomped towards the exit. But Dave just trotted after me, following me all the way to the bus stop.

"So your place?" he asked, clinging to a pole for balance. My mouth fell open. I wanted to bludgeon him with my phone but instead I just stared at him. The whole date had been a disaster yet somehow he thought he was coming home with me. I ignored him and his swaying for the full five minutes it took for him to get the message and leave me alone.

I was still raging when I flopped into an empty seat on the bus. I mumbled under my breath, vowing never to date anyone ever as long as I drew breath, when I looked up out the window—just in time to see Dave whizz by in the back of a taxi.

Chapter 4

My high heels felt like they were made of cement as I made my way up the stairs to my apartment. I put my key in the lock and leaned my forehead against the door. I hoped Charlotte was out because I didn't have anything left in me to deal with her. Sighing, I pushed the door open with my head.

"Yes! Oh! Give it to me, baby! Yes!"

So Charlotte *was* home. And she had company at nine 'o clock on a Wednesday night. I shook my head in wonder, and let's be honest, a little bit of envy, as I kicked off my shoes. Her milkshake brought a steady stream of boys to her yard, right through her, uh, bush. Charlotte had found her bliss early on in life and that was casual sex on a school night. Mine was ordering green chicken curry from the Thai place down the road.

"Oh, Baby! Yeah … Uh … You! Yes!"

Charlotte could always be counted on to be vocal in her exploits—even if she sometimes forgot the name of the person she was under.

I made a mental note to treat myself to a new set of earplugs and hung my house keys on the hook next to my car keys, accidentally kicking the large cardboard box in the hallway—the one on which Charlotte had scrawled 'Lost and Found' in swirly red lipstick letters.

I was still amazed that she had managed to almost completely fill this latest iteration in just the last few months. It was her curiosity box of conquests, containing everything from men's shoes and watches, to handcuffs and ties. A small plastic rugby trophy had even found its way into the box in the last few days. I bent down to pick it up but changed my mind and dropped it, not sure where it'd been.

One quick look in the fridge confirmed Charlotte had found my leftover lasagne, which I'd hidden behind a bag of questionable-looking spinach leaves. Closing the fridge I noticed Charlotte's scrawl in thick black marker across the door: *Your lasagna had too much garlic in it* and underneath that, *Get milk*.

Armed with a soupspoon and a can opener, I headed to the hallway cupboard where I stored the cleaning stuff and my secret food stash. Charlotte was allergic to cleaning so anything in there would be safe. Reaching up onto the highest shelf I grabbed a can of condensed milk for my dinner in the bath.

A few minutes later, with a mouth full of condensed milk, I settled back into the warm water and closed my eyes. The bath was my favourite place. Jules thought it was because it was like being back in the womb. I liked to think it was because I'd been a mermaid in a previous life. Whatever the reason, the amount of time I spent in the bath was directly proportional to how shitty my life was. The water seemed to cushion everything: the crushing sadness, my parents' worried whispers and the weight of my failures. I'd spent ridiculous amounts of time in the bath after my break up with Michael, mascara running down my face, sobbing into packets of soggy salt and vinegar crisps.

It had taken me a good six months hiding at my folk's house to cycle through the five stages of post-break-up grief: Denial, Shopping, Cake, Ice-Cream and Acceptance. After a gentle pep talk from my mum and dad, who'd hinted that they were struggling under the weight of their massive electricity and water bills on account of all my sad midday baths, I'd half-heartedly ventured out into the stupid world. Within a few weeks I'd found a new job and a new place to live. It was good. I'd survived. I hadn't died. And I had been waking up every morning ever since, putting my underwear on the right way round and sticking one foot in front of the other to get me through each day.

"Oh. Yes. Yes! SHIT."

Charlotte's shouts increased in volume and enthusiasm, along with the sound of her headboard banging hard against the wall. I took a deep breath and submerged myself in the bath, the sickly sweet dairy confectionary burning my tongue as I lay there waiting for the sex storm to pass. Under the water I could still hear Charlotte's exuberant, though muffled, exclamations. I swallowed the condensed milk and watched the little bubbles float from my nostrils, trying to hold on a little longer.

I thought about the photo Jules had given me. When I was a child and my whole life stretched in front of me—a gigantic question mark in the sky—there was no way this is what I would have wanted my life to look like. Yes, I'd always wanted to be a writer. But it was the other stuff I hadn't been so sure about. So I'd just let the world tell me what to want, to fill in the blanks for me. And this is where it had gotten me.

When there was nothing left in my lungs I pushed my head above the water. Just in time to hear Charlotte coming in her usual spectacular fashion.

"VICTORY!"

Nope. This is *not* what I wanted my life to look like. I wanted something different. I *needed* something different. Or eventually my body wouldn't know where the bath started and I ended and I'd dissolve in an endless ocean of warm soapy water and become nothing.

* * *

My cubicle was particularly grey the next morning. By ten o'clock I'd already seen four people crying and packing up their desks. Waiting for my inevitable turn I'd chewed off my fingernails and had moved on to gnawing at pen lids like a rat. On top of the stress of my impending retrenchment, every time Smelly Simon heard the next person packing up, he'd rush into my cubicle and press his face close to mine to whisper the bad news. On the bright side (thank you Jules for pointing this out) everyone had forgotten about my 'episode' from the day before.

"Lucy?"

My boss, Rob was standing there, looking more dishevelled than usual. Fiddleshits.

"Yes?" I squeaked.

"Please may I see you in my office?" he asked, raking a hand through his hair.

"Sure." I followed slowly, like an old horse about to be shot in the head.

"Take a seat," he said, closing the door behind us and gesturing to the well-worn chair across from his messy desk. When he sat down on the other side of his desk he looked at me with an expression I couldn't read.

"Lucy, it is my great pleasure to tell you that you have been promoted," he said, his fingers clasped.

"What? Seriously? That's great news! Thank you. Why … I mean … what is the promotion?"

"Online travel writer."

I like to think my brow furrowed delicately in confusion, but really my mouth dropped open and my tongue rolled out.

"Don't we already have a travel writer for Online? Sandy? Mandy?"

"Candy," said Rob. "Yes we did. But she injured herself rock climbing in Canada."

"That sounds about right," I said, nodding. I'd read enough of her work to know that she was crazy. I usually shuddered and skipped right over her articles. If she wasn't jumping out of planes, she was climbing mountains or swimming with sharks. Candy was irresponsible in her portrayal of the world of travel. Not everyone wanted to spend their annual holiday risking loss of limbs or possible death. Some of us just wanted to read a book on a safe, deserted beach. "Is she ok?" I hurriedly added, not wanting to sound insensitive.

Rob coughed. "She broke both arms, both legs, her pelvis and a few ribs. She'll be in a body cast for about six months but, in spite of all that, I hear she's doing okay and is in high spirits."

My eyes bulged.

"Okay, so anyway, your first assignment …"

I held up my hands. "Hang on a second. Sorry, Rob, but I haven't said yes yet." There was no way I was going to take that job. Travel writer? Me? I'd been to Bali with my family when I was 12 and I'd spent most of the trip mainlining Sweet Valley High books and Seventeen magazines in an air-conditioned hotel room.

"I just thought this would be an excellent opportunity for you to stretch yourself and your writing and get out of Classifieds."

"But travel writer? I can't do that," I whispered. I felt like enough of an imposter calling myself a writer as it was, even if it was only in Classifieds. How in the world was I going to be able to pull off tacking 'travel' to the front of it?

"Lucy, do you understand how precarious your position at the newspaper is?"

I nodded.

"I've been up half the night trying to figure out what to do with you because I don't want to get rid of you. It's terrible what happened to Candy but the timing is in your favour. As soon as I heard about it I thought about you. I really think you have potential, Lucy."

I stared at him. It was touching he was so concerned about trying to find me another position, but there was no way I'd be able to run around the world being a travel writer. His confidence in me was misplaced. I didn't have it in me. I opened my mouth to protest once more but nothing came out, so I shook my head instead.

"Besides the fact that you'd be out of a job otherwise, I also think you need this."

Hah! I needed this like I needed Smelly Simon to breathe into my mouth.

"Lucy. I just …" Rob rose from his chair and began pacing the small office. "You've been playing it safe here ever since I hired you. Don't you want to grow as a writer and get back to doing more of what you used to do at that magazine?"

I shook my head. It would have been safer just to stay where I was.

Rob continued to pace. "Years ago my boss gave me an opportunity like the one I'm giving you. I didn't think I was ready either. It scared the hell out of me, but he saw something in me and decided to take a chance. It was the best thing that ever happened to me." He stopped and leaned against his desk. "This could be the making of you, Lucy."

"Or the breaking of me," I countered. Rob didn't respond. "Look, I really appreciate what you're trying to do for me, Rob—"

"Hear me out. Let me tell you about what your first assignment would be before you completely rule it out."

I nodded, shifting my weight in the chair.

"As you know, the newspaper is really pushing digital, so we're trialling a blog on the travel section of the website. You'd be writing blog posts about travelling like a real backpacker. I was thinking something gritty and contemporary to appeal to the younger generation we're trying to tap into."

Rob looked at me expectantly, but when I said nothing he continued.

"Candy had this great idea to backpack the Gringo Trail in South America. So that's what the first series would be about."

"What's the Gringo Trail?" I feigned interest in his proposal, while my mind raced to figure out what I was going to do instead. Like I'd really say yes to South A-freaking-merica. I'd rather get a job blow-drying chest hair.

"It's the so-called beaten track that most of the backpackers heading to South America tend to follow. Gringo is slang for a non-Latin American in Latin America. Candy suggested calling the series '60 Days in South America'."

"60 days in South America? 6? 0?" I asked.

Rob nodded.

60 *Ways to Die* in South America, more likely. I wouldn't last two minutes, let alone two whole months in a place like that. "But South America is dangerous. Couldn't I do 60 Days in the Maldives instead?"

"Candy says it has a bad reputation but it's perfectly safe," said Rob.

Yes, well. Candy had also stuck her hand into a crocodile's mouth. So there was that.

"Anyway, you wouldn't be alone. We've hired a freelance photographer to take the photos. His name is Jack Dawson. Not sure if you've heard of him."

"I think I have. But didn't he die when Rose let go of his hand after the Titanic sank?"

Rob blinked back at me, not a trace of humour in his face.

"When would I be expected to meet this Jack Dawson in South America?" Maybe I could say yes then find another job in the meantime.

"Candy was supposed to meet him in Buenos Aires on Tuesday."

"This coming Tuesday?" My heart sank into my ankles.

Rob nodded.

"But today is Thursday."

He nodded again.

"Rob, I …" My voice trembled and I looked down at my lap.

"You can't do it?" he finished for me after an uncomfortably long silence.

I nodded.

"I'll pack up my desk," I said, avoiding his eyes as I stood and headed for the door.

I flopped down in my chair and looked around my workspace, trying to decide if there was anything I actually wanted to take with me. Maybe I'd just dump it in a pile in the parking lot and set it all on fire. Before I could start the ~~burning~~ packing, my mobile buzzed. It was Charlotte, presumably calling to demand I bring home a pizza she had no intention of paying for. I let it ring off. She called again.

"Listen, Charlotte, now isn't a great time."

"Lucy, I've got bad news."

Chapter 5

"What happened?" I sunk further into my chair and closed my eyes. The last time I'd heard those words coming out of her mouth she'd "borrowed" my car and reversed it into a telephone pole. The time before that she'd flooded the apartment after having a quick nap while she ran herself a bath in the middle of the day.

"Well, I brought a guy home last night. I think his name was Chad. Anyway we had sex twice and he stayed over. Then this morning we kind of started having sex again and he said he wanted to tie me up. And I was all up for it because I've tried BDSM before and it really turns me on and—"

"Charlotte. Please get to the point." I cut her off and poked my head up to see if anyone was lurking nearby.

"And, like, he tied me up really tight and then said he was going to get some chocolate sauce from the fridge and I said that we didn't have any—because remember I told you to get some last week and you didn't—and I suggested maybe some mayonnaise or that pesto stuff you put on your pasta. And then I heard voices, but I just thought maybe he was on the phone."

"Charlotte," I whispered through gritted teeth.

"We got robbed."

"What do you mean, we got robbed?" I spoke slowly, enunciating every syllable.

"Well, like, I was trying to tell you, I shouted for Whatshisname to tell me what was happening and he took a while and it sounded like he was moving furniture around. And then, well … I fell asleep because I was really tired because, you know, we were up pretty late having sex and it was very energetic. And then when I woke up I wasn't tied up anymore and I got up and saw that everything besides all the stuff in my room had been taken. They took your fridge and your bed and like all your clothes. They even took the Lost and Found box. Isn't that like so messed up?"

I dropped my head onto my desk, lifted it, then dropped it again.

"Lucy? Are you there?"

"So when you say *we've* been robbed, what you really mean to say is that *I've* been robbed?" Everything Charlotte owned was in her room. The rest was mine.

Oh my God.

My car.

"Charlotte? What about my car?"

Charlotte hesitated. "Your car's gone too. But you know what the worst thing is? Having sex with someone is like a sacred bond. It is such a violation of trust to rob someone you've slept with, don't you think?"

This couldn't be happening.

"And before you ask," said Charlotte, although by now I was only half listening to her. "I did call the police and I told them the story. The bad news is that because I let this guy into the flat and I can't really remember what he looks like, because I was a bit drunk, there's nothing they can do. But the good news is that you have insurance."

"Charlotte, I don't have insurance anymore. Remember? I couldn't afford the premiums because they kept putting them up after all the claims I'd had to put through."

"Oh. Right. That really sucks for you."

People were now doing drive-bys past my cubicle and I had to get off the phone.

"I have to go Charlotte."

I could have made a plan for a few weeks without a job if I sold my car while I looked for something else. But I didn't have a car anymore. And I couldn't move back in with my folks. Not again. I couldn't borrow from Jules as her and Martin were in the middle of renovating. And my credit card still hadn't recovered from the post-break up shopping rampage I'd subjected it. I'd been backed into a corner and there was only one way out of this predicament.

Chapter 6

"Señoras y señores, por favor tenga su pasaporte abierto en la página de foto. Si usted necesita una visa por favor, asegúrese de que usted haya completado su formulario y tiene el dinero correcto a pagar por tu visa.

Ladies and Gentlemen, please have your passport open on the photo page. If you need a visa please make sure you have completed your form and have the correct money to pay for your visa."

I stood in the immigration queue, clutching my passport in my sweaty hands. To the airport guards I must have looked like I was either suffering from an infectious form of swamp flu or was smuggling drugs into the country in my rectum. Neither of which would result in a warm welcome to Argentina.

While I waited I pulled out the photo of me on the jungle gym, the one Jules had handed me after our drink. At the last minute, I'd shoved it into my journal to keep as a talisman to get me through the next two months. I was hoping it would work its magic soon, because I was about to lose my shit.

For the few days it took me to sort out my life before leaving Australia I'd done an excellent job of denying what I was getting myself into. The trip had been theoretical as I'd packed the three cans of condensed milk that hadn't been stolen into a box to take to my folks. I had run around the shops like a mad woman buying everything I needed. I had broken the lease on my flat and farewelled family and friends. But I'd refused to even crack the spine of my guide book in case it made the trip real.

Except now, standing in a foreign airport on a foreign continent where I didn't speak the language, I could no longer lie to myself, and by the time I made my way through immigration into the arrivals hall, I was beside myself. I wanted to cry, vomit and pass out. I just wasn't sure in which order.

Bent forward, under the weight of the biggest backpack I'd been able to find at the adventure goods store, I was greeted by a sea of strange faces. My chest heaved as I hyperventilated into my hands and spun around in circles looking for a bathroom. Unfortunately, I forgot that my backpack jutted out like a giant tortoiseshell and I nearly knocked over a little old lady.

"Estupida!" she yelled, throwing her hands up. At least I didn't need a translator for that.

"I'm sorry," I said, raising my own hands, tears pricking my eyes. Above her head I saw a sign for the bathroom and made a beeline for it, making sure to give her a wide berth this time. However, in doing so, I knocked into a man who fell, taking his luggage with him. I pressed my lips together, put my head down and rushed towards the bathroom in an awkward shuffle. But my backpack was so heavy and high up my back that to avoid toppling over, I had to widen my stance and run with my legs in a half-squat position. This unorthodox running style would best have been described as "The Granny Crab".

Candy, via Rob, had given me a list of suggested items to purchase on the company credit card, but I'd bought a few more to be on the safe side. Which meant that even though I had the biggest backpack I could find—an 85-litre monster—as well as a smaller 35-litre daypack, I'd still been unable to fit everything. My solution was to wear some of the gear I'd been unable to pack. So as I ran through the crowded arrivals hall to the bathroom I was dressed in the following ensemble:

- Poo-green hiking boots that laced up to my ankles
- Charcoal snow gaiters
- Mustard yellow quick dry shorts (with detachable bottoms— not worn)
- Navy blue Merino wool t-shirt (moisture-wicking)
- Black wind jacket (tied around waist)
- Army camouflage headband
- Wide-brimmed hat
- Neck chain holding red rape whistle and large plastic compass

It was not lost on me how ridiculous I looked as I charged, head down, into the bathroom and squeezed myself into the closest stall. Closing the door behind me was a struggle, which I only managed to achieve by straddling the toilet and reaching behind me to push the door shut. When I was safely locked in I tugged the smaller pack off my chest and heaved the larger bag off my back. Free of luggage, I sank onto the toilet seat and started to bawl. Snot and tears pooled in my hands as I sobbed into them.

The acoustics in the bathroom were so impressive that my wailing sounded good enough to record.

The acoustics in the bathroom at the newspaper and the one at the cinema near my flat weren't nearly as good. Anyone on the other side of the toilet stall would think I'd been through some kind of trauma or was suffering from a mental issue of sorts, but they'd be wrong. Apparently I was "just a healthy human being trying to work through stuff". Or so I'd been told by the therapist I'd seen a year back after my attempts to self-diagnose my particular psychological issue with Google proved unsuccessful. I'd expected her to prescribe medication, or at least refer me to some kind of ten-step program to fix myself. But she'd assured me there wasn't anything to fix. Which hadn't been helpful at all.

During a lull in the sobbing I wondered how long I could stay in the bathroom. I had a muesli bar and half a bottle of water, which I figured could buy me at least seven hours.

"Lucy?"

I stopped sniffling into the soggy wad of toilet paper in my hand and cocked my head.

"Is that Lucy Hart in there?"

It was a man. Who the hell knew I was here? In a toilet stall in the Buenos Aires airport?

"Lucy Hart?" I could see a pair of boots under the stall door.

"I'm Jack Dawson. The photographer?"

Oh my God! In my panic I'd forgotten Rob mentioning that Jack would meet me at the airport. Had he seen me careening through the crowd? How long had I been in here? How long had *he* been in here, listening to my wailing? Whores of Babylon!

I hiccupped. "Hello Jack. Nice to meet you," I said, happy to have a door between us.

"You've been in there for a while. Don't you think it's about time you came out?"

Jack had a plummy English accent. I tried to blow my nose as delicately as possible while wondering if he had a jumper currently tied around his neck.

"Uh, yes. I seem to be suffering from a spot of ... the hay fever, and I was just waiting for the anti-histamine to kick in, you see. I'll be out shortly."

I hiccupped again.

"Fine. See you outside. Please don't be long."

"Yes, okay. Meet you outside. Thank you. Tally-ho."

When I heard the door close I heaved my bags up off the floor, squeezed through the tiny stall door and dragged everything to the basin. I splashed water on my face and looked up to check the damage. My eyes were red and puffy and I had large water blotches on the front of my t-shirt. Great.

"It's all up from here. You can do this," I told my reflection.

To my left someone cleared their throat and I looked up to see a man standing there staring at me. He gestured to the urinals behind me and then pointed at his crotch. The pantomime continued with him pointing at my chest and then at *my* crotch and then at the door.

Right.

After having a breakdown in the men's toilet I didn't see any point in pretending to have a scrap of dignity left. It would have been even more pathetic to pretend otherwise, so I took a deep breath and pushed open the door.

"Hello, Lucy." Jack leaned against the wall outside the bathroom, holding up a piece of paper with LUCY HART scrawled across the page in big, black letters. I peered up at him, since he had at least a foot on me, right into a pair of the darkest eyes I'd ever seen. His hair, slightly lighter than the colour of his eyes, was wild—not quite curly, not quite straight. He was dressed in loose khaki trousers, which hung off his lanky frame, and a fitted navy blue t-shirt.

"Sorry for keeping you, Jack."

Instead of responding he just looked me up and down, his arms crossed tightly against his chest, accentuating a pair of strong, veiny biceps.

"What the hell are you wearing?"

I looked down at my backpacking ensemble, seeing my huge boots, snow gaiters, my bare knees and shins, and the compass and whistle hanging around my neck.

"Never mind. Are you ready to go?"

I nodded.

"Well, come on then," he barked when I didn't immediately follow him. I quickly tried to heave my large pack onto my back, but after a few feeble attempts, Jack rolled his eyes and snatched the bag strap from my hands.

"Jesus! What the hell have you got in here? This must weigh one hundred pounds!"

I nodded matter-of-factly as he pulled it onto his back. "I think it probably does."

"I'm going to have to take a look at what you've got. I bet you've brought shit you don't need."

"I can assure you I have only the absolute essentials. The salesperson sold me only what I needed to survive for sixty days in South America."

"That's what I'm worried about," muttered Jack as he stomped towards the airport doors leaving me to scuttle after him.

Chapter 7

I was lost in the hostel. I was sure my room had been one right turn away, but now I was in what looked like a common room.

"Nöel, I was told I'd be dealing with a professional. She's definitely *not* a professional. She was wearing snow gaiters in the airport for Christ's sake. If I'm going to have to babysit her for the next sixty days, this trip is going to be a nightmare!"

I froze. Jack was in the far corner of the room, his back to me. Part of me wanted to continue to eavesdrop on his conversation, while another part of me wanted to dribble through the cracks in the tiles beneath my feet. He'd sat stony-faced, staring out the taxi window the whole ride to the hostel. I'd wanted to speak to him several times but instead, had shrunk against my side of the backseat, staring out the window at signs in Spanish that I couldn't understand. When we'd arrived at Buen Viaje, our hostel in San Telmo, it was already dark. Jack had stomped upstairs with my bags, pulled out his Mac from a locked cabinet and left me alone in the empty four-bed dorm room without another word.

I'd sat alone on my bed for a while, picking at imaginary bits of lint on my shorts, waiting for him to return. The small room had two bunk beds against each wall and a set of four lockers between the beds. Judging by the clothes and bags strewn across the room our other roommate was a woman. Or a man who wore women's clothes. When Jack hadn't returned after an hour, I'd been so desperate for the toilet that I'd ventured out of the room by myself.

"I'm probably going to spend all my time rescuing her from bathrooms," he complained to the person on the other end of the Skype call.

My face burned with shame. I wanted to shout out that I hadn't asked to be here, but I turned and scurried out, knocking into a chair in my haste. Jack turned and looked straight at me. Bugger.

"Uh, anyway Nöel, uh, …" he stuttered, turning back to face the screen.

Back in our room I lay down on top of the scratchy blanket on my bed and stared up at the wooden slats of the bed above me. Maybe Rob hadn't explained the situation properly to Jack? I wondered if he even knew I'd taken Candy's spot on account of her having fallen off the side of a mountain? I couldn't blame him for being shitty about being stuck with me. I'd probably feel the same if I was in his boots. Although he could at least try to be nice. Someone had drawn a penis on one of the wooden slats, which did seem fitting, since Jack *was* being a bit of a dick.

The door opened and I squeezed my eyes shut, hoping it wasn't Jack.

"Hello there! You must be one of my roommates. I'm Hayley," shouted a redhead with a Kiwi accent.

I sat up. "Hi," I said, lifting my hand in a pathetic half-wave. "Lucy."

"Good to meet you, Roomie. Wow. You look pretty fresh off the boat." She eyed me up and down, though not unkindly, taking in the full effect of my outfit.

"Is it that obvious?" I asked, pulling my bandanna and hat off, followed by my chain with rape whistle and compass. "I landed a few hours ago."

"Don't worry. You'll be fine. I recognise a little of myself in you. I've been backpacking around Latin America for the last year. I actually fly back home tomorrow."

"So what you're saying is there's hope for me, then?"

"Of course there's hope! Why don't we find you an alcoholic beverage?" she said.

Before I could respond she grabbed my hand and pulled me off the bed. Were all backpackers this ~~forward~~ friendly, I wondered, as Hayley chatted away, marching me down the stairs to a bar in the hostel basement. The dimly-lit bar, which was already full at seven in the evening, was filled with the sound of Latin music, happy laughter and the faint whiff of body odour. Groups of people on mismatched chairs huddled together around small tables, their heads bent in conversation. One woman, wearing a luminous yellow scarf that I wouldn't ever have a hope of pulling off, had her head tilted back and was laughing so hard the blonde hair around her shoulders shook. I'm sure she wasn't rubbing her happiness in my face on purpose.

After I'd taken a massive swig of beer I realised my shoulders were up around my ears and dropped them down and rolled my neck a few times.

"That's better, isn't it? Now why don't you tell me what brought you to South America and why you looked like you were about to drown yourself in the nearest toilet?"

I took another gulp of my beer and launched into the story of how my life had gone from beige to brown in the space of a few days. A story I affectionately referred to as The Second Worst Week of My Life.

"Jesus. What a week," said Hayley. "Barman, this chick needs a shot. Immediatamente!"

The barman, whose thick dreads were pulled up into a ponytail, lined up our shots. I downed mine without hesitation, pulling a face and shuddering as the burning liquid slid down my throat.

"Okay, hang on. You said this was the *second* worst week of your life? I'm almost scared to ask what happened during the worst week," said my new friend.

"A month before I was due to marry my ex-fiancé I caught him shagging my boss on her desk. I spent the rest of the week moving my things out of our apartment, cancelling wedding stuff and calling guests to tell them the man I was supposed to marry was a cheating bastard. And then my boss chose not to renew my contract."

Hayley's eyes bulged.

"Barman!" she yelled.

"Let me guess?" He winked before sloshing more tequila into my empty shot glass.

I downed the shot and slammed my glass down onto the peeling counter, marvelling at how much better I was already feeling.

Maybe I could fill my water bottle with tequila and spend the next sixty days in a drunken haze? I smiled at the thought and looked around the bar—right at Jack who was standing near the door looking at me like I'd just farted the chorus of Wham's Wake Me Up Before You (Go Go). My face dropped and I quickly turned away, wondering how much of the conversation he'd heard. When I looked back a moment later he was gone.

"Look on the bright side, Lucy," said Hayley, nudging me with her elbow. "Shit can only get better from here."

Several drinks later I totally agreed with her.

* * *

"Lucy, Wake up!"

I started to open my eyes but it hurt too much, so I gave up and shut them again.

"Lucy," Jack yelled.

How was it possible for his voice to sound even more pompous through the blankets covering my face? He'd probably uttered about five sentences to me since I'd had the misfortune of meeting him, and every word had been dripping with condescension.

"Blerugh," I groaned into my pillow, trying to remain as still as possible. Eventually the toy monkey playing its cheap plastic drum inside my head would run out of batteries and I'd be able to face the world. Until that time I was staying put.

"Come on, Lucy. You need to get up." Jack was such an eggbeater.

"Go away."

"We've got a job to do."

Stupid arse was right. I peeked out from under the blankets. Straight into the bright morning sun that streamed through the window, burning my retinas to dust. I yanked the covers back over my head and jammed my head further into my pillow.

"Too. Much. Tequila," I mumbled into the musty material of my pillow, which smelled like a thousand hung-over faces had been pressed into it.

"Yes, I would have to agree with you on that."

Oh God. What did that mean? After about my eighth shot with Hayley, my mind-tape had stopped recording. I couldn't even remember how I'd made it to bed. I eased myself onto my elbows, and angled my head to look down at my body. Thankfully, I was still fully clothed, complete with my stupid hiking boots. I knocked the boots together and wished to be transported, sans hangover, back to where I'd come from.

There's no place like home. There's no place like home. There's no place like home. When that didn't work I returned my attention to Jack.

"Um. Why would you have to agree with me? I didn't do

anything embarrassing did I?" Eye contact would have been a mistake so I chose to focus on the cockroach scuttling across the floor.

"No, Lucy."

My name sounded like a curse word on his lips.

"You didn't do anything embarrassing."

Phew!

"Well, unless you count stumbling into the room this morning with Red over there," he said, inclining his head toward the opposite bunk, "poking me, then announcing that I was Jack the Self Righteous Prick who frowned upon the wearing of snow gaiters inside airports."

A snorting laugh escaped me and I clamped my hands over my mouth.

Jack cocked an eyebrow. "Do you think that's funny?" he asked.

"Well … it is a little." I shrugged, suspecting I might still be drunk.

I eased myself up to a sitting position and looked across at "Red", who was snoring like a tractor. It hurt to have both eyes open at the same time so I shut my right eye as I adjusted to the light. I focused the left eye on Jack. His dark hair was ruffled and wet and he smelled like peppermint. I chugged down the contents of a water bottle I'd found tucked in my blankets. The water was horrible, warm from hours of being nestled against a body trying to process a large amount of alcohol.

Jack towered above me with his hands on his hips. I could see right up his flared nostrils.

"Listen Lucy, it's clear you don't take your job seriously, which makes me doubt how good you are at it. But I won't have you stuffing up this assignment."

I glared at him. "You don't know anything about me," I snapped.

"I don't have to know you. It's obvious," he said, gesturing at my person, as if to say 'Dur! Exhibit A'.

"What the hell does *this* mean?" I asked, mimicking his condescending gesture.

"You look ridiculous. You hide in airport toilets. You've obviously done zero research into South America. And I don't even know what you've got in that monstrous backpack," he continued, his voice getting louder and louder, making my head hurt even more.

Hayley groaned from her bed. "Shut it! I'm trying to sleep."

I yanked open the zip of my backpack and pulled out my toiletry bag. I didn't know why Jack's words bothered me so much. Any mean thing anyone had ever said to me was a magical theme park ride in a giant teacup compared to how I'd been known to speak to myself. I know "self-love" was the new black but I was still convinced I needed a reason to love myself first, which often proved difficult, especially on days like today.

"Jesus Christ! What the hell have you got in there?" said Jack, as I pulled out a coil of rope and a pair of panpipes from my bag, trying to find my quick dry towel. He looked at me like I'd just released a litter of puppies from its depths.

"None of your business," I retorted. My hands trembled as I resisted the urge to karate chop him in the throat.

"Well I expect you'll make it my business when you can't carry your backpack, or when it takes twice as long for you to get anywhere because it's so bloody heavy."

I ignored him, pulling my clothes and unmentionables out of my stuff sack to look for something to wear. Squinting at the growing pile of clothes on my bed I realised that the colour palette I'd unwittingly gone with for the trip could best be described as Fifty Shades of Poo: dark khakis, light browns, dirty greens and pond-scum yellows. Clutching what I needed to my chest I stomped past him towards the bathroom.

When I returned from my shower I felt about one times better and was in a slightly better mood. I dried my hair with my towel and stared at Jack, who hadn't even looked up from his Mac when I returned. If girls were made of sugar and spice and all things nice, Jack was made from refrigerator coolant and burnt toast crumbs.

"Well," I said, when he continued to ignore me, "are you going to apologise for calling me ridiculous?"

"Why should I apologise? And, anyway I didn't say you *were* ridiculous, I said you *look* ridiculous."

"No you're right. That's *so* much better." I rolled my eyes and gnashed my teeth.

"Listen, I'll make a deal with you. I'll apologise for saying that you look ridiculous if you let me look in your bag."

I narrowed my eyes. "You do realise how creepy you sound, right?"

Jack snorted. "Oh please, I'm not going to sniff your underwear, Lucy."

I pressed my lips together hard to stop myself from laughing out loud. One couldn't glower and laugh at the same time. Jack sensed my amusement and his dark eyes softened, changing from Salem Witch Trial to Igneous Rock Formation.

"I just want to help you. That's all. You can't carry all that around for two months. Will you let me help you?" He waited for a moment. "Please?"

"Fine. But I don't want any attitude about what I've brought with me, okay? Otherwise I'll stab you with these panpipes." I slashed the wooden instrument through the air to demonstrate my point.

Jack didn't need to be told twice. Before I knew it, he was up to his elbows in my belongings, his eyes big and round, just like the lid of the pot he pulled out of my bag. He looked up at me from where he'd sat himself on the floor, his left eyebrow cocked.

"What? The salesperson said I needed a pot. She said she'd been to South America and it had come in handy." I was already regretting my decision to let him poke around.

"You do not need a pot, Lucy. I promise you that."

I plonked myself down on the floor next to him. "Something tells me I'm going to end up with nothing in my backpack."

"If I have my way." Jack placed the pot on top of the rope. "And why the rope?"

"In case I have to scale down a mountain." I would have thought that was pretty obvious.

Jack's mouth curled up slightly and I could tell he was dying to laugh. To his credit he resisted. "And the panpipes?"

"I thought it might make me fit in with the traveller types." I gave the pipes a tentative blow, making a sound not dissimilar to the death rattle of a walrus.

Jack snorted at my logic. "Maybe if you were tramping in France in 1352."

I stuck my tongue out at him. If Jack was going to make me feel like a child I might as well act like one.

"Give me those panpipes," he said, holding out his hand. He chucked them on top of the pile.

He pulled out the next item and I held my breath. "You do NOT need a sleeping bag."

"But what happens if we have to sleep on the side of the road? Or in a church?"

"Why would we have to sleep in a church?" He shook his head. "Okay, so everything you're allowed to keep I'll put back in your bag and everything you're not allowed to keep goes in this pile." On the mountain of discarded paraphernalia went a flare and a portable defibrillator.

"It's criminal how you got taken advantage of by that salesperson," exclaimed Jack as he pulled out a water filtration system.

"Well actually that one was all me. I wasn't sure if the water was safe to drink," I whispered, feeling like if I spoke softly I would be less embarrassed. It didn't work.

A huge bike lock and a money belt followed the water filtration system onto the pile. I leaned across and lifted up my bag, amazed at how light it already was.

"Wow, that's definitely made a big difference," I marvelled.

"Just wait. I'm sure there's more I can take out."

"Really? Can't you just leave the rest?" I rummaged through my bag. "All I have left is my toiletry bag, towel, clothes and my guide book."

"And this monster snow jacket which you don't need," he said, pulling the offending item from my bag. "And what about your snow gaiters? Come on. Hand them over." He held out his hand.

"No, seriously. The salesperson said if there is one essential thing I needed for my trip it was these gaiters." I lunged for the precious articles and clutched them to my bosom.

"Hand them over." He held out his hands and impatiently clicked his fingers.

I scowled. "You're very bossy, Jack." I'd worn the gaiters all the bloody way over here and now I was chucking them out before they'd even seen a single snowflake! But Jack didn't seem like he was going to budge so I threw them on the pile, taking a small amount of satisfaction in the fact that I'd bypassed his outstretched hand.

Before Jack could suggest more things to throw away, I returned what little I had left to the backpack, zipped it, and hoisted it onto my back for a test run. I hopped up and down.

"Amazing," I announced, marching up and down the tiny room, pumping my arms vigorously. I stopped and leaned forward and righted myself again, doing the same to my left side and right. "It doesn't feel like I'm going to topple over. But are you sure I don't need any of that stuff?" I eyeballed the mound on the floor.

"I promise you'll be fine with what you have."

"It feels really empty. Everything is flopping around." I moved from side to side like I was doing the hokey pokey.

"That's because your pack is huge. You could have filmed *March of the Penguins* in that thing."

I pulled the pack off my back and dumped it next to me, flopping back onto my bed, a bit dizzy after all my parading around.

"But what are we going to do with my stuff?" I was puffed. My exertions hadn't done my hangover any favours and I was starting to feel a little sick.

"We'll put it all in the donation box in the common room. I'm sure it will make some panpipe-playing mountain climber very happy."

I watched him stoop to pick up an armful of the things I'd brought to keep me safe on this trip and plotted to rescue a few items when he wasn't looking. Jack must have seen the cogs turning, or at least smelled the smoke coming out of my ears, because he looked at me and said sharply, "Don't even think about it."

60 DAYS IN SOUTH AMERICA

Day 0: An Introduction

Hello there.

I know you were probably expecting Candy, but Candy fell 6m in a rock climbing accident in Canada, broke most of the bones in her body and won't be writing much of anything for a while. (I have been advised that she is in high spirits in spite of her injuries and is planning to be the first woman to sky dive from the moon in a full body cast.) Until she regains the use of her fingers you will have to put up with me instead.

By way of introduction, I'm Lucy Hart, and I eat a lot of cheese. I'm partial to books and very much enjoy the sound of banjos, and the ocean. To ensure that we start this relationship off on the right foot I'm going to tell you a true story: I don't have a clue what I'm doing. And if we are being completely honest, this lack of know-how is not confined to travel.

During the '60 Days in South America' series I will be backpacking a (high speed) version of South America's Gringo Trail. For the uninitiated (i.e. me four days ago), a gringo is a non-Latino person, and their so-called trail is the route most frequently taken by gringos as they travel throughout Latin America. I'll be doing my best to get up to speed as quickly as I can so that I might impart some travel wisdom, but until I can talk with any kind of authority, what I would probably suggest you do is read every word I post and then proceed in the exact opposite manner. I don't want to be responsible for you, dear reader, ending up in a ditch being urinated on by a herd of vicunas, which my guide book tells me are close personal relatives of the llama.

I have briefly Googled what is expected of a travel blogger and it seems to involve quite a bit of sharing the contents of one's backpack. Unfortunately I have recently become acquainted with a very bossy photographer who has deposited most of what I had in my backpack into a donation box. Apparently, I didn't need any of it because this isn't 1895 and I'm not a miner in the Klondike. If you are reading this in the hope of figuring what to take with you on a trip to South America you do not need the following: a camp stove, snow gaiters, panpipes and a flare. Who knew? I certainly didn't. Now that we've got that out of the way, in the absence of me being able to share photos of my 'gear', you'll just have to read the below summarised 60 day itinerary (in case you wanted to follow along at home):

At the moment we* are in Buenos Aires, Argentina where we'll be ~~getting lost~~ checking out the city sights. From there we'll be heading out on a bicycle tour of the vineyards of Mendoza. After Mendoza, it's onwards to Salta in search of cowboys.

In our next country on the tour, Bolivia, we'll be hitting the largest salt flats in the world, then on to Sucre via Potosi and then to the capital city, La Paz. I have been advised that from La Paz we are flying in a very small plane to the Amazonian jungle town of Rurrenabaque where we will be fishing for piranha, hunting for anaconda, and likely praying to see the light of another day.

The next stop is Peru, which will largely consist of the Inca Trail and Machu Picchu, but we'll also be taking in several small towns and spending time on the coast, volunteering at a Hare Krishna eco village where we'll probably be knitting jerseys out of human hair.

If we are still alive by that stage, we will then make our way to Ecuador where we are supposed to be doing all manner of adrenaline activities (yay). And then it's on to Colombia. I would say that here we'll probably be attempting to consume as much coffee and cocaine as possible in at least Salento, Bogota, Medellin, Taganga and Cartagena. The grand finale will involve sailing from Colombia across the Caribbean Sea, through the San Blas islands to Panama (which I am fully aware is in Central America, not South America).

Obviously if we are murdered by drug smugglers we may have to deviate slightly from the above.

Please bear with us if this eventuates.

In closing, I wanted to get mildly philosophical. I have noted that many travel bloggers are partial to quoting Tolkien's, 'Not all those who wander are lost'. I would like to be clear that if I am wandering around, you should bet your macadamia nuts that I am probably lost.

And that is all I have to say about that.
Lucy Hart
*I am joined by the very bossy photographer.

Chapter 8

"Kkgghhhhh."

My head snapped up and hit the back of my headrest.

"W-what happened?" I demanded, looking around the half-full city bus.

"What happened was that you were snoring so loudly you actually woke yourself up," replied Jack, peering at me over the top of his sunglasses.

"Oh." I leaned my forehead against the dirty window and stared out at the streets of Buenos Aires. Jack had been dragging me from sight to sight since we left the safety of our hostel that morning, determined to photograph the whole city while I half-heartedly took notes. We'd been on and off so many buses that I'd lost track of where we were. And by the afternoon my hangover had matured like smelly cheese into a full-blown head-pounding shake-fest. My poor body's only survival mechanism was to fall sleep every chance it got.

The nails-in-a-blender noise that had awoken me, had come from the pack of man-eating llamas who were currently haunting my dreams. They snapped their long yellow teeth as they advanced on me and had just closed in when I woke myself up. Jack was poring over a map circling more landmarks to prolong my punishment. He was so serious about his job that I wondered what drove him. The side eye he kept throwing my way made me feel like a surgeon who'd gotten shit-faced before performing open-heart surgery. I yawned loudly.

"Lucy, don't fall asleep again. We're nearly at our next stop," snapped Jack. I mumbled something rude under my breath just as my head flopped back onto my chest.

* * *

"Kkgghhhhh."

My whole body jerked. Those damn man-eating llamas had almost gotten me that time! Those huge, rabid, frothing at the mouth man-eating llamas. I shuddered. Jack and I had been surrounded by a pack of them. And even as we were seconds away from a violent and bloody death, Jack was still giving me a hard time.

"Oh, if only we had your panpipes now, Lucy," he'd mocked in a falsetto voice. But I got the last laugh. Not long after the words were out of his mouth, a shaggy brown llama with red eyes had chomped off his arm and blood had spurted from his shoulder like a dark chocolate fountain. Ha! I shot Jack a triumphant look, but he wasn't there. I stood and peered around the bus, hoping he was just pretending to hide to teach me a lesson.

But he was gone.

Chapter 9

After I searched for Jack under all the seats in the bus and alarmed the passengers I decided the best course of action was to get off, before I ended up in Venezuela.

As panic clawed my throat, I hopped off and stood with my back against the bus shelter, trying to gather my wits. I had to find my way back to the hostel—without a map or any Spanish vocabulary. Still safely pressed against the bus shelter and without drawing too much attention to myself, I looked left and right for familiar landmarks. Any direction could send me into the path of a mugger or the end of a rusty knife, so I needed to be careful. I didn't know much but I knew that if I continued to stand there, sweating like a racehorse, I was sure to be a target.

But I didn't know which way to go.

"Fucking Jack. When I see him …" I mumbled, grinding my teeth.

I looked to my left. The street was relatively empty. I peered to my right and—holy shit, there was a man standing close to me, reaching out his hand. I screamed and the man took a step back, his eyebrows furrowed with hurt and confusion.

A few people stopped to stare. I clamped my mouth shut and only then noticed the pamphlet in his outstretched hand. He wasn't trying to murder me, he was trying to give me something. I took the paper, with an embarrassed smile, and saw that it was an advert written in English for Spanish lessons.

I attempted to communicate with him with just my eyeballs:

Dear, Nice Man. I am so sorry for jumping to conclusions and assuming that you wanted to murder me, when all you wanted to do was advise me about the half-price Thursday Spanish lessons at Raul's Spanish School in San Telmo. You are kind and I am a shithead. Thank you. Best, Lucy.

When my telepathy clearly didn't work I gave him a thumbs up and jammed the paper into my bag. He shook his head as I scooted away and headed off down the street with all the confidence I could muster. I passed a few people who'd obviously witnessed my little scene and nodded and smiled as they continued to stare.

It took crossing a few roads and ducking around a corner to get a safe distance from the scene of my shame.

The street in front of me was narrow and cobbled and was dotted with restaurants and shops selling ice cream and clothes. Nothing looked familiar.

Get your shit together, Hart.

Across the street a blonde woman stopped to take a photo of a colourful graffiti mural splashed across a wall. She wore a bright, flowing skirt, tank top and luminous yellow scarf and seemed vaguely familiar. I realised she'd been the woman in the hostel bar the night before. I remembered wanting to shove her bloody yellow scarf in her mouth to stop her from laughing. The woman put her camera back in the leather bag slung across her body and headed off down the street away from me.

She looked so confident, so sure of where she was going that I made the split second decision to follow her. She'd know how to get back to our hostel. I couldn't trust myself to get back by myself, but there was something about this woman's swagger that made me trust her instead.

And I'm aware that I could have just walked up to her and asked her for help instead of stalking her like a creep, but what was I going to say? I fell asleep on a bus because I was hung-over, llamas were trying to eat me and I'm a useless individual? I already felt like enough of a tit thank you very much, so instead I followed a safe distance behind her and tried to look normal.

When she pulled out her camera to snap off photos of more graffiti or an interesting street scene, I'd stop and look around. I even sidled up to a teenage girl on the street and nodded my head, pretending to talk to her, even laughing loudly as if she'd said something hilarious. She backed away from me slowly, then ran. The blonde looked up and down the street and caught me staring at her, so I stuck my hands in my pockets and did a little dance on the spot, as if I was just there in the street, enjoying myself. When she continued on her way I waited to put some distance between us before resuming my stalking. I was already exhausted after my day of sightseeing and I prayed she'd lead me somewhere safe soon.

But she kept walking. And walking. Stopping inside a bookstore at one point, and snapping off photos every now and then. Each time she'd stop I'd loiter behind a lamppost and think about how much I hated Jack as I waited.

He was the reason I was in this mess in the first place. I hadn't asked for this assignment and he was taking it upon himself to punish me for choices that had been out of my control. Okay, so yes, my normal life wasn't exactly snowflakes and chocolate-covered strawberries but at least the chances of dying on the street were slim. I was lucky that my life was dead-end dull. Most of the world couldn't say the same.

After about an hour of following her my feet were throbbing and

I wanted to give up. I was about to sink, defeated, to the dirty pavement when she headed into a building with a familiar yellow door. And I spotted a familiar face leaning against the wall on the street near the door.

Jack.

That bastard.

I resisted the urge to shout over to him and watched him from behind a signpost.

He looked at his watch, ran his hand through his dark hair and kicked the wall behind him. If I didn't know any better I would have thought Jack actually looked worried about me.

* * *

I stood in the doorway of our hostel where I'd seen Jack disappear a few minutes earlier. From the look on his face I decided he must have been feeling dreadful about leaving me on the bus. He was probably picturing me dead in a dustbin sans liver. God. If I was him I'd be distraught too.

Maybe he'd be so riddled with remorse that this whole unfortunate incident would actually bond us. I decided if I could be gracious in my acceptance of his grovelling he'd see I was mature. How did one look mature? I needed to practice, so I drew my mouth into a line and tilted my head, patting the tall palm tree in the corner, pretending the large leaf was Jack's arm, outstretched in peace.

"Lucy, are you okay? What are you doing to that plant?" I looked up to see Jack standing there with his laptop under his arm.

"I was just, uh, well never mind," I spluttered, dropping the leaf.

Jack tapped his watch. "It took you long enough to get back, didn't it?"

My mouth dropped open. What? No tear-soaked apology? No over-the-top outpouring of regret? I fumed as Jack turned and headed off, like he hadn't left me to die on the streets of Buenos Aires. I stormed after him, stomping my feet on the tiled floor, suddenly feeling energised.

"I can't believe you left me on the bus!" I hissed, following him to the downstairs common room. While I was red-faced and fuming, he remained calm and sweat-free. Jack shrugged, sat at an empty table, switched on his camera and opened his MacBook.

"Are you not even going to apologise?" I asked, narrowing my eyes. But he just stared at his screen, so I pushed the MacBook closed. He took a deep breath, his hands clenching into fists and the tendons in his jaw twitching.

Usually I pulled away from any emotion stronger than mild irritation. This was probably because whenever I felt even the tiniest spark of anger ignite in my chest I'd hear my eighth grade teacher Mrs Johnson in my head telling me how "unnecessary" it was to lose one's temper.

When I think about it now it seems like such a strange thing to say to a thirteen-year-old kid since that's exactly when you really start to feel EVERYTHING. But what did I know, anyway? Whatever the reason, my comfortable emotional range was somewhere between a three and a half and a six. Anywhere outside that and I was scrambling to get back to equilibrium.

But I'd had a shitty day and Jack had just rubbed my last nerve raw. It therefore felt very *necessary* to make sure he knew.

"I told you not to fall asleep and you did. Okay? As I see it you were in the wrong. So why don't we just drop it?" he said, opening up his Mac again. But I just pushed it shut, this time even harder.

"How mature." Jack was being the model of a zen arsehole and I wanted to scream. My fingers itched to pick up his Mac and smash his perfect white teeth.

We were interrupted by a laugh on the other side of the room. "Holy shit! Look at all this stuff, dude!"

Jack and I looked over in the direction of the voice.

Jack raised his eyebrows. "He's found all your stuff." He nodded at the two guys pawing through the things which Jack had stuck in the donation bin that morning. My heart sank. I knew people would find my discarded belongings soon enough but I'd hoped to be nowhere near them when they did. It was as though someone was reading my journal and laughing at what I'd written. I was the joke who'd brought a portable defibrillator all the way to South America. I gritted my teeth and steeled myself for more derision.

"No WAY, man!" exclaimed the guy's friend, pulling out the rope. They sounded American. Why did Americans have to sound so damned excited about everything? They were going to attract the entire hostel if they didn't keep it down.

"I have to get out of here," I whispered, more to myself than to Jack, and I slunk towards the door with my head down.

The first guy held up my snow jacket, staring at the label at the collar. "Who do you think Lucy Hart is?"

I stopped and stared at them, forgetting for a second that my mum had insisted on sewing labels onto my clothes so that I wouldn't lose them. Like I was five years old at big school. I wheeled around to face Jack and narrowed my eyes as a warning to keep his big mouth shut.

Jack picked up his Mac and waved it at me as if to say 'bring it', his dark eyes glinting like shiny guns in the fluorescent light. "That's Lucy Hart right there," he said, pointing at me.

I wanted the earth to swallow me up.

"Holy shit! *You're* Lucy? But this stuff is amazing. Why are you throwing it out?" exclaimed the guy currently pawing my jacket. I stared at him in confusion.

"I thought—I mean I was told—it was overkill to bring all of that with me, so I dumped it," I said.

"What? Whoever told you to throw this stuff out is an idiot!"

Ha! Payback, motherfucker, I thought as I turned and pointed at Jack who looked completely gobsmacked.

"That guy told me!" I said. In yo' face, Jack!

The second guy threw Jack a look of disgust. "Dude, this stuff is gold!"

"Hey, I'm Benny," said the first guy, then pointing a thumb at his friend, added, "and this is my friend, Steve."

"Lucy," I said, shaking both their hands. "The idiot over there is Jack." I pointed over my shoulder and they nodded.

"We've been driving our motorbikes from Ushuaia in the south and we're heading all the way up to the top of Alaska," explained Benny.

"Yeah. And one of the bags in my pannier got stolen when we stopped off to refuel on our way into Buenos Aires," said Steve. "It was going to cost a shedload to replace and I was freaking out a bit. Seriously. This stuff is amazing. I had rope, a sleeping bag, pot, a filtration unit and lock, all stolen."

I turned and stared at Jack, hoping to turn him to stone with one dirty look.

"Lucy," he said softly. "You're not riding a motorcycle up two continents. You *know* you didn't need that stuff."

I knew he was right. Even if he'd been a complete condescending arse about it.

"Whatever you say, dude," said Steve, sounding unconvinced. "Lucy, are you sure you want to chuck it all out. How much did it cost?"

"I'm doing some travel writing in South America for the newspaper I work for. Jack is taking the photos. So the newspaper actually covered most of the bill. Take it all. It sounds like you need it."

"Can't I at least give you something for it?" asked Steve.

I shook my head. For a single moment I didn't feel like such a chopstick, and that felt like a gift.

"Wow!" Still holding the roll of rope in his hands, Steve wrapped his arms around me in a massive hug. "Thank you, Lucy. You're a legend."

Benny nudged Steve. "Hey, you know what? We managed to get some tickets for the La Boca game and we have two extra. Did you want to come with us, Lucy? To thank you for all this stuff?"

"That's very nice of you but I don't know what a La Boca game is," I said politely.

"La Boca Juniors vs River Plate?" said Jack, his voice strangely high-pitched.

I looked over to see him scrambling up from his seat. Steve nodded.

"How the hell did you get tickets? I tried when I first arrived in BA?"

Benny smirked. "Steve hooked up with the hostel receptionist. She knows a guy who knows another guy."

"Wait. Am I missing something? What game? Why is this such a big deal?" I looked between the three of them.

Jack's eyes were shining like a small boy's at Christmas. "Lucy, La Boca / River games are famous!"

"I'm assuming you're talking about some kind of sport?" I asked.

"Football," said Jack at the same time Steve and Benny said, "Soccer."

"I guess that sounds like fun." I shrugged and nodded. "Thanks guys. That would be great."

Jack cleared this throat. I narrowed my eyes at him, tempted to spite him, but decided to show him *I* could be mature.

"You said you had two tickets. May Jack come too?"

The boys exchanged a look, before Steve eventually shrugged. "If you want him to come he can come."

60 DAYS IN SOUTH AMERICA

Day 1: I came, I saw, I got kissed on the mouth by an old man at a football match

Yes, I've probably given the game away with the title of this post, but you may still be interested in reading the whole thing to find out how this came to pass.

First off, I feel like someone should have prepared me for the mind-bonk that is a La Boca Juniors / River Plate futbol match. My suggestion: Tickets should come with a warning message in large red letters. PELIGRO. DANGER. (And, yes I am comparing soccer to smoking.) Why did no one take this shaking travel virgin aside and gently tell me about just how real shit was going to get?

I mean, yes fine, the signs were there. The Argentines are passionate mofos, after all. I may have only been in this country for a day, but the passion hits you over the head as soon as you step off the plane. You can feel it in the angry-beautiful graffiti scrawled across the sides of buildings, in the way people smile with their whole bodies and talk with their hands. You can even see it in the way the little old ladies curse at you when you trip over them mid-sprint through an airport to hide in the bathroom. It really should have been obvious that this passion would extend to the nation's favourite sport.

So take that passion, multiply it by the fact that La Boca and River have been playing each other for over a century, and what do you get? You get a giant red, white, blue and yellow confetti-filled piñata with a live stick of dynamite up its arse. A hundred years is a long time for a rivalry to mature, for families to take sides, for lines to be etched into the dirt in blood. Literally. And what's a rivalry without a little trash talk? Boca fans call the River team las gallinas, or the chickens, because they supposedly choke when it really matters. River fans are a little more colourful, coining the nickname los bosteros, or pieces of shit.

The Chickens vs The Shit.

I trust I've set the scene sufficiently.

Now, I can't tell you very much about the game. Who kicked the ball to whom, how many tries (?) / goals (?) / points (?) were scored, who kicked who in the shins. This was partly because I spent most of the game pressed against a mob of tall, sweaty men and unable to see anything, and partly because I was too busy watching the sky for projectiles sailing over the ten metre high fence which separated the La Boca fans from the River fans.

One of the guards who had searched us on our way into the stadium had taken my lip balm. "Proyectil," he'd said, waggling his index finger at me like I was a bad dog. Ironic, since he'd behaved like the bad dog, ramming his hands into my front pockets without warning to search for weapons. The search should have reassured me that the crowd would be free of potential flying objects, but it hadn't. Having my beauty products removed from my person meant there was a precedent for women hurling make-up at each other. Something else that should have reassured me was the fact that fans on opposing sides were requested to enter the stadium separately and at different times "to reduce violence". But that hadn't been very reassuring either.

Thank Beyonce's left tit we were in the La Boca section, because they ended up beating River Plate one - zero. We were in the happy winner's camp, instead of the furious "I'm going to tear your face off" losing camp. And I mean that. People in the River section tried to climb over the fence into our section but were unsuccessful after the burly guards beat them off.

All around us people yelled and waved their arms. The roar was deafening, and we were so tightly packed into the stands that I couldn't lift my hands to my ears to block the sound. After the game, fireworks crisscrossed the night, erupting sporadically from random sections of the stadium. Even in the midst of the chaos, I struggled to find the words to adequately describe the atmosphere. The best I could come up with was a cross between a Mardi Gras parade and a prison riot. Blue and yellow streamers and smoke fills the sky and you're not sure who wants to kill you and who wants to kiss you.

Which brings this story full circle. Because we had been shepherded into the stadium first, we were allowed to leave first. And as I shuffled towards the exit, squished against the people in my section, an old man came up to me, pulled my face to his and kissed me full and hard on the mouth, before throwing his hands up in the air in jubilation. And what could I do but laugh at his pure, infectious joy. As he was swallowed up by the crowd, the world seemed a little bit more inviting than it had a moment before.

It's amazing how a gesture so small can replace the lens through which you view everything around you.

That is all I have to say about that.
Lucy Hart

Next Destination: Beginner's Spanish

Chapter 10

Email:

To: l.hart@standard.com
From: j.henry@gbk.com.au

Dear Lucy Hart (Travel Blogger),

I'm writing to you as I recently came across your blog posts in The Standard's online travel section. I wanted to tell you what a huge fan I am of your work.

OMFG, Luce, I'm SO proud of you. And I'm *loving* your posts so far, and from the looks of the blog's comments section, other people are warming to Lucy Hart's take on travel too.

Yikes! That soccer match sounded mad!

I'm glad you have this photographer guy to look after you. Speaking of, you need to tell me all about him! I stalked him online and found a whole long article on him and how fabulous he's supposed to be. I think it's so cool that he decided that photography was his passion and he quit his job in Banking three years ago to pursue it as a career. It's kind of romantic, don't you think? And I have to say he's pretty hunky.

Tell me everything immediately.

Love Jules AKA Your biggest fan x

Email:

To: j.henry@gbk.com.au
From: l.hart@standard.com

Dearest Darlingest Jules,

Thanks, my biggest fan. And yes, people do seem to enjoy the fact that I am scared ninety-six percent of the time and only have my shit together for the other four percent. People are odd. Between you and me I thought if I wrote like I was a crazy person and hardly mentioned travel the whole thing would tank and Rob would send me home. I know. Pathetic.

Now I don't know what articles about Jack you've been reading but they sound like filthy lies. He is the end of a penis. I don't care how dreamy it is that he quit his job to run around the world taking photos. Because if he rolls his eyes at me one more time I'm going to suffocate him in the middle of the night. (Easily achieved given the fact that I sleep about two metres from his stupid face.) Ugh. He brings out a seriously violent streak in me.

What is he like, you ask? He enjoys long walks on his high horse and complaining to his girlfriend Nöel about me on Skype.

*Sigh.

He thinks I am a complete nincompoop, Jules. And I'm trying my best, really I am.

Also, he isn't a hunk. He wears a constant smirk on his face and t-shirts with holes in them and he's all lanky which you know is not my type. And, I don't think he's brushed his hair since before Facebook was a thing. Anyway, even if *I* could get over the fact he's an arse and *he* could get over the fact I am a lunatic, it would be against the laws of nature for him to go for me since his girlfriend is the most beautiful woman that has ever walked on land. (I looked over his shoulder when he was messaging her and might have accidentally Googled her.) Plus she's a Doctors without Borders type who vaccinates orphans and bathes lepers. So there's that.

Guacamole & Good Times. X

Email:

To: l.hart@standard.com
From: j.henry@gbk.com.au

Jack sounds terrible, and I will henceforth despise him on your behalf. Bit of a pity really. He sounded lovely in the article. Anyway, even if he is a complete shit I *am* glad you aren't on your own in deepest, darkest South America.

I miss you.

Love your face off. XXX

P.S. Martin sends his love.

P.P.S. You're not pathetic. You're wonderful.

60 DAYS IN SOUTH AMERICA

Day 2: Spanish Lessons from A Sex Bomb

A rite of passage as a backpacker in Latin America is the obligatory Spanish lesson, or a handful of lessons at the very least.

This makes sense, unlike most of the other activities that will be thrust upon me during this trip. Although I am sure I could get away with playing an elaborate game of charades every time I wanted to order lunch, it is only right that I at least attempt to learn the language. (Please note the emphasis on the word attempt. Don't judge me by the end of this trip if I still don't know my pollo from my pescado.) While I pride myself on being of at least average intelligence, learning Spanish is more difficult than it looks, especially when one is being distracted from the task at hand.

Which brings me to the real topic of this post: Renaldo.

Renaldo is my Spanish teacher. And he is in-the-flesh the hottest piece of ass I have ever clapped eyeballs on.

Seriously.

Renaldo so hot, he's practically a spiritual experience. I now understand what people feel like when they see the Sistine Chapel or taste cheese for the first time.

Renaldo so hot, he moves in slow motion. When he flicks his shoulder-length dark hair, or gesticulates, the world moves in slow motion along with him.

Renaldo so hot, the hills are alive with the sound of his music i.e. the heavy breathing and loud sighing that must follow him everywhere.

Renaldo so hot, he should be sprayed with a hosepipe to cool him down. Preferably while wearing a white t-shirt.

Renaldo so hot, he is actually the cause of global warming. But don't blame him for the melting glaciers. He can't help it. He be born that way.

During my lesson, I even tried to sneak a photo of him with my iPhone so I could post it for all to see, but all I got were photos of my fellow student Pete's hairy arm. I suspect if I had managed to get a good shot of Renaldo's fineness it would have malfunctioned anyway. Jack the Photographer refused when I suggested we ~~stalk~~ *follow Renaldo home in case any photographic opportunities arose, say, like from a tree outside his bedroom while he was getting undressed to have a shower.*

But I assure you the class hasn't all been drooling and panting. Learning a language is serious business. Today, for example, I learned several phrases that I asked Renaldo to translate from English into Spanish. I thought they might come in as handy for you as they would for me.

English phrase: "I want to have your babies."
Spanish translation: "Yo quiero tener a tus bebes."

English phrase: "I want to run my fingers through your beautiful hair."
Spanish translation: "Yo quiero pasar mis dedos por tu bello cabello."

English phrase: "Take off all your clothes immediately."
Spanish translation: "Quitate todo la ropa inmediatamente."

English phrase: "I want to spread you on a cracker."
Spanish translation: "Quiero esparcirlo en una galleta."

You're welcome.

That is all I have to say about that.
Lucy Hart

Next destination: Mendoza

Chapter 11

Email:

To: pamdalehart@pmail.com
From: l.hart@standard.com

Dear Parents,

Just a quick note to confirm, as requested, that I am still alive. (Five days down, fifty-five days to go. Blerugh.)

Jack, the photographer, is STILL an absolute shit. I suspect he stores his tripod up his arse. He thinks your daughter is ridiculous.

Anyway, we're in Mendoza at the moment after a few days in Buenos Aires. (I'm sure you've been reading my blog posts though. **hint hint**) Buenos Aires was nice, the little of it that I saw, mostly through dirty bus windows.

Hope you're both well? Miss you.

Love Lucy x

Email:

To: l.hart@standard.com
From: pamdalehart@pmail.com

Hello Darling,

Thanks for letting us know you're still all right. We do worry about you. I'm sorry to hear this Jack character is being mean to you. Maybe you just need some time to get used to each other. You do tend to judge people too quickly. Remember that time you announced that our neighbour Janie Williams was a real live witch?

And of course we're reading your blog posts. I'm emailing all of them to your grandmother. Well except the Spanish teacher one, as that was a bit risqué.

Everything is the same with us.

I went to book club last night. It was at Sandy's house and she made us a chicken curry and rice but I don't think it was as good as the meal I made when it was my turn to host book club. But obviously I didn't tell her that.

Your dad played golf the other day and Ronald rode over his foot with a golf cart and he thinks it's broken. But don't worry, he's fine. He'll just be hobbling around in a moon boot for the next few weeks.

Anyway. Please let's Skype soon. I got my computer fixed and I got our neighbour Jill's son (the one who is adopted) to set me up with a Skype account and he's written down how to use it.

Love you Lucy.

Please stay safe.

Your mother. X

P.S. Your dad sends his love.

Email:

To: pamdalehart@pmail.com
From: l.hart@standard.com

Well to be fair re: my thinking about Miss Williams being a witch, I *had* just read Roald Dahl's Witches book and I thought everyone was a witch.

XO

60 DAYS IN SOUTH AMERICA

Day 4: Tour de Mendoza

I would so love to report back on my cycling tour of the vineyards of Mendoza to give you an idea of what you could expect should you feel the pull to whimsically wind your way around the dusty tree-lined roads, stopping at wineries to sample their wares. But unfortunately it was a bit of a blur since I got stuck cycling with The Photographer and The Jocks (hi Benny and Steve!) and apparently it was a race to see who could get drunk the fastest. This was achieved by sprinting between wineries, knocking back whichever Malbec was on the menu, before climbing back on to their bicycles and roaring off to the next winery, with me eating their dust.

Eventually I gave up trying to keep up with the peloton and limped my bike back to Mr Garcia from whom we'd hired our bikes at the start of the morning. This lovely smiling man was so kind as to hand me a big plastic cup of his homemade wine and sit with me in companionable silence while I waited for the boys. Every now and then I would sigh dramatically then he would copy me then we'd look at each other and start laughing. We managed a whole conversation with just hand signals and smiles, while I pretended to sip Mr Garcia's battery acid brew, nervous that it might actually make me go blind.

I suspect the boys were trying to prove their masculinity to each other in a language they could all understand: alcohol consumption.
It makes me wonder if this competitiveness comes pre-installed in men, like air-conditioning in a Ford, or if it's a learned trait. I'm

ninety-eight percent sure that the only pre-loaded operating software I came with gives me the ability to cry at the drop of a hat and sniff out a wedge of brie from fifty paces.

I did take a quiet minute to thank Buddha, between getting my toes stuck in the spokes of my bicycle and wiping the sweat from my brow for the seventy-third time, that I was born with a flower garden between my legs instead of the alternative. But it does make me wonder if the way I interact with the world has been learned unconsciously over time or if this is just all me?

Because if this was learned, how do I unlearn it? How does one go about rebooting a human brain?

And if this is just me and I'm stuck like this, then "we're going to need a bigger boat." And I'm going to have to research how to import my new friend's homemade wine to Australia.

And if you're wondering who won the Tour de Mendoza I can tell you that at the end of the day Wine was the winner, because all three boys currently have their heads in toilets and have been that way all morning.

That is all I have to say about that.
Lucy Hart

Next destination: Salta

Chapter 12

My horse was having a bad day.

For the half an hour we'd known each other, he'd chosen to ignore all my instructions and focus his attention on eating grass instead.

Per Candy, one of the activities every discerning backpacker should undertake was horse riding with cowboys, or gauchos as they're called here, in the hills outside the city of Salta, in the north of Argentina. We'd been delayed by a day because Jack had been too sick to leave Mendoza after partaking of too much of the Malbec. He'd been livid when he'd read my Mendoza blog post and was obviously feeling like a right tonsil for doing the exact thing he'd lectured me about—getting drunk on the job—so he'd sharpened his condescending tone accordingly and was poking me with it every chance he got. I hadn't told Jack that I was scared of horses and that I had never ridden one before. Instead I'd hoped to show him I was up to the task. But the half a ton of grumpy animal between my legs had other ideas.

I clicked my tongue and pressed my heels hard into the horse's side like the gaucho had demonstrated, but when this sent the massive animal skittering sideways, I immediately stopped.

Jack was a little way ahead, and I called after him. "Jack, I think there's something wrong with my horse."

"Rubbish. You just need to show him who's boss," he snapped over his shoulder.

I didn't care what Jack said, there was definitely something wrong with Rambo. This wasn't his actual name. But when I'd asked our guide, Santiago, the horse's name, he'd shrugged, so it seemed only right to make one up. I'd nicknamed him Rambo because he looked like a troubled war veteran with something to prove. Whatever his real name, from one mammal to the next, I could tell he wasn't pleased, and I was trying not to take it personally.

"I really don't think his issues have anything to do with my lack of horse riding skills. He's not happy. Maybe we should swap horses? Your horse looks like he's in a much better mood," I said to Jack's back.

"Lucy! Stop buggering around. You're holding everyone up. It won't make any difference if we swap horses. Now move it."

I sighed. It was true. I *was* holding everyone up. Our group included me and Jack, four super-fly Danish guys travelling together, and a German couple. I wasn't making friends with any of them since they'd already had to stop for me several times. But I was sure if I rode Jack's horse, whom I'd nicknamed Tinkerbell because he had the biggest willy I'd ever seen, I would do a better job of keeping up.

"Rambo," I said, patting my horse's neck with one hand while gripping the reins with the other. "You don't mind if I call you that, do you? Now I can only imagine how you feel. I'd also be annoyed if a large woman sat on top of me. But I think we need to make the best of a bad situation, don't you?"

He snorted in response.

I continued, talking to my steed in my calmest spa lady voice. "Do you think I want to be here, Rambo, Sir? I mean. I get it. You'd rather be in the paddock eating hay or, like, shooting bad guys or whatever, but we need to work together on this. The world is *not* against you."

When this didn't work I thrust my hips so violently forward I think I pulled a muscle. But he still wouldn't budge.

"You guys keep going. I'm going to get off and walk," I called after the rest of the group.

Jack yanked Tinkerbell, did a U-turn and cantered up to me before I could get off.

"No you're not! You'll just get lost and then I'll have to come and find you. Just give your horse a kick."

I hadn't told Jack about following the blonde back to the hostel. Unless something major happened to change the trajectory of this relationship I was going to take that information to the grave.

I gave my horse a reluctant nudge with my hiking boot, already knowing it wouldn't have the desired effect. Instead of making him go forward he reversed.

"Harder!"

I nudged him harder as directed.

"Oh for fucksake!" fumed Jack as he gave my horse a loud whack on the backside.

With that, Rambo reared up on his back legs and I grappled for reins, hair, saddle, anything to keep me from sliding off and into the mud.

Jack reached for my horse to calm him down. "Whoa," he said.

But Rambo wanted to get as far away from Jack as quickly as possible, a sentiment I could sympathise with. He bolted off along the trail, whipping through the pack of riders ahead of him. I crouched over his neck, clung to the reins and pressed my legs tight around him, which only made him go faster. The sound of heavy hooves thundered behind us, and although the other riders seemed to be gaining on us, Rambo was faster.

Jack shouted behind me. "Lucy, pull hard on the reins. You need to slow him down!"

"Despacio!" shouted someone else. Slow down? Did they think I was trying to make him go fast? Maybe Rambo only spoke Spanish? That made sense. Unfortunately, the only Spanish phrases I could think of would have made us both extremely uncomfortable.

I desperately yanked on the reins, but that seemed to piss Rambo off even more. He snorted, jerked his head and wrenched the reins from my hands, sending me off-balance. I only managed to right myself by grabbing his mane, just in time to see us hurtling towards a fallen tree in the middle of the trail. I squeezed my eyes shut and clung to chunks of horsehair.

At the last minute Rambo decided he wouldn't be jumping the tree today. He stopped so suddenly that the force sent me flying over him *and* the tree, into the soft, squidgy mud which cushioned my fall. I pulled my face out of the muck and rolled over on to my back, wiggling my fingers and toes to check if I'd broken anything. Finding everything intact, I flopped my head back onto the ground, with a squelch.

Jack knelt beside me. "Lucy, are you okay? God. I'm so sorry. That was all my fault. I'm such a dick. Does it hurt? How do you feel?"

My horse, who by now was behind the tree chewing on grass, whinnied his disdain for Jack loudly—I tended to agree.

I squinted at him. "Rambo hates you."

Jack looked up at our guide, horrified. "Oh my God! She's concussed. We need to get her to a doctor."

Chapter 13

I wasn't concussed. Obviously.

But Jack had insisted on rushing me to the nearest clinic anyway. And it was quite nice to be bathed in his concern for a change so I decided not to clear up the misunderstanding. What was one little secret amongst friends?

It had been a rush to get to the bus on time after getting the all clear from the doctor, but we'd made it.

When I first saw the rusted old bus squatting at the station waiting to take us through the night to the border between Argentina and Bolivia I'd been disappointed, having become quite accustomed to the fancy long distance buses we'd travelled in so far. They'd made me feel like I was touring with Madonna or something. Inside, the bus smelled of stale sweat and dirty metal. Grubby curtains hung from the windows, giving the interior a dark, dingy feel. By the time we'd boarded it was almost full, so we took a pair of seats towards the back.

It wasn't long into our bus trip to La Quiaca—maybe an hour or so—when my stomach grumbled like a monster in a Roald Dahl book. I shifted in my seat, finding it difficult to get comfortable.

Jack looked up, frowning. "What was that?"

Somehow the chickens clucking and people talking over the growl of the old engine wasn't enough to drown out the noises my digestive system was making.

I feigned ignorance as my stomach grumbled again—this time more loudly. "I didn't hear anything."

Jack glanced down at where my hands were covering my belly. "Was that your stomach?"

"No," I lied, as another gurgle escaped. I coughed loudly.

"That *is* your stomach. If you're hungry I've got some snacks in my bag." Jack grabbed the plastic bag of snacks he'd shoved in the side pocket of his daypack. He was just being extra-nice to me since he'd nearly killed me with a horse.

"No, I'm good. I grabbed a hot dog from that stall in the alley behind the hostel."

Jack stared at me. "Really? From the alley with the rats?"

"I didn't see any rats." The judgement was back. "I just needed something substantial to take with my anti-inflammatories. You know, after I was thrown off a horse onto my face? My stomach is probably just struggling to digest it or something." I looked at him and he bit his tongue and looked out the window. Although the doctor had given me the all clear it didn't hurt to remind Jack why I'd hurt myself in the first place.

My stomach rumbled again, this time like a bubbling volcano on the verge of eruption. I focused on breathing in and out while rapidly sliding into panic. Something was wrong. A sharp pain stuck me in my gut and I couldn't stop myself from groaning out loud. I prayed it was just severe indigestion. The man and woman in the seats across the aisle craned their necks and stared at my now doubled over frame. Jack edged closer towards the safety of the window.

It was a seven-hour trip to our stop, where we were supposed to get off and walk across the border into Bolivia, before catching another bus to Tupiza. I took a deep breath and closed my eyes, willing myself to fall into a meditative state that would allow me to hold on for the remainder of the journey. Like a woman in labour, listening to whale music in a hypnotic trance, as she imagines pushing a grape out of her birth canal instead of a watermelon. But no sooner had I shut my eyes when my chest heaved involuntarily.

"Oh God. I think I'm going to be sick!"

To his credit Jack acted quickly, grabbing the plastic bag with his snacks, dumping them onto the floor and holding it in front of me, just in time for me to vomit into it. After nearly filling the small bag with the contents of my stomach, I sat up with my eyes closed and waited. Jack slid his window open. The cold night air rushing in made me feel a little better. I inhaled and exhaled deeply a few times.

"Thank you," I said, grateful for his quick thinking. "I think I feel better."

But the relief was short-lived. The words had barely left my mouth when I doubled over, clutching my stomach in pain with my left hand, my right hand still holding the bag of vomit. "No-no-no-no-no-no-no," I said over and over, rocking back and forth.

I thrust the bag in my hand at Jack and jumped up. "Hold my vomit!" I staggered up the aisle towards the bus driver, willing myself to hold on.

Don't shit yourself. Don't shit yourself. Don't shit yourself. Don't shit yourself.

I crouched down next to the driver. "Please stop the bus! I need the bathroom! El baño! Por favor!" I pleaded. Some of the passengers who'd fallen asleep woke up and started laughing at the wailing gringa at the front of the bus clutching her bum. The driver seemed reluctant to do as I asked, so I dropped to my knees and begged.

"Por favor, señor," I cried, tugging at his pant leg.

I was about to yank the wheel out of his hands and steer us off the road when he took pity on me and pulled the bus over.

"Gracias," I shouted as I raced down the stairs, unbuttoning my trousers and making a beeline in the dark for the nearest bush big enough to hide behind. When my pants were down around my ankles I relieved myself. A sense of absolute joy, like nothing I had ever experienced, came over me. I wrapped my arms around my knees, rested my head on my arms and congratulated myself on making it in time. This relief was temporary though as the gravity of the situation hit me. Food poisoning on a long bus trip was bad. How the hell was I going to get through this? I wasn't built for adventure and embarrassment. I was made for certainty and napping.

My mind flicked back to that night in the bath, when I'd wallowed in the water, trying not to hear Charlotte's sexploits. I'd been so sure that I wanted my life to change. But I'd been wrong. It had all been a big mistake. Bathing myself into oblivion beat shitting myself in Bolivia every single time.

"Lucy?" called Jack from somewhere in the darkness in front of me. Behind him I could hear the bus engine splutter and come to a stop. "I've got a roll of toilet paper. Do you want me to bring it over?"

"No!" I yelped.

"Come on, Lucy. You'll need toilet paper. I'll close my eyes, I promise."

"Close your nose too," I yelled.

I heard Jack stumble in the dark and swear loudly to himself. When my eyes adjusted I saw him over to my left walking gingerly, one hand half in front of his eyes, a toilet roll tucked under his armpit, the other hand holding his nose as directed. He stopped.

"Marco?" he called.

"Polo!" I called back.

"Marco?"

"Polo," I countered and started to giggle at the absurdity of the situation. Jack laughed, which given the circumstances was strangely reassuring.

"Marco?" he continued through his laughter.

"Polo!" I responded, by now almost hysterical with mirth. My chest shuddered against my bent knees as I laughed, resulting in me releasing a loud, gurgling fart. I laughed even harder. By the time Jack found me with the toilet roll he couldn't speak he was laughing so hard. He handed me the toilet paper round the bush, and I ripped some from the roll. In the distance the bus's engine started.

"Shit," muttered Jack.

"Jack, don't let the bus leave without us!" I yelped, hearing him run off.

I wiped quickly, pulled up my pants and sprinted towards the bus that had already started to pull on to the road, all while attempting to squeeze hand sanitiser into my palms and trying not to trip over my feet.

"Come on, Lucy!" said Jack as he hung out the open door. I willed myself to catch up with the old bus, which was beginning to gain momentum. When I was close enough, I leaped onto the bottom step and hoped that Jack would catch me. He easily did, pulling me up as the doors shut behind us. When the passengers saw me, they laughed and clapped. Not knowing what else to do, I waved and bowed.

"Gracias," I thanked the driver, even though I had my suspicions he might have left me with my pants around my ankles given half the chance, and I scurried back up the aisle to my seat. A few rows along a little boy sitting on his father's lap made farting noises into his arm, which his audience thought was hysterical.

"Thanks," I said to Jack, who nodded like it was no big deal.

Back in my seat I prayed the evening entertainment was over, but I must not have prayed hard enough, because the ordeal continued throughout the night. I was forced to de-bus several times and I vomited so much that eventually there was nothing left for me to get rid of—to put it delicately. The driver's patience waned more each time I begged him to stop, and I took to shitting behind the bus so that I was closer, in case he made a run for it. But this came with it's own perils as I had to duck down out of view of the passengers at the back while I squatted.

By the time we arrived at the border, I was completely empty. In Bolivia we caught the next bus to Tupiza, our final destination, without incident, although I did spend the entirety of the three-hour ride pitifully dry retching into my crooked elbow.

At our hostel I collapsed into a weeping heap at Jack's feet in front of the reception desk, which might have prompted him to switch our shared room to a private double room—to save any potential dorm mates from my dramatics. I leaned my head against the wooden desk and attempted to find the will to pick myself off the ground while he carried our bags to the room. And I'd almost succeeded when Jack stooped down and without a word scooped me into his arms as effortlessly as if I'd been an inflatable swan. The gentleness of the action was so overwhelming I leaned my head against his surprisingly sturdy chest and cried into the soft faded blue of his t-shirt.

"Do you think I'm going to die, Jack?" I whispered, my mouth mashed up against his front.

"No, Lucy. I know you feel awful, but I'm going to look after you. I promise you'll be okay."

The way he said this made me know it to be true. I knew I could trust him. But something in his whole manner also just made me crack a little more, so that when he deposited me gently on my bed, I slid down onto the cold floor and sobbed, pausing only to wipe my nose on the front of my dirty t-shirt, which smelled of sick.

While I cried, Jack unzipped my backpack and pulled out my toiletry bag, towel and clothes. "Come on, Lucy. Why don't you have a shower and get into bed?" He stuck my stuff in the en-suite bathroom and gestured towards the shower. "Do you need me to carry you to the bathroom?"

I thought about how he'd cradled me earlier and how it had felt so disgustingly nice to be held, but I didn't feel like I deserved to be carried the three metres to the shower, so I shook my head and crawled to the bathroom instead.

The hot water felt good as it ran over me and washed away the filth, so much so that I decided the shower should be my new home. I curled up into a ball on my new tiled palace and tried to calculate how long I'd been in South America and how much longer I had left, but my brain was mush and it was a struggle to compute.

There was a loud rap on the bathroom door. "Lucy? Are you alive in there?"

"No," I mumbled. "Don't come in here," I continued, a little louder, keeping a wary eye on the door. The last thing I needed was for this man I hardly knew to barge in and find me in the foetal position in the shower.

"Why don't you get out now and get some sleep?" He was being so patient and gentle, having done a complete 180 from the grumpy man who'd greeted me at the airport.

After Jack had coaxed me out from the bathroom I lay curled up in a ball in my single bed while he held a glass of water to my mouth and fed me dry crackers like a baby. It was nice to be looked after. Mike had never looked after me when I was sick, but that was mostly because it made me uncomfortable. I'd always struggled to accept anything that smelled like love from anyone who wasn't my family or Jules. I'd grown up reading women's magazines so I knew that you needed to *deserve* love before you could *be* loved. You needed to be good in bed, be thin but curvy but toned, know how to roast a side of beef, smile with all your teeth (especially when you didn't mean it) and be cool but approachable. And all while still being yourself, whatever that meant.

Even though the times they seemed to be a'changing—Love the woman in the mirror! Your stretch marks *are* beautiful! How can he love you if you don't love yourself *first?*—I couldn't help but wonder if the damage had been done. You can try to remove that regrettable tramp stamp tattoo with several rounds of painful laser treatments but it'll still always be there, won't it?

Right now though I didn't give a shit about any of that, because I was too busy unravelling at the seams. Plus Jack didn't see me like that anyway. I was an obligation, not an option.

"Thank you," I whispered, spitting bits of cracker onto the blanket. Jack patted my arm then put his hand on my forehead.

"You're hot," he said.

"You're sweet."

Jack rewarded my dumb joke with a smile and brushed a piece of wet hair off my forehead.

"It's cold in here." I moaned and shivered, sounding so pathetic to my own ears I didn't even want to know what I sounded like to his. But Jack just dusted cracker crumbs off my bed, pulled the blankets up and tucked me in.

"I'm going to go out to try and find you a doctor. Are you going to be okay while I'm gone?"

I stared up at his mouth but the shapes his lips made didn't seem to match the words that came out, like he'd been dubbed into another language. And then I passed out.

Later when I woke up, the room was dark and my bedding was wet, soaked with my sweat. I shuffled around the bed trying to find a dry patch to lie down, like a dog crawling around in the dirt looking for a comfortable place to die. When I found a spot at the foot of the bed I lay there shaking so violently, it was impossible to fall asleep. It could have been minutes or hours before the door opened and light from the hall flooded the room.

"Lucy? Lucy, are you okay? These sheets are wet," said Jack, patting the bed around me.

My whole body felt heavy.

"Shit. Your clothes are soaked too," he said, his arms on me, lifting me to move me onto his dry bed. I rocked and clenched my fists, doing anything to shift my attention away from the throbbing pain in my gut. Jack's cool hand was against my forehead, and he was swearing.

"No. Ge' off," I heard myself slur. Then I mumbled something like 'Cheese Sticks' and after that it was dark for a while. Until I felt someone pulling at my clothes. I struggled and pushed against the hands, but I was too weak to put up a fight. After that it got weird— there was shivering, possibly the slow clap, more vomiting, shaking, being surrounded by a circle of Care Bears, pain, crying, the Darth Vader music from Star Wars. And then sleep. I think?

Chapter 14

When I awoke, the light was streaming into the room through the netting curtains. The previous day was like a movie whose ending I couldn't recall, hard as I tried. What I did know was that someone was lying next to me on my bed. Craning my neck around, I saw Jack asleep, with his head at the foot of the bed, like we'd fallen asleep at a slumber party. My throat was dry and I reached for a bottle of water on the side table, guzzling it so hard, the plastic crackled under my hands. Jack stirred as I sucked the last drop from the bottle. He sat up and looked at me, rubbing his eyes.

I tried a small smile, unsure of what had happened. "Sorry I woke you."

"S'fine. How're you feeling?" he croaked, getting to his feet and stretching his arms above his head.

"Much better, thank you," I replied, looking up at him from where I lay.

He sat on the bed next to me and put his hand on my forehead. "You really worried me. Thank God I was able to find you a doctor."

I screwed up my face in a bid to remember. "A doctor was here, in our room? I don't remember that."

Jack smiled. "I'm not surprised. You were pretty out of it because of your fever. You hummed the Darth Vader theme and at one point you even said, "Gavin forgot to charge me and now my battery is dead."

I rubbed my temples and stared at him. "Well that makes no sense. Anyway, I feel so much better. What did he give me?"

"An injection in your bum."

I reached round behind me and winced when my hand brushed the tender spot where the needle must have pierced my skin.

"Jack? This might just be my imagination but I could have sworn I wasn't wearing this when I got into bed," I said, frowning in concentration.

"You're not imagining things. I had to change your clothes last night."

I closed my eyes. "Oh my God. Did I shit myself?"

Jack laughed. "No. You didn't shit yourself, Lucy, but you sweated like a pig. Everything got soaked. I changed you and moved you into my bed," he said.

Oh God. I sweated like a pig? The words every girl wants to hear. But hang on. "Jack. I'm still in my bed?"

"I had to change the bed and move you back after you soaked *my* bed. The hostel manager only had a limited supply of sheets."

"Oh my God. Thank you, Jack. I'm so sorry I put you through all that. As if babysitting me wasn't enough already." Ugh. I don't know why he hadn't just let me die.

"Lucy, it's fine. It wasn't your fault you got sick."

"You say that but I *did* eat a hot dog from a rat-infested alley."

Jack yawned and lay down so close his face was inches from mine. "I'm exhausted," he said, closing his eyes. His eyelashes looked like spiders' legs against his skin. We were so close, I could make out the odd freckle on his face and a faint smile line near the corner of his mouth. His breath was warm on my cheek. For a moment I thought he was dropping off to sleep until his eyes flew open.

His eyes crinkled with amusement. "Is it too soon to talk about how funny you were behind that bush when we were playing Marco Polo?"

I laughed and shook my head.

"Everyone wanted to get off the bus and see what you were doing, and I had to stop them."

"Oh God. I must have looked ridiculous!"

"And then you laughed so hard, you farted!" Jack recalled, his body shaking so hard, the narrow rickety bed rattled beneath us. When the laughter subsided we both lay there quietly.

"Seriously though. Thank you for looking after me. I honestly don't know what I would have done without you. I feel like you saved my life." I stared into his now serious dark eyes, our noses almost touching. We stayed that way for a few moments, looking at each other, not moving. I was surprised at how natural it felt to be lying next to this man who only a week before had been a complete stranger. I wondered what he was thinking.

"Lucy …" he said, hesitating. "I …"

Shit. I must have the worst vomit-breath. The poor guy, on top of the night he'd had, was probably trying to tell me that my breath was horrendous and I needed to brush my teeth ASAP. Cripes!

I sat up quickly. "I'm starving. That must be a good sign, right? Do you think it's safe for me to eat something that isn't dry crackers?"

60 DAYS IN SOUTH AMERICA

Days 9-12: The Salt Flats

The Photographer and I have just returned from a four-day tour of the Salt Flats of Uyuni.

For the uninitiated, the Salar de Uyuni is the largest salt flat in the world. It used to be a prehistoric lake, but all the water dried up thousands of years ago leaving behind metres of salty crust that contain about half the earth's lithium stores. This is supposedly enough to make like a gazillion electric batteries, but the Bolivian government has stuck it to all foreign governments showing any interest in exploiting the reserves, choosing instead to wait until they can do it on their own terms. At least this is the case according to our tour guide, Marco, who said that when the country has the resources to mine the lithium, "Bolivia will become as rich as Switzerland."

If you don't care about any of that you could still be blown away by the fact that the salt flats are so vast, they are visible from space. Or, you might be in awe of the coloured lakes covered in pink flamingos. You could be amazed by the kilometres of train graveyard on the outskirts of Uyuni or be dazzled by the islands of rocks and bushes dotting the landscape leftover from when the area was once under water.

But chances are the main thing you care about is the opportunity to take a million forced perspective photos. Especially if your name is Jack.

Forced perspective, you ask? You've probably seen those photos of tourists 'holding up' the leaning tower of Pisa or putting their fingers on the tip of the Eiffel Tower? Forced perspective tricks the eye by making objects look bigger, or smaller, than they actually are. The flat, white, unbroken surface of the salar provides the perfect setting for taking these kinds of photos, because you have no point of reference to put objects into perspective.

Google "Salt Flats + Bolivia" and you'll find pages of these photos—of tourists climbing out of a giant Pringles tubes, boyfriends sitting in the hands of their girlfriends, giant plastic dinosaurs terrorising groups of screaming travellers and people riding on fluffy toy llamas. Few places on the gringo trail rival the Salar de Uyuni for taking photos that'll make your friends and family jealous, because few people can boast about having a landscape in their home country that looks like the moon—if the moon was made of salt instead of cheese.

That last day on the tour our group spent hours taking photos. Constructing photo after photo was like an elaborate team building exercise. Someone had to take the photo. Someone had to direct operations. Someone had to be "the ideas man". Someone provided the props. Someone had to actually be in the photo. And afterwards everyone would huddle around the camera screen looking at what we'd created together.

It was kind of cool. I think I might have even had fun, which is blasphemy because usually team-building exercises give me hives.

And that's all I have to say about that.
Lucy Hart.

Next destination: Sucre, Bolivia

Chapter 15

Ka-boom!

The sound of something being blown up ripped me out of my daydream. I jumped in my seat, the still-cold bottle of orange juice in my hand almost slipping from my grasp. The bus slowed to a crawl and I turned to shake Jack. His superpower was being able to sleep anywhere, an extremely annoying attribute, especially given we were about to be blown to bits.

"Jack, wake up!"

Jack mumbled and shook his head, but kept his eyes shut. A little spot of drool dribbled from the corner of his mouth.

I shook him again. "Seriously. Didn't you hear that? Someone is trying to bomb us!" There were no signs of anything exploding outside the window. Just the same dusty dry landscape I'd been staring at for the last twenty minutes since leaving Potosi. Fact: Bad things happened on buses. At this rate ~~if~~ when I got home I was going to need treatment for bus-related PTSD.

Jack sat up, wiped his mouth with the back of his hand and peered out the window. "It is highly unlikely someone is trying to bomb us, Lucy."

Our fellow passengers *did* seem a bit more blasé about the whole situation. Maybe this was a regular weekly occurrence? Bombs away

Monday? I leaned down to make sure my shoelaces were tied in case we needed to make a run for it. No one likes to be caught unawares when there are explosives involved.

While I was hunched over there was another explosion—a lot closer than the last one. This was happening. I took a massive swig of orange juice. Running for your life required energy.

KA-BOOM! Another one. My hand jerked in fright, wrenching the bottle I was holding and splashing orange juice in my face. The sticky nectar dripped down my hair and neck. I wiped myself with the bottom of my t-shirt. "Those were bombs, Jack."

Jack scoffed. "They can't be. Why would there be bombs going off in the middle of Bolivia?" He was trying to appear calm, but he was nervously rubbing the back of his neck. A definite tell. The bus lurched to a stop in the middle of the road, and around us, people stood up calmly and moved towards the door in an orderly fashion.

"For any number of reasons, Jack." I held up my hand and started to list the possible reasons with my fingers. "Reason one—."

Jack stood and held up a hand to stop me. "Before you unleash that wild imagination of yours and get yourself all worked up, let me check with the driver."

Before I could say another word he joined the flow of passengers edging towards the door and I smiled in spite of my worry. Even though he was still a bit prickly at times it was alarming how well he knew me already. This was inevitable given how much time we'd spent together. After spending almost every waking hour together in the two weeks we'd been travelling we were so far past small talk that I found myself saying anything that popped into my head, not because I wanted to fill the silence but because I was so comfortable with this person that it just seemed appropriate to empty my brain out loud. I'd never had that with anyone. Jules and I had spent hundreds of hours together over the years but never this many joined together in a row.

Out the window I could see a few passengers milling around in the sun. Men stood around smoking cigarettes and talking amongst themselves. From my vantage point I could even see a chola taking the opportunity to squat behind a large rock, her tilted bowler hat sticking up above it, giving her away. The cholas in Bolivia were fascinating, with their ornate shawls, tiny bowler hats, petticoated skirts and long plaited hair. They looked like extras in the Bolivian adaptation of Pride & Prejudice.

Jack returned a few minutes later. "There's a big group of men just up the way there. The bus driver thinks it's a strike. He's gone to check."

"And he's left the bus in the middle of the road like this? To get rear-ended? And that's not the worst of it. What happens if he gets blown up? Who'll drive the bus?" The number of questions I asked in any given situation was directly proportional to how nervous I was in said situation.

Jack gave me a look.

"What? Fine. Okay, I'd feel bad if the driver got blown up, but I'd feel worse about having to walk all the way to Sucre. Can you drive it if he dies?" Jack was like a human Swiss Army knife, so disgustingly capable that I bet he could.

Jack's face was serious but his lip twitched like he wanted to smile. "No one is getting blown up, Lucy. This isn't a Nicholas Cage movie."

I laughed in spite of my nervousness. The buses we'd been on in South America thus far had played a disproportionate number of Nicholas Cage movies dubbed into Spanish. Mr Cage's movies had somehow started to seep into the fabric of the trip, along with bus rides and empanadas and that catchy reggaeton song that played on repeat wherever we went.

"I'm going to see if the driver is back," said Jack.

I grabbed my bag and stood. "Fine. I'm coming with you."

Outside, the bus driver was talking to the small crowd that had formed around him. I noted that he still had all his limbs and no one seemed to be wailing and beating their chests. I wondered if we'd stumbled across the set of a Nicholas Cage movie and if the bombs were just cars being blown up? I'd never met anyone famous before.

Jack wandered off to talk to him while I passed the time writing the word 'HELP' in big letters in the sandy dirt with the toe of my hiking boot. Maybe my character had been kidnapped and I needed to MacGyver an escape plan using only my wits and the underwire from my bra?

Sometimes I wished that someone *would* actually just write the screenplay for my life so that I at least knew what to do. Because this whole improvisation thing was *not* working out for me. Stage directions would be excellent right about now.

When Jack walked back to me his hands were shoved deep into his pockets and his mouth was pressed in a grim line. "What's going on?" I asked.

"Miners' strike. The bomb sounds are actually sticks of dynamite they've managed to get hold of from the mines. They won't let the bus through."

"Why the hell not?"

He shrugged. "It's just what they do. Every year or so, they decide they've had enough and they strike."

I looked past Jack at the bus passengers already offloading their boxes and bags like they'd practiced it before in a drill.

I asked the obvious question. "Why can't the driver just drive the bus super fast through the strikers?" That's what Nicky Cage would have done.

Jack shook his head. "The driver said he's been in this situation before. A few years ago he tried that and the strikers threw rocks at the bus and some of the passengers got badly hurt. It's safer just to walk through. He said there should be another bus a few kilometres up the road that will take us on to Sucre."

That didn't make any sense at all. "He wants us to walk through the protesters? Surely that's more dangerous than us driving through in a bus made of metal?"

"Yep. The protesters won't hurt us if we walk. Come on. Let's get our stuff."

I wasn't going anywhere. "Why doesn't the bus just turn around?"

Jack pointed behind me. Only about twenty-five metres away, a large group of men were shouting and shaking their fists as they walked towards us. The sight of them made me want to hide under the bus.

Jack grabbed our big bags, which had been dumped in the dirt, and helped me strap my pack to my back. But even as our fellow passengers headed off, I couldn't move.

"Jack, I'm scared." My voice wobbled in time with my chin. Without even looking at the striking mob I felt their anger fizzing like lit fireworks. Jack clipped my bag around my waist and did the same with his own, then reached for my hand. His grip was firm and reassuring, making me feel instantly better.

"I've got you and I won't let go. I promise." He squeezed my hand and I nodded with a grateful smile. The bus driver was in front of the group and the passengers trailed behind two by two. I watched as the strikers reluctantly stepped to the side to open up a narrow passage.

I whispered to Jack as we trailed behind the others. "At least they've stopped letting off dynamite."

KA-BOOM!

I jumped and screamed, clapping a hand to my mouth a fraction too late. Men jeered at me and I closed my eyes for a moment, hoping to shut everything out. I thought back to a conversation I'd had with a guy we'd met at our hostel in Uyuni.

His name was Dan, and he was travelling north to south, in the opposite direction to us. He'd just arrived after spending a few nights in the mining town of Potosi, the town we'd left that morning for a bus change on the way from Uyuni. One night over pizza, Dan had told us about the tour he'd done down a mine. I would never forget how he said he'd cried for an hour after emerging from that dark hell. The conditions so appalling, they weren't fit for any kind of life form, let alone the children and teenagers who were often forced to work there. Many of Potosi's residents were so poor, it was either mine or starve. What had struck me about my conversation with Dan was that here was a guy, the size of a small truck, with hands to match, someone who could've eaten dinosaurs for breakfast if they were on the menu, and his tough-guy heart had been broken by what he'd seen.

I tried to think about this as Jack and I inched through the blockade of angry men. They were desperate. Desperate men did desperate things. With dynamite. They'd come to the end of what they could bear and they just wanted to be heard, to take back what little power they had. And I could relate to that. I was still knock-kneed with fear, though, and it was all I could do to focus on the warmth of Jack's hand and the road in front of me. But the understanding did dull the sharp edge of my terror.

Uno, dos, tres, cuatro, cinco, seis, siete, ocho, nueve, diez.

I counted to ten in Spanish. And when I got to ten, I started again. And again and again and again.

Uno, dos, tres, cuatro, cinco, seis, siete, ocho, nueve, diez.

Uno, dos, tres, cuatro, cinco, seis, siete, ocho, nueve, diez …

Eventually I felt the pressure of Jack's hand lessen and I looked up in surprise. The road before us was silent and free of angry mobs. I glanced behind us to check that we weren't being followed—the men just a cloud of dust in the distance—and I gently released my hand from Jack's.

"Thank you," I whispered, peeping at him. He offered a small smile and a nod.

"How long do you think it will take us to walk to Sucre?" The rest of the group had powered on and we trailed behind like fat kids at camp.

"It was supposed to be three hours by bus from Potosi and we were only about twenty minutes out before we were stopped. So I'd say about eight hours walking, maybe less, maybe more."

"Eight hours? But hopefully another bus is already on its way from Sucre to pick us up? Right?" I asked, my voice pitched high with worry.

Jack nodded. "But we're already falling behind the pack, Luce. We need to pick up the pace so they don't leave us behind."

I nodded, shifting the pack on my back to get more comfortable, and tried to walk faster while watching the group drift further and further away.

After about two hours of walking in the hot afternoon sun, Jack and I had slowed to a crawl. I couldn't see anyone in front of us.

"Please can we stop, Jack? I'm knackered."

"I know, Luce, but we're already so far behind. We need to stay close in case a bus comes."

I stopped walking. "Jack, at the rate they were going they've probably already reached Sucre on foot by now." Which was embarrassing given that thirty percent of the passengers were old women and small children.

Jack stopped a little way ahead of me, slumped his shoulders and hung his head.

"I can't keep this pace up much longer. I'm about ready to collapse." They bred them tough and strong in Bolivia. I, on the other hand, was soft and squidgy.

"Okay, let's stop for a bit. Hopefully they won't forget the gringos and they'll send another bus or a taxi or something to get us."

We walked a short way into the scrubby bush and found a shady spot on the ground behind a large bush. I sunk down to the earth in the shade and knew immediately I wouldn't be going anywhere for a while. But I did try to kid myself by leaving my big pack strapped to my back. With my pack wedged against a small rock, I leaned back to rest my head on the top of the bag and closed my eyes. Jack groaned on the ground next to me. I opened my eyes and saw that he hadn't taken his pack off either and was draped across it like a movie star in the middle of a death scene. His eyes were shut.

"The plan is to have five minutes of shut eye and then we'll get up and keep moving."

Jack grunted in agreement and I settled back behind the bush.

Chapter 16

When I woke up, what felt like five minutes later, everything was black. My breath stuck in my throat. You know that feeling you get when you're in the middle of a dream and you're so terrified you want to scream but you can't? Well, that. It was so dark around me that I could have been in a box buried ten feet deep. Except for a snoring Jack next to me, which was at least enough reassurance for me to resume breathing.

I waggled my feet in front of me and after a while could just make out the outline of my boots. Everything around me was still. The night sky had been Photoshopped with a billion more stars than usual and I sighed deeply as I stared up at it.

Jack stirred. "Bet you wish you had your camp stove and sleeping bag now."

I laughed and swatted him with my hand. His arm was warm, and my skin prickled in response, making me aware of how cold I was starting to feel in the cool night air. I could hear the hitch in his breath and knew he was looking at me, even though it was too dark to see.

"Lucy, I owe you an apology."

"For what? Throwing away my portable defibrillator?" I joked.

He cleared his throat and I pictured him in the dark, making his

Serious Face, the one he usually reserved for checking maps or fiddling with the settings on his camera. A soft breeze rustled the leaves in the bush as I waited for him to respond.

"For everything."

"It's fine. I would have been a dick too if I'd been lumped with someone like me."

Jack let out a short, sharp laugh.

"It's not fine. I could see how out of your depth you were. You were hiding in the men's bathroom. And instead of being kind, I was a shit."

"Jack. You were put in a difficult situation, having to look after me ..."

"... and I behaved appallingly." He shuffled closer to me before continuing. "Being a photographer was my dream and I quit this supposedly amazing job in banking to pursue it even though everyone—and I do mean everyone—told me that it was a mistake. I've been trying to prove myself to them ever since. And sometimes I just take it all too seriously."

"But you love being a photographer. Your excitement shines out of your eyeballs like mania. Every time you have that camera in your hand you look like I'd look if I was an ice-cream flavour tester at Ben & Jerry's. Surely that's enough proof that you made the right decision?"

"Nöel thinks it's a phase." He let what he'd just said hang in the air. "But we're getting off track. This started off as an apology, not a sob story."

"I understand how much this means to you, Jack. And as I see it, I've only made it this far *because* of you. I've put you through heaps. So I'll only accept your apology if you accept mine."

Jack protested, but I continued. "It can't have been easy having to look after me like you've had to. You didn't sign up for me."

Jack waited before responding. "You know you're not as useless as you think you are, Lucy."

I snorted. I was so useless that I might as well have been the dead Bernie in the movie *Weekend at Bernie's* the way Jack had been carrying me around South America.

"Really, Lucy. You're so …" He stopped. "You're very …"

What? Strange? Nice? Character-building? I held my breath but he didn't finish. If I didn't know better I would have said he was holding on to what he thought of me like it was a secret he wasn't yet ready to share, which was infuriating.

"Anyway it doesn't matter. I accept your apology," he said.

We sat in silence for a few moments, before I piped up.

"So now what do we do? I mean do you think they've waited for us?"

Jack snorted in response, then shuffled off his backpack and unzipped it. I unclipped my own backpack and shrugged it off, shivering as the wind hit the sweat patch my bag had left on my back.

"We'll share my last snack bar, get warm and try to get some more sleep, because we can't go anywhere in the dark. Tomorrow we'll get up and start walking again and maybe someone will pick us up."

I heard the snack bar packaging crackle in Jack's hand and my stomach rumbled on cue.

"Where's your mouth?" he asked, reaching out and running his hands over my face before poking me in the eye instead.

I laughed. "Ouch! That's my eyeball."

"I was looking for your mouth," he said, finding my mouth and shoving half a snack bar inside. I yanked it out so I didn't choke on it as I laughed.

"You could have just handed it to me like a normal person, you know?"

Jack chuckled. "Where's the fun in that?"

From where I was sitting, I could see the faint outline of his face. I reached for him, looking for a soft squishy eyeball. I grabbed his face and he tried to pull away, laughing.

"That's my mouth!" He laughed so hard he started coughing on his mouthful of snack bar.

"Oh sorry. I was looking for your eyeball."

I unzipped my pack and fumbled around looking for my jacket until Jack flicked on his head torch.

"That would have been a big help when you were jabbing your finger in my eye," I said.

Jack smiled while he looked in his pack.

"Stop your whinging, woman, and get your jacket. I think the temperature is going to drop even more and I don't want you freezing to death."

"I think that's the sweetest thing you've ever said to me, Jack Dawson," I said, first pulling on the woolly llama jumper I'd bought in Uyuni, then my wind jacket. I also pulled out my stuff sack full of clothes to use as a pillow and cradled my filthy daypack to my chest. When I was hunkered down in the dirt, Jack lay next to me. My back was turned to him but I could feel his breath on my hair, which felt oddly comforting. He edged closer to me, then switched off his torch so that we were blanketed by black.

I'd never been spooned in the bushes on the side of the road like that before. The way I drifted off to sleep, with surprising ease, you'd think I'd even felt *safe*.

* * *

The sun was awake, and I think it wanted me to wake up too. Although it was bright, the air was still cool, so I knew it must have been early.

A throbbing pain in my hip reminded me that I'd spent the night on the cold, hard ground. Jack was behind me, making strange snorting noises in his sleep. I shifted to relieve some of the pain in my hip, being careful not to wake him.

Blerugh. The inside of my mouth was covered in a layer of dirt, dirt that wouldn't budge when I gingerly spat onto the ground. I ran my dry tongue along the inside of my mouth and thought about things I wanted to sink my teeth into to help wash away the scum. Triple-cream brie. Red wine. Chocolate fudge cake. Ice cream. The hard naked butt cheek of that hot Swedish actor whose name I couldn't remember. My stomach rumbled, angry that I'd switched it on with thoughts of deliciousness, ravenous after our meagre dinner the night before. Joyous saliva quickly flooded my mouth and I swilled around the dusty residue before attempting to spit it out while still lying on my side. That didn't work very well and I mostly ended up with a thick splodge of spit suspended from my lips, which refused to budge.

(Form an orderly queue gentlemen, because it doesn't get sexier than this. Oh, and you want me to talk dirty, do you? You got it. Sand. Mud. Grime. Dust. Earth.)

How the hell did I get here? Like seriously. And I didn't mean, here on the side of the road in Bolivia, but HERE, on the side of the road in Bolivia. I was just about to get existential while lying in my patch of dirt when Jack moved behind me and began making snuffling sounds into my hair. The gesture felt oddly intimate, weird but not entirely unpleasant. I craned my neck around to check if he was still sleeping, but my head snapped back before I could see anything. It felt like Jack was yanking at my hair. Hard.

I yelped in pain. "What the hell? Jack! What are you—" I stopped just as Jack appeared from behind a bush, his eyes as wide as flying saucers.

"But—" I started before my head got snapped back even harder, the snuffling sound behind me getting louder.

"Uh … Lucy … Jesus." Jack bent slowly to pick up a stick, never taking his eyes off whatever was behind me.

"Jack? Jack!? What the fuck is it?" I was too scared to move. Yank. Yank. Yank! My hair felt like it was being pulled from my skull.

"Llama."

"What?"

"Big fucking llama," hissed Jack, waving his stick at me.

The pulling stopped momentarily, and I managed to inch my face around and found myself nose to nose with a big shaggy llama. Out the side of the beast's mouth I could see a large clump of what looked like … my hair. I pushed myself up and away from it so fast I think I broke the sound barrier.

"Shiiiiit!" I shouted, flapping my hands in front of me like I was shooing away a bee, instead of a big hairy llama with a mouth full of teeth. But the llama wasn't the least bit put off by my girly squeals and flapping about, and just stared at me through the longest set of eyelashes I'd ever seen. No wonder he thought my hair was a bush; he couldn't see anything through those things. A bush that tasted like orange juice, I thought, remembering the juice I'd spilled on myself the day before.

Thankfully, he lost interest in me pretty quickly and moved to another bush, one that probably tasted less of zesty citrus and unclean backpacker. I patted the back of my head gingerly, and found the beginnings of a soggy dreadlock. Gross.

I angled my head towards Jack. "How does it look?" When he didn't respond I looked over at him and saw his lips pressed tightly together, the corner of his mouth twitching. I rolled my eyes. "You can laugh if you want."

And with my permission, he lost it completely, doubled over laughing, his hands on his stomach. Jack had a lovely laugh and I smiled and shook my head as I watched tears roll down his face. I didn't tell him I thought that it was him nuzzling the back of my neck, though. That would have been embarrassing. Instead I busied myself looking for the half-jar of peanut butter I was sure I'd stashed in the bowels of my backpack a few days ago. By the time I pulled the jar out with a flourish, Jack had stopped laughing.

"Are we done?" I asked, raising my eyebrow at him, watching him wipe away the tears. When he nodded I waved a small bottle of hand sanitiser at him.

"Hold out your hand." I squirted large blobs of sanitiser onto both our hands, and once we'd cleaned up, offered the open jar of peanut butter to Jack. He stuck a finger in and hooked a generous scoop then shoved it eagerly into his mouth. But as we chewed Jack started laughing again, turning around quickly so that all I saw were his shaking shoulders as he laughed silently. I rolled my eyes, calmly stuck two fingers in the jar and smeared peanut butter onto the back of Jack's head.

"Hey," he said, touching the back of his head, feeling the gooey paste.

"Let's see if that llama likes peanut butter shall we?" I laughed. "Here llama, llama. Where are you?" I called.

Jack lunged for me and the jar in my hands and I managed to twist out of his grasp, but not before he smeared peanut butter on my cheek.

"Noooo," I screech-laughed, giving him a push, immediately looking around for a leaf or something to wipe it off, worried the llama might actually come back for round two.

After hooting at his handiwork Jack held his hands up. "I'm sorry, Lucy. Come on, let me get it off." He gestured me over and pulled up the front of his t-shirt, revealing his flat, hard stomach.

I inched closer and tried not to stare at his abs. A smile twisted his lips as he held my face in one hand and his t-shirt in his other hand. My breathing hitched as he seemed to inch his face down to mine. Oh my God. Jack was going to kiss me. My heart thudded as he licked his lips, his face so close to mine I could see how the sunlight made his dark eyes look almost navy blue.

But he turned my face at the last minute and ran his tongue along my cheek, from bottom to top.

I pushed him away with a shriek and ducked my head so he wouldn't see my face burning. That was the second time in ten minutes I'd thought Jack was coming on to me. I needed to pull myself together.

Jack pulled out his half-full water bottle and handed it to me, still chuckling. I drank half and handed it back, before I nodded towards the road.

"Back to the road?"

"Back to the road."

* * *

We'd been on the road for about an hour, when a car screeched up alongside us and squealed to a stop in a cloud of dust. As Jack and I coughed, out of the haze I saw a young guy lean out of the window with a sideways baseball cap on his head. He looked like a disciple of Snoop Dogg.

"Estan ustedes caminando debido a la huelga?" said the guy. To me this sounded like '*something something walking something something strike*'.

Jack nodded. "Si, claro."

"Vas a Sucre?" said Snoop.

I nodded, this time understanding that he was asking if we were headed to Sucre. Along with Snoop Dogg in the passenger seat, there was another young guy in the driver's seat and an elderly couple in the back. The car was clearly being held together with rope, duct tape and hope. My gut twisted a little, which could've meant that I was either starving or my intuition was trying to tell me not to get in the car. I didn't have the best track record listening to my gut, because I just didn't trust that the organ that digested my food knew better than the organ that was actually designed to think.

Okay, yes, so fine, I'd sensed that I should have gone with the nerdy computer programmer over Charlotte when I'd interviewed for potential flat mates. And maybe my stomach knew that my ex-boss Laura had it in for me when my brain clearly didn't. And that Mike had been pulling away ever since we'd got engaged. My *gut* hadn't been surprised when he'd cheated. But I'd also trusted it when it told me to eat the poisoned hot dog from the alley with the rats, so until I could learn to differentiate between hunger pangs and an actual message that I could interpret I was just going to keep going as I'd always done.

"Si," said Jack.

The driver named his price. "200 bolivianos para ir a Sucre?"

He could clearly see we were desperate. Two hundred bolivianos, the equivalent of about forty US dollars, was a princely sum by Bolivian standards. But I would have paid fifty-three times that to be whisked the rest of the way in his chariot.

"Si!" I shouted. Jack gave me a look that said, 'Woman, you should have left this to me. I was going to negotiate.' But I just shrugged and gave him a look in return that said, 'Jack Bigglesworth Dawson, I'd have given this man my first born son to take me to Sucre.' His frown said, 'You know that's not my middle name.'

Oblivious to this telepathic conversation, Snoop Dogg sprung out of the car to help us with our bags. He untied the rope that was threaded through two holes that held the boot in place and dumped our big packs inside. Their vehicle was one of those big old American cars that could have easily carried the entire Adams Family in the back. Jack slid in first, kindly wedging himself up against the elderly couple's cage of guinea pigs, and rested his pack in his lap. I squeezed next to him, wedging my left butt cheek onto Jack's right thigh so we could shut the door. Cosy.

And as we reached for the non-existent seatbelts, Snoop Dogg roared off down the road. That freaking car was as speedy as it was old. My eyes watered as the wind blew sharply through all four open windows. The rusted window handle meant I couldn't even wind up my own window and the wind whipped my hair around my face like jellyfish tentacles, stinging my eyes.

Instead of whining, I pulled my scarf from my daypack and wrapped it around my head like I was trying to mummify my face. I tucked the end of the scarf in under itself, making sure to leave a space to look out and a breathing hole. I rested my face down on my daypack in my lap and tried to sleep. And I think I would have got there had the driver not hooted loudly as we swerved wildly to avoid a llama plodding across the road. I dug my fingers, nails bitten to the quick, into Jack's leg.

"How long do you think we'll take?" I shouted at him over the wind.

"About twenty minutes, at this rate!"

I peered past him at the older couple. They had serene looks on their faces, as if they had made peace with the idea of death and were ready to meet their maker. I wasn't ready to meet my maker. I was too young to die. Dammit. There was so much I still needed to do with my life. I needed to learn how to do a French plait. I needed to punch someone in the face. Heck, *I* needed to get punched *in* the face. And I couldn't die before I at least had sex one more time.

I glanced over at the guinea pigs. The way they were scrambling in their cage, they hadn't yet made peace with death either. A couple were scratching at each other like meth addicts. Another pair seemed to have the same idea as I had and were humping like mad.

I leaned over Jack and tried to get a better look at the little critters, but as I did the car swerved again and my head was thrown against the back of the seat in front of me, flicking my scarf loose. Slightly dazed from hitting my head so hard I wasn't quick enough to grab the material before it whipped off my face and flew out the window.

Whatever. I wasn't fussed about losing the scarf. I was more worried about how I was going to untangle my hair when I reached Sucre. But seeing the scarf fly out of the car Snoop Dogg gave a shout and the driver slammed on the breaks. I waved my hands at him.

"No te preocupes por eso," I said, trying to tell him not to worry. But he chucked the car in reverse anyway and roared backwards. I turned to Jack. "Tell him it only cost like ten dollars and I don't need it."

But when Jack told them they were horrified. The cost made them even more determined to find it. Even the elderly couple became more animated at the possibility of the lost scarf. But before we could reach the scarf Snoop Dogg shouted, his head sticking out the window.

"Mira!" Snoop said, pointing down the road.

We all turned and peered through the rear window as another car stopped in the middle of the road. Someone opened the door, jumped out, picked up my scarf then jumped in the car and drove towards us.

"Oh, that's nice," I said. "They're bringing my scarf back."

The car drove up, then quickly accelerated past us. Snoop Dogg lunged across to the driver's side and slammed his hand on the horn. But that just made the car accelerate more.

I tried again to placate them. "Esta bien. It's fine." But while I was amused that my scarf had been stolen right in front of our eyes, the car's other occupants were appalled. The driver shouted what I imagined were swear words strong enough to strip paint, because the elderly couple flinched violently at every second word. When he was done shouting, he whacked the car into gear and set off after my ten-dollar scarf.

I must have aged about twelve years in the time it took for us to pull close behind the other vehicle. As we roared along I screamed at the driver to slow down, but the more I yelled, the faster he went.

I leaned over to Jack and through my halo of flying hair yelled at him. "Tell him to slow down. I don't need the scarf!"

Jack jerked his head away from me and pulled a few strands of my hair from his mouth. "I don't think he's going to listen. I think you should just hold on and wait it out."

Every time we gained on the car it pulled away, which made Snoop even more determined. He shouted at our driver to drive faster and leaned out the window, yelling at the car in front of us. When this didn't work, the driver veered the car wildly to the other side of the road and jammed his foot on the accelerator, inching us alongside the thieves.

Snoop leaned out the car window, yelling and gesticulating to me in the back. I think if I wasn't so scared that they were going to flip the car, I might have been touched by their kindness, that I doubted came with any ulterior motive.

A kindness that had followed me since the beginning of the trip but which I'd just realised now—as I hurtled towards my death. The man handing me that flyer for cheap Spanish lessons when I was lost, Benny and Steve and their football match tickets in exchange for the ridiculous junk I'd carried with me all the way from home, Jack and I playing a random game of Marco Polo after I'd been two seconds away from shitting my pants. It felt strange to hold something good in one hand and something bad in the other hand *at the same time*. Kindness in my left hand and vehicular homicide in the right. Before this trip my view was that shit was either snow cones and eskimo kisses *or* binge-eating twenty boxes of after dinner mints seven months past their expiry date. Dark or light. Glass overflowing or glass smashed into a million little pieces. This made me smile a little at what felt like a very grown-up epipha—

"Car!" Jack pointed ahead, his eyes wide.

The driver slammed on the breaks and scrambled to get the car over to the right side of the road. But we didn't make it in time and the oncoming car clipped the driver's side. Jack threw his arm across my body, but the car wasn't going as fast as we were, and while the angle of the connection made us spin around, by some miracle we didn't flip.

"Are you okay?" asked Jack with a worried look on his face, scanning my body for injuries.

I nodded and opened my mouth but nothing came out.

"What the hell, dude? Casi nos mataste!" Jack shouted. I hoped he was telling him that he almost killed us. The driver shrugged, leaned outside his window to assess the damage, turned to Snoop and shrugged again. Before he could even put the car back into gear I opened the door and fell out onto the road, my knees buckling beneath me as I thought about how I should have listened to my gut.

"Que estas haciendo?" Snoop asked.

Jack got out behind me and helped me to my feet. He pointed to the open road. "Vamos caminar."

Thank God he was onboard with us walking the rest of the way. There was no way I was getting back in that car. Down the road I saw the driver of the other car, get out, assess the damage, shrug and calmly drive away. I fumbled my way round to the back of the car and with shaking fingers untied the rope holding the boot together. Jack and I pulled out our packs and dumped them on the road.

"Qué distancia hay a Sucre?" Jack asked Snoop.

"Quizas diez kilometers mas," said Snoop. Jack pulled out his wallet, handed him the full fare and they roared off.

Jack shifted his pack on his back and without another word

started the trudge towards Sucre, but stopped when he realised I wasn't following him. He raised his eyebrows and nodded his head in the direction we needed to head, as if he hoped a little encouragement might get me going.

But I shook my head. "I give up, Jack," I whispered, all thoughts of being a grown-up having left my brain when my life flashed before my eyes. "It's too much and it's too hard. And I give up."

"What do you want to do instead?"

"What do I want to do instead?" I repeated, completely mystified by the question. No one had ever asked me that before. And I'd never thought to ask that of *myself.* I wanted my life to change but I'd never thought to actually ask myself what I wanted instead.

"Yes. If you don't want to walk to Sucre what do you want to do? Right now?"

I wanted to lie down and not get up for a week. I wanted someone to spray ice-cold gin and tonic into my open mouth with a water pistol and press a cool towel to my forehead. But most of all I wanted to drop to my knees and scream out of frustration, because I felt so utterly powerless and out of my depth that I was shaking.

"Right now?" I took a deep breath. "I want to scream."

Jack didn't look the least bit surprised. "So scream then."

"What?"

"Go on. You said you want to scream, so do it," he replied, like it was the most natural thing in the world to want to shout on the side of the road in the middle of Bolivia.

I started to protest. "But—"

Before I could say anything more Jack threw his head back and shouted so loudly and with so much force I was surprised his face didn't pop clean off his body.

"Now you go," he said when he was finally done, his face red from the exertion.

So I took a deep breath, opened my mouth as wide as I could and screamed until my throat itched and my eyes watered. It was so fucking liberating I couldn't believe how much better I felt after letting it all out. When I got home I was definitely buying a sound proof booth on eBay.

"Are we good?" he asked.

"We're good," I laughed.

Chapter 17

A few hours later, Jack and I arrived at the hostel in Sucre looking like we'd just crawled through a goddam post-apocalyptic desert wasteland. And, as great as our need was for a shower, our desire for a cold beer was even greater. So smelling like sweaty balls and petrol, we marched into that hostel bar, parting the crowd like Moses did the Red Sea.

"Jaysus, you've got to be making that up?!" exclaimed Celia, my new Irish friend, after hearing our story.

You see, our appearance had garnered much attention and we'd quickly amassed quite the curious crowd around us, even though they couldn't stand too close on account of the fact that we smelled so bad. We were only supposed to have a beer each, but when word spread that we'd got caught up in the strike, the bar quickly flooded with more travellers gagging to buy us alcohol.

One beer turned into four.

"That's a fecking mad story!" What was it about the Irish accent that made swear words sound like beautiful music?

Her friend Nancy, on the other hand, had been frowning for a good ten minutes at the dreadlock that had taken up residence at the back of my head.

"You know, love," she said eventually, fingering the crusty clump, "I'm a hairdresser back home and I've got my scissors with me. I could probably fix this up for you, if you'd like?"

I jumped off my bar stool and squealed. "Yes, please!"

She laughed and held up her beer glass. "Let me just finish my beer."

Beside me on another bar stool, Jack sniggered. "Just the words you want to hear from your hairdresser moments before they take scissors to your hair."

"Don't listen to him." I nudged Jack with my shoulder to tell him to be quiet and he surprised me by pulling me close to him so that he could fiddle with the back of my head.

"It looks like a stoner started dreading your hair and lost interest," he said, still with his arm wrapped around me like it was the most natural thing in the world.

"Come on, love, let's get that hair sorted out," said Nancy. "Celia, I need your help. I have a plan," she continued, giving me a wink. I didn't want to pull myself away from Jack's embrace, but I also wasn't going to pass up the opportunity to get my hair fixed, so I reluctantly hopped off my stool.

The girls suggested I have a long shower and shampoo before the cut and disappeared to their room, and half an hour later I was clean, dressed, and sitting in a chair in the communal bathroom with a sarong around my shoulders. I yelped as Nancy worked up a sweat trying to brush out my deadlock, so much so that Celia left deciding more beer was required to raise morale—returning just in time to watch Nancy chop off the last bit that refused to come out.

I'd have to say, it was the most fun I've ever had having my haircut. It was great "craic" as Nancy and Celia would have said. Usually I dread having my hair cut. All that staring at my floating head in the mirror and answering probing questions about my ovaries is not my favourite way to spend an hour. But the girls made it fun, cracking jokes and striking up conversations with anyone who wandered into the bathroom.

The camaraderie amongst backpackers had been something that took me by surprise when I'd first been transplanted into a hostel common room. I recalled how Hayley had been so friendly my first day in Argentina and had pretty much saved me from having to drown myself. Travellers were always keen to strike up conversations with the nearest stranger and were usually interested in hearing whatever you had to say. It was strange, but I think I liked it.

When my hair was cut and blow-dried I tried to take a peek in one of the bathroom mirrors, but Celia insisted on doing my make-up first. When they were done they stood back to survey their work.

"Well, how do I look?" I asked.

"We're not done yet," said Celia.

"What do you mean?"

"We had a feeling you didn't have any clothes that aren't all similar to what you're wearing," said Nancy, waving at my sensible ensemble of a mustard-yellow merino t-shirt and zipped off khaki shorts. Celia wrinkled her nose.

I plucked at the moisture-wicking material. "What's wrong with what I'm wearing?"

"Well this doesn't really go with that," said Nancy, pointing at my face and then the rest of my body, sounding thoughtful rather than mean.

"We think that might be part of your problem," she continued.

Celia nodded in agreement.

"What problem?" I stared between the two of them.

Celia replied like it was completely obvious. "You know. The whole sad, hapless, 'I'm a big scared mess and nothing ever seems to go my way and I don't know why' thing you've got going on."

"O-kay." I mean, they'd met me just over an hour ago so really they didn't know anything about me.

"You dress like someone who doesn't give a shit about herself," said Celia, and I winced at how close to the mark she was.

"Yeah. We think you need a makeover," said Nancy.

I rolled my eyes, hoping to cover my reaction to their spot-on assessment. "A make-over? Hello? This is Bolivia, not Beverly Hills."

"We've already started getting a few things together. You'll see. You'll feel so much better about everything when we get you out of those horrible clothes."

Can you say 'movie montage makeover'?

Because, apparently, while I was showering, Nancy and Celia had begged and bartered with obliging females throughout the hostel to amass a pile of clothes for my makeover. They'd found me leggings, tank tops, dresses, shorts and jumpers, none of which were the slightest bit moisture wicking. They'd even scrounged up an assortment of accessories to complete 'my look'. Their room looked like a hundred backpacks had exploded, with clothes strewn across every surface. I even noticed a bra hanging off the ceiling fan.

I was touched at how generous everyone had been. Even though they didn't know me, all the women they'd asked had refused payment, especially when they'd heard what I'd been through.

"Seriously. You're doing me a favour," said one woman when she stopped by to see how the makeover was progressing. "I've been travelling for a year and I am so sick to death of everything in my bag."

Another woman had just been on a three-week holiday and had packed too much stuff. "I overestimated how many clothes I would need by about ten kilos. If my boyfriend complains about how heavy my bag is one more time I'm going to lose it."

Someone else was flying home from La Paz in a week's time and was happy to help. She told me that she'd been just like me eighteen months earlier when she'd started her trip to Mexico with a bag full of boring.

Celia even swapped her favourite scarf for a long black maxi-dress for me to wear, and Nancy gave away a pair of sneakers she said she didn't wear for a pair of jean shorts that were just my size.

When I was dressed in my final reveal outfit Nancy clapped her hands excitedly and Celia pretended to wipe away a tear as she surveyed her work. Nancy pushed me in front of the full-length mirror and, with a flourish, Celia yanked off the blanket they'd draped over it.

"Ta-da," shouted Nancy.

Gasping is so clichéd after a makeover but I couldn't help myself. I stepped closer. "Holy shit!"

Nancy had cut my hair into a messy bob that made my face look thinner. Beneath Celia's artfully applied eye makeup, my hazel eyes looked huge and green and, honestly, kind of amazing. The girls had dressed me in the long black maxi, and accessorised it with a bright blue scarf, half an arm of jangly bangles and huge gold hoop earrings. The dark material was tight and clung to my curvy body, accentuating its twists and turns.

"One last thing," said Nancy before she yanked the front of the dress down to reveal more of my cleavage.

Celia approved. "Yes, much better. You have ace boobs. You need to show them off more."

I really looked ... lovely. And I couldn't remember the last time I'd thought that about myself. Or if I'd *ever* thought that.

The words caught in my throat but I choked them out. "Thank you. I feel amazing."

"You *look* amazing," they chimed before wrapping their arms around me in a group hug.

"Come on, let's get back to the bar. Those men are going to be dead bored without us," said Nancy with a wink.

Back at the bar, and much to my embarrassment, Celia insisted on making me the centre of attention. "Everyone shut up! Oi! We'd like to present the new Lucy!"

Nancy nudged me. "Do a spin," she said out of the side of her mouth.

I spun around tentatively, feeling the whole bar's eyes on me. Everyone clapped and hollered. I got several hugs and high fives from people I was sure hadn't even been in the bar an hour ago and didn't know me from a bar of soap. I searched for Jack in the crowd, hoping he'd roll his eyes and immediately make me feel less awkward.

But when I finally met his eyes, he didn't roll them. He was close enough that I could see they were the colour of dark wood. He'd showered and his hair was wet and messy and I breathed in deep, hoping to catch a whiff of his pepperminty Jack smell. The way he was looking at me was making me nervous, and I fidgeted, tugging at the top of my dress while flashing him a self-conscious smile.

"Don't you dare," shouted Nancy, lunging at me to yank the dress's scooped neckline back down. I swatted her hand away just as Jack's eyes flicked from my chest back to my face. Colour was slowly rising in his face, and he swallowed, his Adam's apple bobbing as he held my eyes. He opened his mouth as if to speak, but closed it just before turning to the bar and ordering another drink.

60 DAYS IN SOUTH AMERICA

Day 14: Travellers are crazy

Travellers are crazy.

That's right, I said it. But I'm sure everyone was already thinking it anyway.

And yes, I mean you with the tattered hostel wristbands sitting cross-legged on the floor.

And you with the passport that's run out of blank pages, the one you accidentally managed to flush down the toilet in Ushuaia.

And I'm definitely talking to you in the yoga pants with the crazy-eyes, eating questionable-looking street food off a crusty sheet of tin.

Why do you look so pleased to be here? How are you not lying on the ground gnawing on your fist?

It is complete and utter madness.

Seriously. I have been in more awkward, uncomfortable, horrible situations in the last two weeks than in all the thirty-something years of my life put together. And I've had enough of it.

- *I have been thrown off a horse who I may or may not have named Rambo. (You'll never know.)*
- *My shampoo bottle has ejaculated over the entire contents of my backpack. (Thrice)*
- *I nearly soiled myself on an overnight bus.*

- *A llama ate my hair.*
- *I have been lost approximately forty-nine times.*
- *I can't pass urine without at least four people hearing me. (Because: communal bathrooms)*
- *I've slept on the side of the road for a night.*
- *I almost got blown up in a miners' strike. (And I'm only half exaggerating.)*
- *And I was involved in a car chase, which ended in a car crash (that had nothing to do with shooting a Nic Cage movie.)*

Why would anyone choose to feel like you constantly don't know which way is up? To knowingly put yourself in situations where you're forced to interact with strangers every day? To sleep in different beds night after night and trusting that you won't wake up to one of your dorm mates licking your face? To guarantee you can only ever understand thirteen percent of what's happening at any given time because everything is written in Spanish?

Why do you do it? What is the point of it all?

People talk about "getting out of your comfort zone" like it's a pill. But I just feel like I've boarded a one-way train to Crazy Town and I'd like to get off please.

And that's definitely all I have to say about that.
Lucy Hart.

Next destination: La Paz, Bolivia

Chapter 18

My phone buzzed and I picked it up to find a WhatsApp message from Jack—even though he was sat directly opposite me.

Jack: I'm hungry. Let's go get some food before we Skype your folks.

I rolled my eyes and looked at him over the top of my laptop. We were both sitting at a long table off the courtyard of the Wild Roger Hostel in La Paz, along with several other travellers who had their heads buried in their respective electronic devices.

Lucy: Are you seriously WhatsApping me? Edit your photos and stop bothering me.

Jack's phone chimed and he picked it up like he couldn't possibly know who it was. He typed out something and put down his phone, and then started to pretend to type on his keyboard. I knew he was pretending because he was making a stupid constipated face. My phone buzzed.

Jack: My editing is done.

Jack: Also, I feel it's my duty as your travelling companion to tell you that the guy next to you is creeping on you.

I peeked at the guys on either side of me. I knew which one I was hoping was doing the creeping.

Lucy: Really? Irish Hottie or Sweaty German?

Lucy: Also, travelling companion? Really? Who am I, Maid Marian? It was weird that Jack was giving me the heads up on some guy creeping on me, since I suspected he'd been creeping on me himself two nights ago when the Irish girls had worked their magic on me in Sucre. He hadn't said a word to me about my make-over or the look he'd given me, so I'd taken his lead and pretended that it had never happened. Denial was both a river in Africa and my religion, after all.

Jack: Irish Mountain.

Yes!

Lucy: I wouldn't mind climbing him. *wink face emoji *eggplant emoji *ice-pick emoji

Jack: Gross. I said I was your travelling companion, not your BFF. This is not a sleepover.

Jack: And why do you insist on writing out your emojis instead of just using the actual emoji?

Lucy: What? You said mountain, I said climb. Do you think *he'd* be interested in a sleepover? Should I talk to him?

Jack: You can try but by the looks of him he probably only communicates via grunts and chest beating.

Lucy: Yes, well he's extremely hot. He can communicate with me any way he likes.

Jack: If you're into the whole bearded manly look …

Lucy: … which I very much am.

Jack: Anyway, as previously mentioned, I'm hungry. And I can hear your stomach grumbling from here. You probably shouldn't hit on the mountain on an empty stomach.

Lucy: You're right. I need to carbo load.

60 DAYS IN SOUTH AMERICA

Day 16: La Paz Love Potion #9

Today a witch offered me a love potion.

There I was, in the middle of the infamous witches' market in La Paz in Bolivia, minding my own business, perusing all manner of dried llama foetuses and rat skulls for sale, when a bottle was thrust into my hands like it was some kind of emergency.

I have mixed feelings about the fact that she singled me out as the sad sack who was obviously living a loveless life. Out of all the tourists wandering the dark alleys and dank smelling stalls, I was the one who obviously needed magic to make a man fall in love with me.

But rest assured, men who may be terrified that I'm coming for you to spike your beverages. You can stop taking your tea with you to the little eligible bachelors' room. This isn't a drug. It's more like a talisman, one which needs to be buried in the dirt, with rose petals and goat placenta. (I'm guessing.) I suppose it might work even better with a little prayer or a spell, chanted naked during a waning balsamic moon. (Off the top of my head maybe something like: Matching Underwear and Strawberry Flan. Do me a favour and find me a Man.) I can't be sure, though, because it didn't come with any directions.

Floating in a clear viscous liquid inside the bottle (which possibly contains traces of asbestos and the hanta virus) are a little plastic man and a little plastic woman. Moving amongst this pair of lovers are all the elements that make up a life together:

A bean (symbolising how their love would grow like a beanstalk up into the sky to where there are giants),

A yellow star (symbolising a Bon Jovi love song, but not the one that ends with that crazy chick burning down the building),

A gold shoe (symbolising being grown-ups who wear shoes on their feet),

A green ball (symbolising the circle of life as depicted in the Disney classic The Lion King), and

A hot pink car (symbolising the mistakes we make in life because who the hell would ever choose to paint their car pink).

Before the witch disappeared back into the shadows I'd wanted to ask her if the potion would guard against a broken heart, if she could promise my hopes and dreams would not end up shattered on the pavement, but mostly I wanted to make sure that if I found a man to love me he wouldn't wake up one Tuesday morning and decide to shag my boss on her desk.

I'd wanted to ask her all these things but my Spanish is terrible, so instead, I saluted her like she was a major general—not a toothless old lady—and hoped for the best.

And yes I'm aware that asking for a money-back guarantee on love is like reserving the right to demand a refund for a movie you watch all the way through. If I buy a ticket for the roller coaster I've got to deal with the screaming and vomiting.

(I wonder if there's a spell for bravery?)

Anyway. For those of you with the balls to try, you can now buy love in Bolivia for two dollars, which I'm sure y'all will agree is a freaking bargain.

And that's all I have to say about that.
Lucy Hart

Next destination: Rurrenabaque, Bolivia

Chapter 19

"Hello? HELLO?" said my mum, her voice booming from my Mac. Jack quickly pressed the volume button down.

"Hi, Mum!" My parents had insisted they be introduced to Jack, so we'd set up a time to have a Skype call to "meet" him. Unfortunately the wifi connection was so weak I'd had to start the call without video.

I heard my mum shuffling around. "Dale, I clicked the green button but I don't hear or see anything. What do I do now?"

"Oh shit. Here we go." I took a deep breath and clicked the video button so they would see my face, but my image didn't appear right away.

"I don't know, Pat. You're the Skyper," my dad said. More shuffling, sounding like one of my parents had stuck the microphone up their nose. "Now, just so I know, where is Lucy again?"

I picked up my laptop and spoke into the microphone. "Dad, I can hear you. Turn up the volume so you can hear me."

My mum replied after a moment. "I think she said Burundi, no wait, that doesn't sound right. It was something beginning with a B. Wait, let me think for a moment."

"Mum! Dad! I can hear you guys. I'm here." I waved my hand over the camera, but the video was still struggling to connect.

"Belize?" I heard my dad ask.

"Jesus!" I huffed, snatching up my phone to text my mother.

"Burma maybe? No, that's not it. Oh, wait, someone just texted me. Oh dear. I can't read that. Dale, do you know where I put my glasses?"

My dad was relentless. "Was it Bosnia? No that's not in South America. Let me Google it. Pat, what's the code for this iPad again?"

I turned to Jack, who was chuckling. "I'm glad you think this is funny. I'm actually going to lose it."

"Oh, the text is from Lucy. She says she can hear us," said my Mum. At that exact moment the video popped up and I could see them both on screen.

My dad's eyes widened. "But how can she hear us?" He looked around the room, completely mystified, everywhere except at the screen in front of him. I waved my hand in front of the camera, hoping the movement would alert them to the fact that the call was live. I texted mum again.

"Oh. She says that she's on Skype. And that we must turn up the volume. Dale, how do you turn up the volume on this thing?" She stuck her face right up against the camera giving us a lovely view of her eyeball as she tried to adjust the volume. I picked up my laptop and pretended I was going to throw it across the room.

Jack laughed. "Lucy, it'll be fine," he said, rubbing my back to calm me down. The gesture felt comforting, like when he'd held my hand walking through the strike, but this time it was also confusing. It made me wonder how his hand would feel elsewhere.

"Let me see," said my dad, his ear suddenly looming large in the screen. "Wait, lend me your glasses, Pat."

Jack's warm hand stayed where it was, sending a flood of heat out from the spot between my shoulder blades to the rest of my body, which I was trying desperately to ignore. I didn't need any sexual feelings muddying the waters of our relationship. He was being a good friend and I was getting hot and bothered.

"Lucy! Can you hear me now?" screeched my Mum.

We jumped and Jack slid his hand from my back. I bit back my disappointment at the loss.

"Oh look, it's Lucy on the screen."

"Yes Mum. I can hear you. You don't need to shout. Can you hear me?" I said, grateful we were alone in the dorm room.

"Oh goodie! We can hear you! And we can see you. Oh dear, your face looks very red. Did you get sunburnt? Oh wait, is that Jack with you?" My mum waved. "Hello, Jack."

Jack returned the wave. "Hi, Mrs Hart, Mr Hart."

My mum's laugh tinkled through the speaker. "Oh, what lovely manners, but please, Jack, call us Pat and Dale."

It had taken about five seconds for Jack to win her over.

"By the way guys, we're in Bolivia," I clarified, ignoring her comment about my red face and shoving my desire for Jack into the black box I reserved for all feelings I wanted to ignore.

"Yes, that's it! I knew it. Bolivia!" said my Dad. "Didn't I say Bolivia, Pat?" he turned to my mother.

She frowned. "No, you didn't, actually. Lucy, we still can't believe you're in South America. You're so brave!"

My face burned and I looked down. I was the complete opposite of brave. And Jack knew it.

"Oh, Mum. That's sweet. But I'm not brave at all. I still don't know what the hell I'm doing,"

"Don't listen to her. Your daughter *is* brave," said Jack. "She's been through a lot in the last two weeks and she's still here. Lucy's a real trooper. You should be proud of her."

I looked at him in surprise, started to mumble a response before I even knew what to say, and then stopped.

I looked up at the screen to see two very proud parents staring back at me. My mum's hand was on her chest, her eyes glistening with emotion. "Oh, isn't that sweet?"

"We are, Jack. We are," said my dad, his voice gruff. "But we're glad that you're there to keep her company."

After a few minutes of chitchat covering everything from what we had for breakfast (toast) to Jack's favourite thing on the trip so far (the soccer match) Jack shifted on the bed next to me.

"Well, Pam and Dale, it's been my pleasure. It was great meeting you, but I'm sure you've got stuff you want to catch up on so I'll leave you to it."

"Lovely to meet you," said Pat.

"Jack." My dad nodded his goodbye.

Jack turned to me. "I need to head out and get a few things before we all go out for dinner. I won't be long. See you later, Luce."

I nodded as he stood and picked up his stuff.

"Where are you going later?" asked my Dad.

"We're going out for curry with a few people we've met in the hostel." The group we were going with included the hot Irish mountain man whose name I'd recently learned was Conor. I'd invited him after talking to him when Jack and I had returned from lunch, carbed up as Jack suggested. I was quite looking forward to it. Although I obviously didn't tell my folks their daughter was hoping to get some later. I wondered if *that* was why I'd reacted so strongly to Jack's hand on my back. Because my body was anticipating action? Be still, my beating hormones.

Mum looked thoughtful for a moment. "You know Lucy, I really don't know what you were going on about in your last email. Jack really seems lovely. He's not a shit at all."

Fuuuck! My face burned as I looked up at Jack's retreating back as he walked out of the room. "Mum! You're on speaker! Jack can still hear you," I whispered through gritted teeth.

She clapped her hand and mumbled through her fingers. "Whoopsie."

* * *

That night we sat at the curry restaurant, menus in hand, trying to decide what we were going to order. Jack sat to my right and Conor sat directly across from me.

Before my mum's earlier faux pas, I'd been looking forward to seeing how the night went with Conor. But that excitement had dulled a little, worrying about whether Jack had heard my mum refer to him as a shit. The first time I saw him after the call was in the hostel courtyard where our group had assembled. He'd offered me a small smile as he spoke to the Austrian couple we'd met at breakfast. Along with Jack and I, hot Connor and the Austrian couple, we'd recruited a German woman and a Swedish guy to come along for a meal. (I had to keep reminding myself that this wasn't real life and back home I wouldn't be able to get away with asking random groups of strangers on dinner dates as I went about my day.)

"So, Conor, what do you think you're going to order?" I asked him, resisting the urge to reach across the table and stick my fingers in his mouth.

He flashed a smile. "I haven't decided yet."

"It says here if you order the world's hottest curry and finish it you get a free t-shirt," said Daniel, the Swedish guy.

I looked at Conor's biceps, noting how they strained against the fabric. "Do you think they'd have a t-shirt with sleeves big enough for your arms," I said, fluttering my eyelids as though bugs had just flown into my eyes. I could actually hear the sound of Jack's eyeballs rolling in their sockets. My flirting skills were rusty as hell, but I was still rewarded with a laugh from Conor before he was drawn into conversation about cycling Death Road with Daniel.

"Jack?" I whispered out of the side of my mouth.

"Lucy," Jack whispered back, playing along.

"You know how I bought that love potion?" I asked, flicking my eyes at Conor to make sure he couldn't hear me.

"Yes?" he replied, raising his eyebrows.

"Well?" I cocked my head towards Conor, hoping Jack would get my drift. "What do you think?"

Jack snorted and rolled his eyes. "I don't know what's more sad. That you believe in love potions or that you want that meathead to fall in love with you," he said, returning his attention to his menu.

"Whatever. He's hot like a korma. You know that New Zealand chick I was talking to this morning? She said her friend bought a bottle of love potion when she was travelling in Bolivia last year and she met the love of her life the very day she bought it. What do you call that?"

"Really, Lucy. Aren't you a writer? You should know that's called a coincidence."

I stuck my tongue out at him, before taking a peep at Conor over the top of my menu. He had a thick head of dirty blonde hair, a very impressive beard and extremely white teeth. What a view. Connor caught me looking at him.

"Lucy, where are you heading after La Paz?" he asked.

"We're going to Rurrenabaque then back to La Paz and on to—where are we going next?" I turned to Jack.

"Arequipa."

Connor frowned.

"But you two aren't *together* together?" he said, nudging his head towards Jack, who didn't respond.

"Nope. Definitely not. Jack has a girlfriend and I am single to mingle." Single to mingle? Ugh. Could I be more desperate?

Conor laughed and winked at me. I looked over at Jack and waggled my eyebrows, but he didn't look impressed. If I didn't know any better I would have thought he was jealous. But that was ridiculous since he had a beautiful girlfriend. The more likely scenario was that he was grumpy because he *had* heard what my mum had said. Surely he knew that I didn't think he was a shit anymore? We were such a good team together, now that we'd gotten over ourselves.

I looked at my menu when the waiter started taking orders at the other end of the table. I needed to make sure whatever I ordered wouldn't give me serious curry breath.

"And for you, señor?" the waiter asked Jack.

"The World's Hottest Curry, por favor," he replied. I snorted.

"I'll have the mild butter chicken, please," I said when the waiter turned to me.

"And for you, señor?" The waiter looked at Conor expectantly.

"Chicken korma, medium."

"You're not giving the World's Hottest Curry a go?" said Jack.

"Yeah, I don't think so. That guy over there was crying," Conor replied, pointing at a table behind us. "Crying wouldn't be a good look," he said, giving me the "glad eye" as my gran calls it. Yes! It was on like a donkey's kong. I conjured up my sexiest smile by trying to picture what he looked like with no clothes on.

Jack shook his head. "Damn. I really thought that of everyone at this table you'd be the one to man up with me."

Conor stiffened and sat up straighter in his chair, obviously smarting at Jack's comment.

They stared at each for about four seconds before Conor snorted. "Bring it on, dude," he said, sitting back in his chair, folding his arms to make his huge biceps look even bigger. "I'll change my order to the World's Hottest Curry. Extra Hot."

* * *

Email:

To: l.hart@standard.com
From: j.henry@gbk.com.au

Lucy Loo, how are you?

Tell me things are going better for you and that you don't currently have the shits and/or are in the process of getting blown up.

I loved your Love Potion post by the way. Is the love potion working? Any dirty backpacker men sniffing around you? Tell me everything and don't spare any nasty details. And if there is nothing to tell just make it up. You know I'd be none the wiser. I need some excitement. At the moment my life is all sofa swatches and paint samples and I feel like I'm seventy-three years old.

Love you. x

P.S. Seriously, though, re: the love potion post. You're going to find someone to love you as much as you deserve to be loved. I know it was tough with Mike but you are stronger than you realise and you got through that. You can get through anything and love is so worth it. Don't give up!

(End of pep talk. Fade to black.)

Email:

To: j.henry@gbk.com.au
From: l.hart@standard.com

Hi, my Jules,

Thanks for the pep talk. The love potion *almost* worked. But alas, my backpacker cherry is still intact and in its dusty baby-moth filled plastic packaging.

I met this hunk of a man called Conor (he's Irish!) at the hostel I am staying at and I was getting my flirt on like a disco queen (which as you know means saying the most ridiculous things and being extra dorky). But stupid Jack had to ruin any potential action by challenging said hunk to eat the Hottest Curry in the World. In the end Jack and Conor both got very sweaty and spent all night running to the toilet, neither of which is conducive to getting jiggy in any shape or form.

And now we're off this morning into the wild jungles of Bolivia to Rurrenabaque, where I'm probably going to end up mauled by a jaguar or similar.

Love you bye. X

* * *

"Wow, my wrist still hurts. On the plane ride back to La Paz remind me not to sit next to you," said Jack, making circles with his wrist.

We were in a jeep bound for the Beni River, where we would be with our tour group for the next few days. Jack and I had just arrived in Rurrenabaque, having flown from La Paz in the smallest plane I'd ever seen in my life. It was so tiny that when I boarded I was surprised to actually find seats. And because it was the size of a mosquito, I could feel every vibration and spent most of the short flight squeezing the blood out of Jack's arm.

I whacked him hard on the wrist. "You'll live."

Jack yanked his arm away from me and made a face. "Ouch! Are you still pissed because you think I ruined your chances with Conor?"

I swiped at my sweat moustache with the back of my hand. The sun was hot and the air was thick with humidity, so different to La Paz. The dirt road we sped along was bordered by a wall of lush green, the sight a welcome change from the thirsty landscape we'd become used to in Bolivia. "I don't *think* you ruined my chances with him, I *know* you did."

"How was I supposed to know that he couldn't handle a little spicy food?"

I narrowed my eyes at him.

"What?"

"You couldn't handle it either. I could hardly sleep with you groaning all night in the dorm room and running to the toilet every four minutes," I snapped.

"Fine. It was stupid. I'm sorry I ruined your chances with him, but I think you'll thank me. I didn't like him."

"You don't have to like him." I looked out the window so he couldn't see my face. "If I didn't know any better I would've said you were jealous."

Jack hesitated. "I was being protective."

"Ugh. Whatever," I said, turning back to see him rubbing the back of his neck, which made me wonder if there was something else he wasn't telling me.

"Now Lucy, I don't care for the tone of your voice," he said, making his voice extra pompous and silly, which he knew was my favourite.

"Well Jack, I don't care for the tone of your face," I retorted, trying and failing not to smile.

The jeep pulled up under the shade of some trees that looked out onto the river bank. Men loaded supplies and luggage onto a long boat painted in the colours of the Bolivian flag, one of several boats moored there. Our driver helped us unload our backpacks from the jeep.

"Gracias," I said, smiling.

"De nada. Your group is there." He pointed towards the long green, yellow and red boat.

There were three women standing next to it and I squinted to get a better look at the people we'd be spending time with in the jungle. They were probably sizing me up too as I picked my way down the muddy bank, trying not to land on my guava. One of the women, a blonde in a summer dress, turned and looked back up at us. I stopped dead.

"Jack," I hissed out of the side of my mouth.

Jack stopped and looked at me warily.

"Yes, Lucy," he replied, patiently.

"Don't make it obvious but you see that blonde chick in the dress?" I said through gritted teeth like a deranged ventriloquist.

He looked down the bank at the group. "Yes."

"Remember I told you about the time you left me on the bus and I had to stalk that backpacker all the way back to San Telmo so I could find our hostel?"

Jack sniggered, before remembering he'd been the cause of me needing to stalk her and stopped. "Yes."

I held my hand in front of my mouth like I was scratching my face so she couldn't see my lips move. "Well that's her."

Jack laughed. "I wonder if she'll recognise you."

"You tell her what I did and I will hit you over the head with an oar."

"Hello," said one of the women in a thick French accent as we approached the group.

"Hi. I'm Lucy," I said, shifting the weight of my pack and staring at the ground.

Jack waved. "I'm Jack."

"I am Sylvie," said the French woman.

"Veronique," said the woman standing next to her—also French.

"I'm Carol," said the blonde, sounding American or possibly Canadian. Now that I was up close to her, instead of hiding behind a lamppost, I could see she didn't look Scandinavian at all. She was still very blonde though.

Our guide Victor stood at the back of the boat and motioned for us to get in. "Vamos."

Jack and I quickly dumped our bags over the side into the boat and scrambled aboard with the others before Victor pushed off the bank. Victor had a kind, smiling face and a large no-nonsense moustache i.e. everything you wanted in a man who was steering you down a river filled with piranha.

As he steered he pointed out large rodents called capybara sunning themselves on the banks of the river. I'd read about them but was surprised at how big they were. They didn't resemble the over-grown hamsters I'd imagined and were more like a generous meal than a bite-sized snack for the predators that lurked in the depths of the murky brown river. Capybara were definitely going on the list of animals to fear while in South America.

"Mira," said Victor. "Look." He pointed at the steep riverbank ahead to a large congregation of caiman sunning themselves. I removed my fingers that were curled over the side of the boat and jammed them under my butt. Sure, caiman were supposed to be smaller than their alligator cousins, but they were still big and toothy enough to take a chunk out of a body part that I'd definitely miss.

As we glided past, the biggest caiman slithered into the water and like a scaly submarine, slowly submerged before disappearing completely from sight.

I'd read that the Beni flowed into another river and eventually all the way to the Amazon. Watching all these animals make themselves known to us while we buzzed up the river to our camp, I couldn't help but muse that these predators of the Beni were the ones who didn't want to go out into the world and see what they were made of, following the river all the way to the bright lights, big city. They were like me. Sticking to their safe patch of river bank because they were worried they'd be chewed up and spat out by the mighty Amazon. This made me feel better about being such a scared little sausage, and I leaned back in my wooden seat while taking in the scenery as we travelled up the river to our accommodation.

Dark green jungle climbed high up into the blue sky, a sky criss-crossed with brightly coloured birds who put on a show for the tourists. Everything buzzed with life and I sighed deeply as I took it all in, for a second almost forgetting my fear. Bolivia really *was* special—minus the mining strikes and kamikaze drivers. It was raw like an uncut diamond. The country was poor and there was a suffering that rubbed at a privileged First Worlder like me. But it was as beautiful as it might be brutal.

I felt compelled to share the moment and looked around at everyone on the boat, immediately locking eyes with Carol. Damn.

"You look familiar, Lucy. I'm just trying to figure out where from."

"I don't know," I said, bringing my hand up to my face, pretending to shield my eyes from the sun.

"Did we do the Death Road cycle trip together?" she asked. I shook my head, feeling Jack's eyes on me now.

"What about Spanish lessons in Sucre? Were you in my class?"

"Nope. I didn't do Spanish lessons in Sucre," I said.

"Lucy did do Spanish lessons in Buenos Aires though," said Jack, placing emphasis on Buenos Aires. If he'd been closer I would have kicked him.

"No, that can't be it. Oh well. I'm sure it will come to me."

She turned to face the front of the boat and I gave Jack the finger, but he just sniggered. There was no way in hell I'd be volunteering to Carol that I had stalked her in my moment of pathetic need. Every time I thought about it I cringed and batted away the memory. I would rather invite an anaconda to wrap itself around my face than confess.

* * *

Our home during the tour was a ramshackle wooden building that looked out over the river. A large dormitory ran the length of the building, with a dining room and kitchen making up the rest of the space. I was dismayed to learn that the bathrooms and showers were in a separate building out back, my mind immediately thinking about going to the loo in the middle of the night. Other than that, our quarters were cosy and I would have been happy to sit with my feet up and watch the river with a beer in my hand.

Instead, we offloaded everything from the boats, had a quick look around and jumped back on-board for a spot of piranha fishing, something I didn't even know was a thing. Back on the boat Carol sat next to me.

"So Lucy, what do you do?" asked Carol.

"I'm a writer. And you?" I replied. I was quite used to these conversations by now, after several weeks of meeting new people every day. I smiled inwardly, wondering if when I was home I'd forget where I was and attempt to strike up conversations with strangers on the bus.

"I'm a nurse. Are you and Jack together or just travelling together?"

Jack and I usually made faces when someone posed that question to us, like five-year-olds who'd been forced to hold hands, but this time we just looked at each other. When Jack cleared his throat and looked at his feet I turned back to Carol.

"We work together on a travel blog actually. I'm a writer and Jack does the photography." The words popped out of my mouth, because the truth sometimes has a way of doing that. But as soon as I told her I realised now I *really* couldn't admit to stalking her through the streets of Buenos Aires. Travel writers were supposed to be awesome and have GPS built into their bones, weren't they?

She nodded like she was impressed. "Cool."

Exactly Carol. *Cool.*

Carol told me she was on sabbatical from her job in Vancouver and was travelling from Ushuaia in Argentina all the way up South America and Central America through Mexico and into the States, then back home. The way she talked about this epic trip, so damn relaxed without even a hint of uncertainty, made me feel, strangely, jealous. I was more nervous about getting a bikini wax than she was about a whole year of travelling by herself.

"Wow, that's amazing. I definitely couldn't do that kind of a trip alone. Don't you ever worry about something happening to you?"

"Nah. There's no point in worrying about something that may or may not ever actually happen. Worry is like asking for trouble."

God, I admired her. She was a proper badass. Worry was like my true north. I wasn't sure I would know how to function without it.

Her and Candy, the newspaper's original travel writer, would have got on like a bungy cord on fire. If she knew the "real" me she'd dismiss my ass in a heartbeat. Right before her and Candy laughed about what a dork I was and knocked back twelve suicide tequila shots.

"Look!" said Sylvie, pointing a little ahead of the boat at several large swirls in the water.

I popped my head up in horror, half-expecting to see a Piranhnaconda. "Dolphins!" squealed Veronique, clapping her hands.

So, not a Piranhnaconda. I let out a sigh of relief like a deflating balloon, and stuck my head up to get a better look. Victor slowed the boat to a stop a little way back from the swirls, and I waited to catch a glimpse of a famous pink river dolphin. One by one they surfaced from the muddy brown water and poked their little snouts up to greet us. They were more of a dusky sand colour than pink and were definitely smaller than any dolphin I'd ever seen, but still. They had teeth.

"If you want, you can jump in and swim with them," said Victor.

"What? That can't be safe," I yelped, horrified at the thought of dipping even my least favourite toe into the Beni.

"Oh, come on!" said Carol as she whipped up her dress, revealing a colourful bikini that was sure to attract predators, and dived right in. The French girls quickly followed her lead and joined her.

"Tell me you're not going to jump into that water too?" I asked Jack. He was already on his feet and pulled his t-shirt off, tugging it from the back and over his head like men tend to do. Which I'd always found kind of hot.

But this was Jack. So I tried to push that thought aside as soon as it surfaced.

"Lucy, you'll be fine. Victor wouldn't let us swim if it wasn't safe."

I blinked up at a shirtless Jack, grateful I was wearing sunglasses. His body looked hard and strong, and for a moment I forgot what I was saying. Something about being scared—right, yes.

"We're supposed to be fishing for piranha in this very water and you've seen the caiman on the banks. God knows what else is in there."

Carol smacked the water. "C'mon, you wimps! Get your butts in here."

"Shh," I hissed at Carol in a stage whisper. "Stop drawing attention to yourself. You don't know what's down there." I turned to Victor. "Are you sure it's safe?"

"Sure," Victor replied, his just-lit cigarette dangling from his lips.

"Then why aren't *you* swimming?"

"Because I have to stay with the boat," he replied, before pulling out his mobile phone.

Jack crouched down to press his hard front up against my back and whispered into my ear, his voice rough and growly. "Lucy, get into the water now or I'll tell your new friend your little secret."

"You wouldn't?!" I hissed, turning my head to look at him, the movement pressing me harder into his back. His body was hot against mine.

He pressed his lips to my ear. "I fucking would."

My body jerked a little as I felt the heat of his words against my ear. I was enjoying having Jack up against me a little too much for my liking, so I spun around to get away from him and stood up, my hands on my hips.

"I'm not wearing swimmers. I didn't realise we were all going to commit suicide this afternoon or I would have dressed appropriately," I hissed at Jack. What was worse, I wondered. Carol knowing I was the lamest travel writer in the world or being eaten alive by piranha?

"It doesn't matter. Just jump in like that," he said, nodding at my jean shorts and t-shirt. "I'll give you five seconds."

I looked up at the girls swimming. They looked happy enough. I could jump in and dive back into the boat immediately. After the car crash outside Sucre I was practising following my gut—or at least attempting to. But although my digestive system wasn't throwing up any alarm bells my brain was going haywire. I looked over at Carol, who waved me in.

"Come on, travel writer!" she yelled, not realising her words felt like a punch to the tit. I had to do this. She couldn't know.

"Fine. But I hate you!" I snapped at Jack, before pushing him backwards into the water. I yanked off my sunglasses and jean shorts, revealing a pair of black underwear, and jumped into the water wearing my t-shirt. The water was cold. That, combined with the fear already shooting through my veins, made my heart beat like the little engine that could.

"Look at you, Lucy. You're an animal," said Jack, swimming up to me with a big smile on his face.

"Fuck off," I breathed, trying not to smile as I pushed his face under the water before paddling back, feeling proud of myself for jumping in (even though it was on account of the loaded gun to my head). I heard him laugh behind me after he surfaced, but I waited until my arm was safely hooked over the side to look back at him. The rest of the group were treading water a little way off from Jack, and were closer to the dolphins, which were about ten metres away from the boat. I tried to pull myself up, but wasn't strong enough and Victor was talking on his phone with his back to me. I was about to try to heave my arse into the boat again, when something brushed past my leg. I stiffened and opened my mouth to scream, but nothing came out. This was it. I was about to die, a late afternoon snack for a family of piranha. I should have listened to my brain.

And then, right in front of me, a dolphin popped out of the water and stared at me. When I realised I wasn't going to be eaten, I reached a hand out. The dolphin squeaked, waited a bit, almost daring me to touch it. And I did. I grazed my fingers gently across the side of its face before it squeaked then dropped back underwater.

Holy shit! I smiled, feeling as though my insides might just explode with joy. I looked up to see Jack staring at me.

"There she is," he said with a knowing smile.

60 DAYS IN SOUTH AMERICA

Day 19: I went anaconda hunting today

Dear reader, do you know which sentence, out of all possible sentences, is the most unlikely to ever have come out of my mouth? Ever?

I went anaconda hunting today.

I mean, come on!

Those words, strung together, would have been just as likely for me to say as any of the following five-word sentences:
I have a lop-sided testicle.
My hero is Donald Trump.
I don't like chocolate ice-cream.
This good earth is banana-shaped.
(This post is sponsored by The Hyphen, without which my sentence experiment would have been 1400 times more difficult.)

Okay, so.
Yes.
I went anaconda hunting today.
I pulled on a pair of mud-encrusted black gum boots, two sizes too big, tied a bandana around my forehead like The Karate Kid and spat chewing tobacco into the dirt. Okay, so I didn't do that last thing. But that would have been cool if I had.

In the late morning before the sun had warmed the air too much, our group marched behind Victor into the swampy overgrown pampas. Our eyes peeled for the anaconda that had starred in that movie with JLo. But we didn't find it. (Thank you Elvis.) Some members of the group saw the end of one as it disappeared through the grass, but I missed it, too busy getting stuck up to my elbows in the swampy swamp. Don't ask me what we were actually going to do with one if we saw it up close. But it was more the intention behind the exercise i.e., that we were brave adventurers on the search for dangerous reptiles in the wilds of Bolivia.

Meanwhile the closest I came to any kind of reptile, dangerous or otherwise, was being defecated on by the biggest gecko I'd ever seen in my life. The beast had been hiding in wait for me in the wooden shower behind the cabins. But that is neither here nor there.

The point of this post is to posit the following: If I can do this, there must be other stuff that I've filed under "Don't Try This At Home" that I could do. I could sign up for Bollywood dancing lessons. I could eat dinner in a restaurant all by myself. I could smack people on the ass in the street. I could try hula-hooping. I could eat tripe. I could wear white! I could glue false eyelashes to my eyelids.

You're probably seeing a bit of a theme with these posts of mine. I tell you nothing about South America and you have to listen to me rambling on about my life. Because what is this travel blog if not a place for me to work out my personal issues? And you thought you came here for useful travel advice! Phfffff. For shame.

Anyway. Even though I'm telling you nothing about actually travelling on this amazing continent, I am hoping you might still be taking something away from my words. Like maybe the reassurance that if I can do some of the things, you can do some of the things too?

Maybe you have 537 travel-themed Pinterest boards, pinned with images from every inch of the world, but the thought of actually booking a plane ticket anywhere makes you feel like your insides are being squeezed by a sixteenth-century corset.

Maybe you bought yourself a travel magazine subscription with last year's birthday money from Great Aunt Gert, and each month you pour over the pages, determinedly dog-earing the ones that make your heart thud just that little bit faster. But you've already written yourself off as an armchair traveller and would never actually put that birthday money where your heart is.

Maybe you tell anyone who will listen that travel is a frivolous endeavour while you doggedly knit wonky beanies for orphans in Lithuania, all the while secretly wishing you could hand deliver said wonky beanies to the orphanage yourself.

Whatever your thing may be, before you write yourself off, maybe you book that ticket/cruise/tour/road trip/excursion/outing/adventure? Because if I can do it, then you sure as shit can too.

And that's all I have to say about that.
Lucy Hart

Next destination: Arequipa, Peru

Chapter 20

Jack and I made our way through the Arequipa market eating local Peruvian food in a bid to lessen our hangovers. I was never falling for 2-for-1 margaritas ever again. Carol, who'd been travelling with us since Rurrenabaque, had chosen to take her hangover for a hike in Colca Canyon. What a weirdo.

"Mmmmm, this is so good," I said through a mouthful of queso helado—cheese ice-cream—while ducking my head so Jack wouldn't try to get a photo of me with my mouth full. Cheese and ice-cream were two of my favourite things so I knew the treat would be a hit, but it was more like a sweet milk sorbet than any kind of cheese I'd ever tasted. We'd tried spicy stuffed peppers called rocoto rellenos. And before that alfajores, shortbread cookies sandwiched together with manjar, a thick type of caramel. The food was all so delicious the thought of stomach parasites burrowing out through the wall of my gut into my internal organs hardly bothered me at all.

Jack laughed at me. "You look like you're enjoying that," he said, eyeing the ice-creams stains down the front of my tank.

"I am, but only because I'm being paid to," I replied as I pawed my breast, trying to wipe away the stain. I licked my thumb and rubbed the spot.

"Lucy, stop fondling yourself," said Jack, his voice a little gruff. I rolled my eyes, pretending I didn't notice the weird sexual tension that had been building between us.

Jack steered us to a stall selling something called anticuchos. He handed over some money in return for the little squares of meat on a skewer. I pulled a chunk off and chewed.

"Mmm ... these are good. Kind of juicy," I said with my mouth full. "What kind of meat is this?"

"It's cow heart," said Jack, his eyes twinkling. I coughed and he whacked me on the back.

I punched him in the arm when I'd recovered. "You shit!" I said, before shrugging and biting off another piece.

We walked in silence for a moment, weaving through the stalls, taking in the people and smells. I stopped suddenly.

"Oh God. There's that creepy dude from the hostel. What's his name?" I tilted my chin and Jack followed my eyes.

"Bob, or Crazy Bob apparently. He's actually a nice guy, you know. You'd like him if you spoke to him for five minutes."

I doubted that. Word on the street was that Bob had tried to pull out his eyeball during a bad acid trip. "You like everyone, Jack," I said, lingering at a stall selling beautiful woven blankets, rubbing the thick material between my fingers. I could feel Jack's eyes on me.

"Lucy, I know that look. What is it?"

I dropped the blanket in my hands and looked straight into his eyes, noticing that they resembled black coffee that afternoon. "You like everyone. Except you didn't like me. At least in the beginning. Why is that?"

He hesitated and picked up the blanket I'd just dropped. "I didn't not like you, Luce. You were just ... different to most people I've met." Jack moved to the side to let a young couple with a baby pass us.

I smirked. "You mean you don't know any other weird hot messes?"

"You are seriously one of a kind."

I nodded. "Should I take that as a compliment?"

He opened his mouth to expand on his cryptic response, but didn't speak, reminding me of the time he'd apologised to me in the dark, on the side of the road in Bolivia. He'd stopped short of telling me what he thought of me. His secret opinion of me.

I decided to leave it alone and pulled the sleeve of Jack's t-shirt instead. "Let's just pretend we didn't see Bob please. Seriously, that wonky eyeball is enough to put one off one's cow heart," I said, waving my half-finished stick of organ meat at him.

We just managed to get out of sight of Crazy Bob with the wonky eye when Jack stopped, his eyes suddenly lighting up.

"Uh-oh. What is it?"

"Well, in the name of research for "the blog," and also because we're being paid to, I spy a rack of roasted guinea pigs that have your name all over them." Jack grabbed my hand and pulled me to the stall in question.

I shook my head and dug in my heels, but Jack just pulled me harder. "No way Jose. You play with guinea pigs. You don't eat them."

Jack ignored me and turned to the lady serving the once-fluffy pets up for lunch. "Buenas dias, señora."

"Buenas dias, guapo," she replied, calling Jack handsome. She was as feisty as she was old and Jack seemed more than happy to engage in some flirty banter, most of which I still couldn't understand.

He turned to me. "She definitely wants me. And also she says her guinea pigs are the best in the whole market."

"I don't care if she serves the best guinea pigs in the entire universe, Jack. I'm not eating Mr Snuggles."

I could see Jack's mind-cogs turning as he tried to figure out how to convince me. But by now I had his number. Under his sometimes crusty exterior he had the sweetest heart and the best intentions, and when I looked back I was able to recognise all the times he'd tried to nudge me along: leaving me on the bus, whacking my horse on the ass, blackmailing me to jump into the river. He thought he could trick me into being brave and adventurous—sometimes with mixed results.

"What about if—"

I held up my hand to stop him. "I'll eat pig if you eat ceviche."

Jack abhorred ceviche. I knew this because I'd had to listen to him go on about it for an hour yesterday when a few of us were trying to decide where to go for lunch.

Jack shuddered and puffed out his cheeks like he was about to throw up. "You know how much I hate that stuff. Plus they always pile coriander on it. Parents feed ceviche to their children when they've been naughty. I'd actually rather eat poo. Or a maggot crawling in poo." He glanced at a crusty-looking dog turd that had wedged itself between the cobbled stones.

"Deal," I said, reaching for his hand and shaking it before he could pull it away.

"What?" said Jack, his face pale and rigid with terror. "You want me to eat poo?"

I threw my head back and laughed.

"Nope. Just a maggot."

Jack thought for a moment before shrugging his shoulders.

"Okay, fine," he replied, like I'd requested he eat a cheese and tomato sandwich.

Jack reached for his wallet and pulled out a few soles, and handed it to the señora who was giving me the stink eye. With my pig in hand, we set off in search of maggots. Which, in the end were almost too easy to find. It only took us a few minutes of wandering around before we found a few fresh maggots wriggling under a meat stall.

"Buen provecho," said Jack, giving my char-grilled rodent a nod, as I gingerly gnawed off a piece of meat. It was tough but inoffensive, like dry chicken that had been cooked for three days. But then didn't everything taste like chicken?

"Buen provecho," I said, trying not to gag as I watched him place the maggot on his tongue and quickly shut his mouth so the creature didn't wriggle out. After pretending to chew and swallow he opened his mouth wide, throwing out a pair of jazz hands as he did.

"And you kiss your girlfriend with that mouth?" I asked, wrinkling my nose, before quickly turning away from him. Because I'd just caught myself wondering what it would be like to kiss him with that mouth *myself*.

60 DAYS IN SOUTH AMERICA

Day 27: Machu Freaking Picchu

I'll forever remember the day I saw Machu Picchu. The memories will be etched in my brain like symbols carved into stone.

Jack and I had spent the previous four days hiking on the trail before arriving in the town of Aguas Calientes. That morning, we woke up before the sun to walk to the gate with the rest of our trekking group. Even at that early hour our group was wide awake and wired. With headlamps strapped to our foreheads and hiking boots tightly laced we were ready to make the climb up the million or so steps to the gates.

And those steps, let me tell you, were no joke.

By a third of the way I'd decided I was relieved we were stumbling up the steps in the dark, my headlamp lighting only a metre or so in front of me. Because I couldn't see the path, I was only able to focus on the next two steps I needed to climb to make it all the way up to the sky. Anyway, I'm quite used to stumbling around in the dark. Before we knew it, the sun was coming up and I was at the gate amongst the clouds.

The grounds at Machu Picchu were still covered in mist when we entered. Slowly throughout the morning the rising sun revealed the ruins little by little—as though Pacha Mama didn't think we could handle the heart-splintering awe in one go. So she drip-fed us the splendour little by little to stop us from cracking open. ("You want the truth? You can't handle the truth!")

Everywhere we walked, people seemed to talk in hushed tones. Like they could feel the sacredness. And how could they not? The Incans built a city in the sky. A city that was lost to time for so long, the jungle reclaimed it. The only way it could be more spectacular was if the city was levitating above the ground.

As I sat at the top of Wayna Picchu and stared down at the manicured greens and partly reconstructed stone walls, I thought about the people who had first come upon it, blades in their sweaty hands, hacking at the dense undergrowth, trying to figure out what they were seeing.

That's what I've felt like over the last few weeks. For so long, my soul, my mojo, call it whatever you like, has been covered in weeds. Large, thick weeds that blocked out the light and made me forget that being alive was a gift not a chore. I've suffered through life like a woman with carpal tunnel performing a four-hour hand job. This makes me sad. I want to enjoy it again. Life—not hand jobs. Hand jobs are for the birds.

And that's all I have to say about that.
Lucy Hart

Next destination: Cusco, Peru

Chapter 21

"I can't believe this time yesterday we were at Machu Picchu."

No response.

"Jack, are you listening to me?"

Grunt.

My cheeks ached from smiling—like a newly crowned Miss World with Vaseline smeared teeth, making me almost want to raise my hand and wave elegantly at the plants in the courtyard. If anyone had told me a month ago that visiting ancient Incan ruins was in the stars for me, I would have insisted they put down their crack pipe.

Jack and I were lying in hammocks in our hostel in Cusco where we'd been working for most of the morning. The courtyard was a big open square in the middle of the hostel and I could see big fluffy clouds drift across the pastel sky above us. It was a welcome change not to have to tear off to catch a bus, and I was enjoying basking in the glow of my accomplishment before hurling myself into the next planned activity. Jack was still engrossed in his photo editing, but I'd convinced myself that part of my job included people watching and I was allowing myself a short break.

"Hello. Please may you give me a push?" I called out to a short guy with a towel slung over his shoulder. He gave me an odd look but pushed me anyway, before heading to the bathroom.

Jack looked up from his screen, shaking his head. "You're a weirdo, you know that?"

But he couldn't fool me. I smiled as I thought about how he'd high-fived me and told me how proud he was of me as we'd stared down at Machu Picchu from where we sat at Wayna Picchu, our feet dangling over the edge of our rocky perch. I was still on a high from the experience—either that or I was suffering from altitude sickness given that Cusco, where we now were, was over 3000m above sea level.

"Did you feel the energy when you were standing on the top of Wayna Picchu? It was definitely a spiritual experience, don't you think?" I asked.

But Jack had already gone back to his work and merely grunted in response.

"Hello," I said to a pretty blonde walking past with a bag slung across her body. "Would you mind giving me a push?"

"Don't push her," said Jack, his eyes glued to his screen. "You'll just be encouraging her." He looked up just in time to see the blonde stop and give me a push. I stuck my tongue out at him as I swung through the air. The woman giggled at our exchange and stopped to chat.

"Where're you from?" she asked Jack in what sounded like an American accent.

"England."

"Pity. For a second there I thought you might be from Scotland."

"Nope."

"Do have some kind of Scottish fetish?" I asked.

"Something like that. I want to sleep with a Scotsman and I haven't yet come across one in my travels. I've already had an English guy," she said, all matter of fact—like she was telling us the time.

"What do you mean you've already 'had' an Englishman?" My interest was piqued.

She shrugged. "I mean I've had sex with an English guy. I think he was from Manchester."

"Do you have some kind of sexual bucket list?" asked Jack, suddenly more interested in the conversation than his work.

She smiled and shrugged mysteriously.

I gestured to the wicker chair near us. "Sit down and tell us everything. I'm Lucy. And this is Jack, by the way."

"Misty," said the blonde, sitting cross-legged on the chair.

"What else have you got on your bucket list? I mean, is it all sex stuff?"

Misty laughed. "No it's not all sex stuff. There are other things. I just don't buy into having a conventional bucket list with the same stuff as everyone else. We're all different so why should our Bucket Lists look the same? I want to shave my head and perform a marriage ceremony, donate my eggs, perfect my handstand, bath in custard—stuff like that."

"But tell me about the sex stuff," I asked, waggling my eyebrows.

Misty tapped the side of her nose and winked.

"Oh come on! Tell me something."

"Well, I do have a list of nationalities I want to sleep with."

I leaned so far forward in my hammock that I almost spilled out. "So when you find someone with the appropriate nationality to tick your, um box, so to speak, you immediately tell them to take off all their clothes?"

"Pretty much. If you don't ask you don't get."

"I suppose if I looked like you guys would be lining up to sleep with me."

Misty was petite and beautiful. She was one of those annoying girls that seemed to rock the whole backpacker look so well—nose stud, messy plait and obligatory travel bangles halfway up to her elbows. She even looked gorgeous wearing jean shorts and a faded hostel t-shirt. Even post makeover, without a shred of moisture-wicking fabric in sight, I couldn't hold a candle to her.

"Please, girl. You have curves and boobs." She gestured at my chest. "You're hot!" I looked to where she was pointing and saw a brown stain on the top of my tank. I lifted the tank to my nose and licked the stain.

"Coffee," I said.

"Now *that's* hot!" said Jack, imitating Misty's drawl. I threw him a dirty look.

"Excuse me, Jack, but I can see your nipple through that hole in your t-shirt and you seem to have misplaced your razor?" I retorted with a raised eyebrow, having noticed that he hadn't shaved since La Paz. The stubble suited him, something I was trying and failing to ignore. Jack frowned as his face went red.

Misty giggled. "You guys are super cute."

"Where are you headed after Cusco?" I asked.

"I'm off to the jungle to see a shaman about some Ayahuasca. And then after that I'm headed to Central America. What about you guys?"

"To the coast then up from Peru into Ecuador then on to Colombia. We're finishing off with a boat trip into Panama through the San Blas islands." I hoped I sounded as though I'd chosen to be here instead of being dragged, kicking and screaming.

Misty shuddered. "I met a couple in Arequipa who know a guy whose boat was attacked by pirates while sailing through the San Blas Islands. He got stabbed and almost died!"

"What?" I snapped, my eyes widening.

"I don't know,' said Jack, looking unconvinced. "That sounds like a backpacking urban legend to me. Like the Japanese backpacker who rode his bike off Death Road."

"Or the one about the police raiding that bus for drugs and deporting backpackers in Banos," I offered.

"All I know is what this couple told me. You guys need to be careful in that area."

I looked at Jack and he gave me a reassuring shake of his head.

Misty looked at her watch. "I need to meet some people in town. It was great chatting with you guys. Good luck with everything."

When Misty left, Jack turned his attention to his laptop, but I couldn't stop thinking about the possibility of pirates in the San Blas. I pulled the sides of the hammock around me as though they would somehow protect me from what was about to come.

"Jack?" I whispered from the depths of my cocoon. "Are we going to be attacked by pirates?"

"No, we're not, Lucy," he said.

"Are you sure?" He didn't sound as convincing as I would have hoped. I squeezed my eyes shut to push away the worry. A shadow fell over my face and I looked up to see Jack standing over me.

"Lucy Agnes Hart, we are going to be fine." When I didn't look convinced, he changed tack. "Come on, who do you trust more: me or Bucket List Barbie?" he asked.

My laugh was a short, sharp, goose-like honk. "You, Jack Mansford Dawson," I said, squinting up at his face.

"Good. Now do you want a push or what?"

"I thought you'd never ask."

Jack pulled me up high and gave me an almighty push. I laughed, almost forgetting about the knot forming in my gut.

60 DAYS IN SOUTH AMERICA

Day 28: Make that Bucket List your bitch

Guys.

To get you into the travelling vibe, I am going to list the phrases I come across on a daily basis while on the gringo trail.

- *Does this hostel have wifi?*
- *How long have you been travelling for?*
- *I didn't like [insert town] because it was too touristy.*
- *Where are you from?*
- *Do you know what the wifi password is?*
- *I'm on a sabbatical.*
- *What do you do back home?*
- *Is the wifi working OK for you?*
- *Do you want to be friends with me on Facebook?*
- *Where are you headed to next?*
- *Can I borrow your iPhone charger?*
- *This wifi is shit, and*
- *[Insert activity here] is TOTALLY on my bucket list.*
- *South America is a bucket-list bonanza.*

You've got Machu Picchu, Iguazu, the Salt Flats, Atacama Desert, the Galapagos and Carnaval, to name a few.

The sound of fellow travellers furiously ticking off bucket list items follows me everywhere on this crazy continent. (The sound is a cross between grasshoppers mating and fingers tapping on smart phones.)

I've never been particularly interested in having a Bucket List. Most of the usual suspects seem to involve life-threatening activities like running with the bulls or swimming with sharks. I know Bucket Lists are so-called because they are all about doing things before you kick the bucket, but I think most of these items only seem to increase your chances of kicking said bucket.

But I met someone today (Hi Misty!) who taught me that it's okay to have a Bucket List all my own that doesn't look like everyone else's, that it's okay to have a life all of my own that doesn't look like everyone else's. And that made me feel happy. Which made me want to drink many cervezas in celebration. Which made me drunk. Which made me want to lie down. Which made me want to sleep.

I challenge you to make your bucket list your bitch—not the other way around. You don't have to climb mountains or run marathons if you don't like climbing or running. Knit the world's longest scarf if you want. Snort cocaine off the buttock of a supermodel if you'd prefer. Heck, ride a tricycle blindfolded through a ring of fire. Eat a kilogram of sherbet for breakfast. Or craft the perfect origami vagina. Or don't have a bucket list at all and slurp gravy through a straw like it's a smoothie.

And as always, that is all I have to say about that.
Lucy Hart

Next destination: Hare Krishna Village, Peru

Chapter 22

Hare Krishna Hare Krishna Krishna Krishna Hare Hare Hare Rama Hare Rama …

Chanting wafted out of the temple and into my earholes.

"I can't believe you talked me into coming here," I hissed at Jack. It had been a few days and a thousand kilometres after the high of Machu Picchu and I had very much come back down to earth. Jack and I had arrived at a Hare Krishna settlement just north of Lima where we would be volunteering. A privilege the village folk kindly offered backpackers in exchange for a small fee.

Elena, the volunteer manager, showed the arriving volunteers the ropes.

"And once you have made the shit in the bucket, you cover with sawdust and put the lid back on."

I glared at Jack but he didn't dare make eye contact with me. I'd been sceptical about coming here, but Jack had sold volunteering at the village to me as a health retreat. I had pictured practicing yoga and washing vegetables—not shitting in a bucket.

"What do you do when the bucket is full?" I asked, petrified to hear her response.

"Everyone takes turns emptying it." Her face, when she said this, was serene and not at all like she'd just told me I'd be required to carry around other people's poo. "Let me show you now," she continued, "where you have to take the bucket when it's full."

The settlement, which extended across several acres of land, was sandwiched between a sad-looking beach and a freeway. When we'd arrived at the bus stop that afternoon, we'd hailed a tuk-tuk driver to take us to the village. The driver had offered, unsolicited, that the nearest town was but a ten-minute tuk-tuk ride north. It was as if he'd known, then, that we'd want to escape. I was tempted to run away immediately, up the dirt track that ran parallel to the main road, and never come back. Instead, I traipsed behind Elena and the other volunteers, past a fruit orchard, empty paddock and workshop to a large excrement pit that had mushrooms growing on top of it.

"That's a long way to have to carry a bucket of shit," said Ruby. She was English and a smart-arse and I liked her already.

Elena nodded gravely. "That is why you should not wait until the bucket is too full. Now we will all go back to your rooms so you can wash yourselves because you are all unclean."

I discreetly lowered my nose to my right armpit and sniffed. She couldn't be talking about me, could she? Nonetheless, I followed her back towards the compound, where the men and women had been allocated separate sleeping quarters.

In addition to Jack, myself and Ruby, the other volunteers included Ruby's girlfriend Emily, Marla, a sweet, grey-haired hippy from California and Angel, a Dutch woman who I already wanted to kick in the shins. Angel was one of those self-righteous backpackers convinced she was travelling the right way and everyone else was travelling the wrong way. She looked down her nose at everyone from a height that suggested she brushed her teeth with leaves and had rowed here all the way from the Netherlands. She'd even laughed at my 80-litre backpack when I'd dumped it in the dorm when we arrived. Apparently, she was travelling with only a handkerchief tied around a stick.

There are those people who are put in your path to make you feel bad about yourself. You know the one. You're in a yoga class. You're wheezing after your third sun salutation—please God make it stop—and the woman in front of you, with the butt that's so perfect it looks like it was manufactured by Mattel, is doing all the hardcore yogi variations and you can't even reach your bloody ankles. That's what Angel was. The reminder that as much as I tried I would never get it right, the embodiment of just how much I thought I was fucking up.

I fell into step next to Jack. "We weren't made to shit in buckets."

Angel, who was walking just ahead of me, turned and laughed. "You know we weren't made to shit in toilets either?"

I rolled my eyes. What kind of a name was Angel anyway? And why was she wearing that floor-length poncho and sticks in her hair?

"I know that!" I snapped, stomping ahead so I didn't have to look at her stupid face.

"Oh dear," I heard her say. "I think I've upset her. I just think it's sad she's forgotten our true nature."

"Don't worry about Lucy. She's probably just embarrassed," Jack said as I slowed my pace to hear the rest of their conversation.

"I didn't mean to embarrass your girlfriend. I think it's because I'm Dutch. We're just direct, you know."

"She's not my girlfriend. And don't worry about it. She'll be fine."

"If you're not her boyfriend you're obviously looking out for her. That's so nice of you. She looks like she needs all the help she can get. That backpack of hers is enormous. You could fit a whole fridge in it."

"Maybe not a fridge, but at least a portable defibrillator," chuckled ~~Judas~~ Jack.

Angel giggled. "No! You're kidding me."

* * *

"That was so good I could lick the bowl," Marla said.

We'd just finished our dinner of black-eyed peas, steamed vegetables and homemade tomato sauce, all grown right there in the village. While the food *was* good, I'd somehow ended up at the back of the queue when dinner was served, meaning the dregs had been dumped onto my metal prison plate. And, before I could even ask for a slice of bread, the chef, Alejandro, had rushed off to the temple to join the others for worship. I'd worked like a dog all day digging in the veggie patch and was starving.

"You know what we need now?" Marla said.

"A steak?" I replied.

"No."

"Pizza?" I tried again.

"Weed!"

I swallowed hard, never having smoked weed. I'd skipped out on experimenting with drugs during my younger years after hearing about a girl at my high school who'd ended up with a handbag full of dead rats and her fingers chewed off to the knuckle after a bad trip. That, and the consumption of drugs didn't really go with my people-pleasing good girl look.

Angel leaned over and pressed her forehead to Marla's. "It's like you're inside my head," she said, pulling the elderly woman into a hug. Ugh. Go away.

Angel had come to dinner wearing dungarees over a small tie-dye boob tube. A large feathered crown on her head completed the hipster shaman princess look. She smelled like sandalwood and rust.

"I'm up for some weed," I said, surprising myself. But fuck it all. I was tired of being good. I wanted to be adventurous instead.

Angel looked as surprised as I felt, and I resisted the urge to jump on top of the wooden table and yell that I could be cool and worldly too—even if my version of sandalwood and rust was soap and deodorant.

"Great!" said Marla, jumping up from the long wooden table. "I'll get the weed. You go make yourselves comfortable around the fire pit."

We ran our plates under the cold tap outside the kitchen and stacked them on the table before trooping back to the fire pit in the centre of the compound. The open-air, earthen compound housed the men's dorm on one side, the women's dorm directly opposite, and the bathrooms along the wall between the dorms. The common room/library made up the last side of the structure.

As we filed through the archway into the compound Jack pulled me aside.

"Have you smoked weed before?" he whispered, concern etched on his face.

"No, but I have to start sometime," I replied, jutting my chin out in defiance and sounding way more confident than I felt.

"You don't have to do this. You don't have anything to prove," he said.

I looked at Angel, who was stood barefoot in the middle of the veggie patch, her eyes and arms open, face tilted towards the moon. At any moment I half-expected her to start howling.

"I know. But I want to."

I squeezed Jack's arm and walked to the fire pit, taking a seat on a log and waiting with the others. Marla didn't keep us waiting long. In no time at all, she rolled a big, fat spliff, lit it, took a few drags then sent it on its way around the circle. When it reached me I took a tentative puff, and when I didn't embarrass myself, went a little deeper.

"That's right, honey," said Marla. "Now, inhale and keep it in your lungs before letting it go."

I held the heat in my lungs before exhaling. But as I let it out, the smoke caught in my throat and I coughed violently as my eyes streamed with tears. I held out the joint to Jack, avoiding his eyes while I coughed into the crook of my arm. When the coughing subsided, Marla smiled at me kindly—or at least I think she did, it was hard to tell through the tears. Then I waited to feel the buzz.

But nothing happened.

The fat blunt burned to a tiny stub after a few rounds and when it had been snuffed out Emily got out her ukulele. We sang along to Beatles' songs and I didn't feel any different. Everyone shared stories, and still I didn't feel any different. We tried to come up with a catchy name for the poo pit at the back of property, and still I didn't feel any different.

Maybe the weed wasn't strong enough? Maybe I hadn't smoked enough? Or, maybe I just sucked at being stoned? All I felt was hunger. So, during a lively rendition of "We All Live In A Yellow Submarine", I excused myself and headed to the dorm to scrounge for snacks. I was crouched down, rummaging through my bag looking for a chocolate bar when someone came up behind me.

"I just came in to check on you. How're you doing?" asked Angel.

"I'm fine," I said, pushing myself to my feet with my hands on my hips to demonstrate just how fine I was. But I got up too quickly and had to sit on my bed to stop the black spots from dancing across my eyeballs.

"You don't seem fine," she said, sitting next to me on the bed.

"I am. Just stood up too quickly," I huffed. Couldn't I just look for my chocolate bar and shove it into my face in peace?

"Or you're just high," she said with a knowing smile.

"I'm not high. I didn't smoke very much at all."

"Well, how do you feel?"

I considered her question. "I'm a little lightheaded I suppose. And I'm hungry."

She giggled, the feathers on her head rustling as her shoulders shook.

"Honey, you're *definitely* stoned."

I frowned. "Do you really think so? I don't *feel* stoned," I said, wiggling my fingers and toes to check.

"Have you ever smoked weed before?"

"No," I admitted. "But I don't feel any different." If this was what it felt like to be high I don't know why everyone was so excited about it. I felt like I was lost in a supermarket on an empty stomach.

"You know what, I have some cookies with me. You can have a few if you're hungry?"

I nodded, and from her bag she pulled out a small plastic bag with four or five cookies in it.

"Are these chocolate chip?" I asked, with a mouthful of cookie. They tasted like chocolate chip, but also like someone had rubbed them in the dirt.

"Yep. Chocolate chip and, uh … oat," she replied, with a big smile on her face.

After I'd eaten two cookies, I tried handing her the bag, but she shook her head, insisting I eat the whole lot. "Seriously. Lucy. I remember the first time I got stoned I was absolutely ravenous. I don't mind if you eat them all. Plus I feel bad for making fun of you earlier. I was just joking, but I know I probably came across as mean."

"Thank you. And it's okay," I said, before shoving a third cookie into my mouth.

"Friends?" she asked, holding her arms out for a hug.

Let's not get carried away here, Ladybird, I wanted to say. She still gave me a bad vibe, but I nodded, flicked cookie crumbs off the front of my shirt and succumbed to the hug. "Sure, why not?"

We rejoined the others and for the next half an hour we sang songs, told jokes and talked around the fireless fire pit. It was the most fun I think I'd had the whole trip. And they were all so funny. Even Angel, who I had by now come round to, was amusing.

"I wish we could light a fire in this pit," said Angel, which made me cackle with laughter.

Jack glanced at me. "Lucy, are you okay?"

"I'm fine. Hey guys. I know! Why don't we go into town? It'll be an adventure. And maybe we can get some pizza and a steak and ice cream." I stared at the group, not blinking.

"I don't know. I'm kind of enjoying just being here," said Emily.

"Come on, that's lame. We only live once in this life. Let's make the most of it," I exclaimed, stumbled to my feet and punched the air to a chorus of half-hearted nods and shrugs.

"Okay you guys, get your wallets and meet me outside the village. I'll go round up some transport," I said, heading back to the room to get my wallet and coming out again a few moments later because I'd forgotten what I'd gone into the room for in the first place.

I stood there for a bit, remembered that I needed my wallet and went back into the room to get it. The night was going to be epic. For once, *I* was going to be the ringleader of an adventure. I'd decided I was going to wrangle a few tuk-tuks, so I tramped out behind the village, where we'd seen a few of them parked the day before. I imagined everyone thinking how cool and fun I was, and how they'd probably tell their friends about me when they got back home.

When I got round the corner, I came across a handful of tuk-tuks parked in a clearing under a tree. I walked up to a few and peered in, but they were all empty.

'Hola?" I called out into the darkness. "Hola?" I said again, a little louder this time. I jumped into the back of the nearest one and decided to wait for one of the drivers to arrive.

But no one did.

That couldn't be the end of the adventure—before it had even started. I couldn't go back, tuk-tuk-less, and tell the others what could possibly have been the biggest adventure of their lives had been cancelled. The Legend of Lucy couldn't be over before it had even begun. I was not letting myself down this time.

I stumbled out of the tuk-tuk and fumbled around with the key in the ignition. The drivers had probably all clocked off for the night so they wouldn't mind me borrowing their vehicle for a little while, I thought. Once we returned from having the best night of our lives, I'd leave some money on the seat. I jumped in the front, turned the key in the ignition and shimmied in excitement when the engine puttered to life.

The tuk-tuk was an automatic and I quickly learned that when I turned the handle, the machine lurched forward. With some expert manoeuvering, I turned the little vehicle around and tore off down the dirt road to fetch the others.

Chapter 23

"Tah-dah!" I shouted, throwing my hands in the air when I pulled up to them.

"Lucy, what are you doing?" asked Jack.

"Where did you get that tuk-tuk? And where is the driver?" asked Angel.

"He said I could borrow it for the night. What a nice man … erm … Pepe, is. Hop in, gang! I know it'll be a bit of squish but the trip shouldn't be too long."

Marla, Emily, Ruby and Angel all exchanged looks. No one moved.

"What's wrong? This is going to be fun. Come on!" I was shouting but I couldn't help it.

"I'm not going in that thing with you driving?" said Ruby.

"Yeah, I don't think it's safe," said Emily, backing away from the tuk-tuk.

"Safe shmafe," I yelled. Why was everyone being so boring? Marla also retreated.

"Whatever. Jack? Angel? You guys are coming, right? You're not lame like these lame-o's?!"

"Usually I don't get into tuk-tuks because they're for tourists. And, like, I'm a traveller. But since this is a special occasion I'll make an exception," said Angel, with a weird glint in her eye.

I rolled my eyes. "We're all just visitors, Angel. Just like that chicken is only visiting your head," I said, pointing at her feathered headdress, making a flapping motion with my arms. "But that doesn't mean it can't still feel the wind in its feathers."

Jack smothered a smile. "I'll come too, Lucy. But can I drive?" he asked.

"No, Jack." I shook my head firmly. "I want to be the master of my fate, the captain of my soul, the driver of my own tuk-tuk."

"Okay, fine. But I don't want to feel the wind through my feathers please," he said, climbing into the back. "Make sure you drive slowly."

I revved the engine but it wasn't loud enough for my liking so I added my own engine noises to the mix.

"Let's ride, bitches!" I yelled. With a flick of my wrist, my hand slipped off the handle and the tuk-tuk jerked forward. Then the engine puttered out.

I turned the key in the ignition. "Okay, now, let's ride. Adios Amigo, bitches!" I shouted, accelerating and sending us roaring down the path, the little engine whining.

"Isn't this fun?" I shouted, turning around to look at Jack and Angel.

"Yes it is. I can't wait to see what happens next," said Angel, her mouth twisted into a smile.

"I think it's supposed to take like ten minutes to get into town," I shouted into the wind. "But at this rate we'll get there in no time."

We caned it along the dirt road and I smiled into the wind, pretending I was Nicholas Cage in *60 Segundos*, the Spanish version of *Gone in 60 Seconds*. I had boosted a tuk-tuk and was driving for my life to get away from the cops. I must have been going at least eighty kilometres per hour. But, when I glanced down at the odometer it only read five. I tapped the screen and frowned. It *had* to be wrong. It felt like we were tearing along.

"I think the odometer's broken," I shouted back at Jack and Angel, who appeared remarkably calm in the back seat, considering I was driving like a bat out of hell. I tilted my head to the moon like I'd seen Angel do earlier in the veggie patch, closed my eyes and laughed at the night.

"Lucy, maybe you should keep your eyes open while you drive," said Jack, popping his head through from the back.

"Isn't this fun, Jack? Aren't I just the craziest?" I yelled.

"Yes Lucy, you are the craziest," said Jack, squeezing my shoulder. I turned to smile at him and noticed something that looked like a donkey cart coming up behind us.

"Shit, there's a donkey cart on our tail!" I shouted, facing forward and checking my rearview mirror. The cart was gaining on us fast. "What the fuck? That is one fast donkey," I yelled, jamming my hand onto the accelerator to keep ahead of them.

"Uh, Jack. There's another tuk-tuk behind the cart and the driver is shouting something at us," said Angel. I turned to look behind me, the wheel still in my hands, sending the tuk-tuk lurching right as I did.

"Lucy, why is that guy yelling at us? Did you really just *borrow* this tuk-tuk?" asked Jack.

But, I couldn't concentrate on him with the cart roaring up alongside us on our left. I looked over at the donkey that was now almost neck and neck with me, and for a second I could swear its eyes flashed red. The donkey snorted and its eyes definitely flashed this time, glowing hot embers, like it was possessed by a demon. My God! I had to get away from it. I pressed down on the accelerator.

"Lucy?" Jack tried again.

"Jack, forget I stole the tuk-tuk. That demon donkey wants to eat my soul! Like the dirt cookies Angel gave me," I yelled, swerving the tuk-tuk over to the right up against the bushes that lined the dirt path and separated us from the main freeway. Branches flicked at the little vehicle as we hugged the bush. I kept my mouth shut to stop any leaves from flying into it and peeked to my left to check on the donkey. It was still there, steam rushing from its nostrils, hot like the pits of hell. It gnashed its dirty yellow teeth. The driver seemed to spur the evil animal even closer towards us.

"What did you give her?" I heard Jack shout behind me.

Angel mumbled something I couldn't hear in response.

"No!" I screamed. "You can't have me," I shouted at the donkey and driver.

"Okay, Lucy. Why don't we stop the tuk-tuk?" said Jack, stepping round the side of the vehicle from the back partition.

"No, Jack. He wants to take me to hell for stealing that tuk-tuk," I screamed. Jack tried to ease the handlebars out of my grasp, but I wrestled with him.

"He doesn't want to take you to hell, Lucy. It's just a normal donkey. Angel's cookies were weed cookies and you're just really stoned right now," said Jack, throwing Angel a dirty look in the rearview mirror.

"But his eyes are red! And he's so fast. A normal donkey can't run at ninety kilometres per hour, pulling a cart like that," I said. This couldn't be the weed could it? Maybe the *donkey* was stoned.

"His eyes aren't red and he's only going ten. It just feels faster to you," Jack said, giving the broken odometer a tap. "Come on, everything's going to be fine. Now why don't you let me drive?" I shook my head and shoved him off the handlebars.

"Lucy, listen to Jack," said Angel. "You're not thinking straight."

"Shut it, Angel," snapped Jack.

"No, I don't want to die," I shouted. I needed to get away from the evil stoned donkey and the tuk-tuk driver and I was going to drive us all the way to Ecuador if I had to. But when I looked behind me the cart was almost on top of me, so in a panicked last ditch effort I wrenched the tuk-tuk—right into the massive bush that jutted out in the track.

Somewhere deep in my brain I realised that I *was* stoned. Extremely stoned. But that didn't make things any easier though. So I stood there, with the hoody of my llama jumper pulled over my head, while Jack tried to placate the driver of the stolen vehicle.

"Lo siento," I whispered over and over again, so quiet I was sure the driver couldn't hear me over his angry tirade. I peeped out from under my hoody and caught Jack looping his index finger near his temple and mouthing the word loco. And I must have helped substantiate my insanity plea because I realised that the donkey cart driver had stopped alongside us and I suddenly shrieked at the sight of the donkey. Jack quickly handed over some cash to the tuk-tuk driver and pulled the sleeve of my jumper.

"Come on, Lucy. We're going," he said out of the corner of my mouth, dragging me off down the road back to the village, with Angel trotting a safe distance behind us.

60 DAYS IN SOUTH AMERICA

Day 36: Lady Gaga rides a llama

Hello from Ecuador!

And no, I haven't visited the equator yet.

Instead, I'm in the beautiful city of Cuenca and I've decided to take a few more Spanish lessons.

I have grown tired of communicating via hand puppetry so with the little time I have in this UNESCO World Heritage listed city, I signed up for several intensive lessons.

Think: Rocky IV movie montage when Balboa is training to fight Ivan Drago—the scene where he chops wood and milks cows. Meanwhile over at the Big Brother house Ivan is doing his best Science experiment impression getting injected with 'roids and leaking on the treadmill like a fat man in a sweat lodge. Okay, so I'm not carrying the large rocks on my back, but trust me, I'm doing just as much grunting.

(And yes, as research for this post, I watched that montage on Youtube twenty-three times. Because, I'm a professional. Unlike Ivan Drago, who needed chemical assistance to even have a chance of beating Rocky)

My one request to the manager of the language school: a teacher who wasn't aesthetically gifted, so that I'd be sure I paid attention to the lesson at hand and not to the teacher's arse that I wanted in my hand. She obviously thought I was odd and had I not been holding a fist full of dollar dollar bills, she would have told me to take my strange elsewhere.

I am happy to report that my teacher was as unattractive as he was kind, and the lessons went swimmingly. I have now progressed from sounding like a dim-witted caveman to a dim-witted three-year-old. I do find it frustrating, though, that when I speak Spanish, I have no personality or sense of humour to speak of. Unless you count the jokes I make about riding on llamas, which my Spanish teacher did seem to enjoy.

Aside from llamas, I also always seemed to involve Lady Gaga when constructing sentences in Spanish.

I was all:

Lady Gaga iba al mercado. Lady Gaga used to go the market.

Lady Gaga tiene un hermano. Lady Gaga has one brother.

Lady Gaga lleva un vestido echo de carne. Lady Gaga wears a dress made of meat.

Lady Gaga se monta en una llama. Lady Gaga rides on a llama.

And so on and so forth. Which no doubt will prove super useful during the rest of my travels through Ecuador and Colombia. Because, right now, Jack and I are into the home stretch. We've passed the half way mark, the point of no return. There's no going back now.

If this trip was a house party, right about now everyone would be on their sixth shot of vodka and people would already be hooking up in cupboards because fours are starting to look like sevens and sevens are starting to look like a shirtless Brad Pitt in Legends of the Fall before he went cray-cray. No one's called the cops yet but your neighbour has told you that he likes wearing ladies underwear.

Like I said, there's no going back now.

Y eso es todo lo que tengo que decir.

Lucy Hart

Next destination: Banos, Ecuador

Chapter 24

I opened my eyes and looked around me, feeling like a soggy cucumber that had been left out in the sun. Another day, another bus ride. It was the silence that had awakened me from my slumber. The bus was quiet and empty, which made me think we'd arrived in Montanita.

My cheek rested on Jack's shoulder, his head against mine. I could feel his chest expand and contract with each breath. He'd have to wake up soon, but for a moment I enjoyed the closeness with the person who felt like my whole world at that moment. We spent so much time together that we were almost like one person. LucyandJack. I tried to match his slow, steady rhythm with my own.

We'd been travelling all day to get to the town. I couldn't wait to have a shower and eat dinner and as if on queue, my stomach grumbled loudly and Jack stirred.

"Mhmgmmm," he mumbled, lifting his head.

"Hi," I croaked.

"Hi," he said, his eyes still closed, a sleepy smile on his lips.

"Your bony shoulder is surprisingly comfortable," I said.

He looked down at his t-shirt sleeve and nodded at the map of Italy shaped blob of moisture I'd left behind. "I can see that."

"Oh shit!" I reached out and attempted to rub away the drool with my fingers.

Jack laughed. "You know you're just rubbing your spit in more?"

I unzipped the top pocket of my daypack to look for a tissue.

"Hey. It's fine. Don't worry about it."

"Are you sure?"

"Yeah. I'll spit on you and we can just call it even," he continued, deadpan.

My eyes widened. "Don't you dare!"

"An eye for an eye. A spit for a spit," said Jack, reaching towards me menacingly as I shrunk back against the bus window. He made a gross gobbing sound in the back of his throat and grabbed my arms, his hands warm against my skin. He pulled me towards him and I squealed. But honestly? It didn't feel all that bad to have his hands on me that way.

God, I needed to get laid. It must be the reason I was having all these sexual thoughts about Jack.

"Bejan del autobus!" someone shouted from the front of the bus. We both jumped.

"Someone clearly wants us off the bus," said Jack.

He ducked his head into the aisle. "Lo siento, señor," he called, before turning back to me with a wicked smile on his face and waggling his fingers. I rolled my eyes and leaned my head back against the seat to get a better a look at him and all his dishevelled glory.

"You've got the indent of my clip on your cheek." I smiled and reached to cup his face with my hand, running my thumb along the grooves the metal had left on his skin. The gesture was instinctive. We'd spent so much time together that it felt normal to reach for him like that. But suddenly the air in the bus felt too still and the air in my lungs wouldn't stay put. Jack swallowed hard and—

"Ahora!" roared the man. Now!

Standing outside the bus station, after we'd been yelled at because the driver needed to get the bus back to the depot, I watched the throngs of people clog the streets of the beach town in the fading light of the day.

"Uh, Lucy, do you want to lead the way?" Jack was struggling to make eye contact with me. Probably because I'd just fondled his face like a crazy person. Well done, Lucy, You made it weird.

"What do you mean? You booked the hostel in Montanita because I booked Banos and Quito."

My pack was heavy and my back was already sticky with sweat.

Jack frowned. "No, I didn't. You said *you* would."

"No, Jack," I said, readjusting my daypack on my front. "Remember you spoke to those guys in our hostel in Lima who recommended that awesome hostel, and you said you'd book it?"

"What? That doesn't sound right. I said that they ..." He stopped, and I raised an eyebrow. "Whatever, we'll just have to find a hostel now then," he muttered starting off towards the town. But I didn't move.

"Hello? Remember they also said there were supposed to be insane waves this weekend, which is why the town is so packed. That's why you were definitely going to book ahead. Look around, Jack."

The town was pumping. It was going to be a nightmare trying to find two spare beds.

"Don't worry. We'll find something. You wait here and I'll go find somewhere for us to stay," he said, pulling off his bags and dumping them at my feet, before heading off into the crowd.

Sighing, I dragged his pack like a dead body over to a nearby bench and sat down. I could smell the sea in the air and even though the town was buzzing with activity, I could just make out the sound of the waves. The town looked cute with its little wooden huts and thatched roofs, blocks of colour dotted throughout in the forms of umbrellas and painted shop fronts. Unfortunately for us, judging by the number of people wandering around, Jack was never going to find a place and we were going to end up sleeping on the bench I was sitting on. Ha! My sleeping bag would have come in handy for the second time on the—

"Lucy?"

I looked up in surprise to find Conor, the hot Irishman from La Paz, standing in front of me, a surfboard tucked under his muscled arm. He was shirtless and shoeless, and he looked sexy as hell in a pair of board shorts that hung low on his hips. Grrrrrrr.

"Conor!" I jumped up to hug him, and may have held onto him for a little longer than necessary.

"It's great to see you." He looked around. "Where's your bodyguard?" he asked, smirking.

"Jack? Ugh. There was a mix up with our hostel booking so he's gone to find us a place." I wiped away the beginnings of a sweat moustache, hoping Conor hadn't noticed.

"Conor!?" shouted another guy, also with a surf board under his arm, heading towards the beach.

"I've got to run. I'm supposed to be doing a lesson. But listen, I'm staying at the Wild Roger hostel if you want to come find me later for a drink. I'd be more than happy to share my bed with you if you don't end up finding one. I have a private room." He punctuated that last bit with a hot look that made my reproductive organs do the can-can. "Think about it," he called, jogging off.

When Jack returned half an hour later I was still thinking about it. I'd decided that the feelings I was developing for Jack could be explained by good old fashioned, garden-variety horniness. People got horny all the time. There was no reason to freak out about it. I just needed to channel this energy towards Conor instead of Jack and everything would be fine. Once I'd scratched that itch we could go back to normal.

"I've found us a place," he declared, with a massive smile on his face. "Come with me if you want to shower."

I laughed and rolled my eyes. "I thought for sure you wouldn't find anything. I thought I was going to be sleeping on this bench." I hauled my pack on and clipped it round my waist, deciding not to tell Jack about running into Conor. He wasn't a big fan of the Irishman.

"I didn't think I would either," he said, fastening his pack into place. "But I ran into Crazy Bob. Remember that guy with the messed up eye from Arequipa?"

I shuddered and stopped.

"That dude creeped me out. What does Crazy Bob have to do with you finding accommodation?"

"Calm down, Luce."

"You know I love it when you tell me to calm down."

Jack closed his eyes and sighed. "Crazy Bob is managing the Luka hostel for a few months. He remembered me and we got talking. When I said we were stuck for a place to stay he said he'd make a plan."

"What kind of plan?"

"I don't know yet. He just said to get our stuff and when we got there he'd have something."

When we arrived at Luka, Crazy Bob greeted me like a long-lost friend, enveloping me in a massive bear hug. It made me nervous, and I prayed Jack hadn't pimped me out for a place to sleep.

"Good news, guys! We've had a last minute cancellation," he announced in his Northern accent, his wide smile accentuating his bad eye, making him look creepier. He seriously needed to consider an eye patch.

"Awesome," Jack and I exclaimed in unison. I wouldn't have to sleep on that hard bench after all.

"Come on." He gestured for us to follow him. "I'll show you to your room."

He marched us down a path to a bright blue door, through a garden sheltered by palm trees with coloured hammocks strung up between them. He unlocked the door and handed Jack the key. "You can just check in when you're ready. Thought you'd want to dump your stuff first, yeah."

I gave his arm a grateful squeeze. "Thank you so much."

"No worries mate. Wifi password is 'surfs up', one word," he said, before heading back to the reception.

"Jack, I'm just telling you that I'm going to have a forty-minute shower—" I stopped when I saw the cosy-looking double bed in the middle of the room. We both stared at the bed until I cleared my throat. "Uh, now what?"

We'd shared a private room in Tupiza when I'd been struck down with the squirts, but other than that we'd been in dorm rooms with other people. Jack's tired shoulders had slumped down around his toes.

He took a deep breath. "Can we just deal with this later? We can both have a shower and maybe eat something and then we can sort it out." He rubbed the back of his neck and looked at me. The poor guy *did* look exhausted. Babysitting me seemed to be taking its toll on him.

"Okay, no worries. You know what? We passed a few hammocks in that garden when we walked from the reception. Maybe we can take shifts tonight or something? I'll go chat with Crazy Bob now to see if we can get moved tomorrow. People are bound to be leaving."

"Thank you. That'd be great." He was visibly relieved we didn't have to go marching back round town searching for room at the inn.

I left him riffling through his daypack and went back to the reception to ask about getting separate beds. Bob wasn't at the desk so I explained our situation to the receptionist and enquired if anyone was checking out the next day. No one would, she explained, but she said she'd let us know if anything came up. After us checking in to so many hostels together I'd memorised Jack's passport details by now (and basically everything else I needed to commit credit card fraud) so I checked us both in and went back to the room.

There I found Jack sitting on the far side of the double bed, back to the door, laptop on his knees and earphones in his ears.

"You don't know how good it is to hear your voice. I miss you so much, Nöel."

I didn't want to intrude on their private moment so I quickly yanked my stuff out of my bag so I could leave. I'd run out of shower gel the day before, so I threw my stuff on the bed and walked over to Jack's bag, which sat in front of him. I waved my empty shower gel bottle at him, but he just flicked his eyes at me then returned them to the screen without acknowledging me.

I unzipped his pack anyway and pulled out his toiletry bag, waving his half-full shower gel bottle at him. He still refused to look at me. "*Stupid arse*," I huffed as I stomped off to the communal showers Bob had pointed out on the way to our room. The shower felt good, but I was still put out by Jack willfully ignoring me. I didn't want to be included in his Skype call with his girlfriend, but it would have been polite to at least dignify my request with a nod.

He was still talking to Nöel when I returned, more determined to ignore me, making that crystal clear when he didn't budge, even when I slammed the door.

"Oh, it's nothing," he said, inching further along the bed towards the wall, angling the screen away from me.

This infuriated me and, like a bratty child, made me even more determined to get him to look at me.

"You sound like you're doing some amazing stuff over there. I just wish you weren't so far away." He raised his voice to cover the sound of me violently zipping and unzipping my pack several times and rattling my toiletry bag.

Still no reaction.

Ugh. Whatever. By now they'd been at it for over half an hour and they didn't sound like they'd be stopping any time soon.

"Yeah, I miss you too."

I needed to leave before my ears started to bleed, so I jammed my wallet inside my bag, slung it over my shoulder and blew out of the room.

If Jack was going to ignore me then I could ignore him right back.

* * *

I'd spied the Wild Roger hostel on our walk to Luka so I knew exactly where I was going when I stormed off. By now the sun had set, and throngs of people wandered the streets with no particular place to be, laughing and smiling, their faces illuminated by the odd street light and the neon signs of bars and restaurants. Their happiness pissed me off.

It didn't take me long to find Conor lounging on a cheap plastic chair by the hostel pool, drinking beer with a group of guys. I noticed how his face lit up when he saw me, and he pulled a chair close to him for me to sit in.

"Guys, this is Lucy."

I raised my hand in a wave until I became self-conscious about the possibility of sweaty pits. I needed something cold to drink— preferably something that was seventy-five percent alcohol.

"I'm going to get myself a drink. Does anyone else want anything?"

The other guys shook their heads, but Conor jumped to his feet.

"I'll come with you," he offered.

When he'd ordered us both a round of beers he ushered me to a corner table.

"Are we not going back to the pool?"

"Nah. I want you all to myself." He watched me down half my beer in one gulp. "So, where's Jack?"

"Skyping his girlfriend." The beer felt good going down.

"Lucky for me." He winked before launching into an update of everything he'd been up to since we'd last seen each other. Making conversation with him was easy in that he did most of the talking and I did most of the listening. But I didn't mind. His accent was hot, no matter what the subject, and letting him talk gave me time to think about Jack and how much he'd pissed me off earlier.

It was ridiculous really. He was allowed to talk to his girlfriend. Although I wasn't sure why he needed to pretend that I didn't exist while he did it. Maybe we just needed a break from each other. Maybe it wasn't a good thing that I felt like we were one person. Plus, the pace of the trip had been relentless. When we weren't on buses, we were exploring markets or museums or ruins, and if we weren't doing that I was writing posts and any extra copy that Smelly Simon needed and Jack was editing photos.

Conor interrupted my thoughts. "Another beer?"

I looked at the empty bottles in our hands and realised I hadn't heard a word he'd said. I jumped up. "Why don't I get the next round?"

Even though I knew Jack hadn't meant to shut me out, his actions still stung. As the stoned backpacker behind the bar took his time to get me my beers I looked over at Conor, who threw me a sexy smile. He really *was* easy on the eyes. And for some reason he was into me. I was happy I'd thrown on the short, sleeveless dress with the scooped neck I'd picked up in Lima. The dark navy material clung to my body, showing off my assets to the *breast* of their abilities. I'd even managed to run a brush through my hair and stick in my hoopy earrings before I'd left the room.

By the time I sat back down, I'd pushed all thoughts of Jack from my head, already deciding that I would definitely be having sex with Conor by the end of the night.

Cut to Conor pushing me up against the wall outside his room later on as he fumbled in his pocket for his key. He was doing a good job of cupping my boob with his free hand and grazing his teeth across my neck. Who said men couldn't multi-task?

"Mmmmm … you smell good," he mumbled into my hair.

"Really?" I was pleased I'd showered earlier then—even if I did smell like Jack's stupid minty body wash. "That's good because usually I smell like sweaty old bus pleather and hand sanitiser."

Conor pulled my mouth roughly to his, indicating it was time for me to stop talking. Right. More kissing, less talking. I could do that. He was a damn fine kisser, giving me just enough tongue to leave me wanting more. He finally unlocked the door, and when he flicked on the light I was able to clearly see the bulge in his pants, making it clear that Conor was looking forward to getting me under him as much as I was.

Keys, bags, wallets were discarded on the floor. He grabbed my face to kiss me and I reached for the button of his jeans, eager to get a better look at what I'd be working with. My hands quickly acquainted themselves with what I found in his boxers.

Clothes started to come off, and very soon I found myself naked, rubbing up against the hot Irishman. And Conor was hard in ALL the right places. I was about to break my self-imposed 'no talking' ban and ask him if I could bounce a coin on his surfboard abs when he picked me up, walked me over to his bed, and threw me down. Goodnight! All thoughts evaporated from my mind, making way for desire. For a brief moment, it was just him and me and hands and mouths.

Until the thoughts rushed back as they inevitably do.

The fan was pretty noisy. Why was Conor attracted to me? Must buy new toothbrush. What day of the week was it? What was the name of that book the woman in Quito recommended? When had Conor last had sex?

I hadn't had sex in, oh, seventy-seven weeks, four days and three hours. In guy time that was probably about forty-three years. Let's be honest—Conor had probably fornicated that morning before breakfast.

"Do you have a condom?" I asked, praying to the sex gods that he did. He nodded and fumbled for one, retrieving a foil packet from his wallet, then hesitating momentarily. The room was dark, but moonlight streamed in through a crack in the curtains and I saw him frown. He cupped my face, still holding the condom packet, and the edge of the foil square scratched at my skin.

"Lucy?" He stared down at me, his face serious. "Tell me you love me."

A laugh escaped before I could catch it.

"I'm sorry. I think I might have heard you wrong. Did you say you wanted me to tell you that I loved you?" Wires did tend to get crossed in the bedroom once all the blood began pumping away from the body's auditory system to a person's nether regions. Add alcohol to the mix and before you know it, instead of hearing, say, 'speed up' you hear 'stick your finger up my butt'. Things can go pear-shaped very quickly from there. That's why I felt it was important I repeat his request to make sure I'd understood it.

"Yes. Tell me you love me. I mean, I'm not stupid, I know you don't love me. But I just want to hear you say it."

I pushed him away. "But why?" Sticking my fingers up his butt might have been preferable to me telling him I loved him.

"It's fine. Just forget I mentioned it," he said, roughly pawing at a boob and pulling me back to him. But as I kissed him, my enthusiasm waned. All the important parts of me had lost interest.

My options were to suck it up and have sex with him or politely excuse myself and exit with my balled up knickers in my hand. I decided to go with a third option, choosing to pretend to fall asleep and snore loudly into his open mouth. Conor went still.

"Lucy," he whispered, shaking my shoulder gently.

I snorted in response.

"Lucy," he repeated, louder and with another shake. When it was clear I was sound asleep, he pulled away. I lay there, naked on my side, and hoped he'd fall asleep quickly so I could make my getaway. But he had other plans.

After a few moments of silence I heard a weird slapping noise, followed by gentle grunting sounds. Conor was jerking off. I half-opened one eye to see him crouched next to me, his eyes clamped on my chest area. When it was clear he had no interest in my face, I opened both eyes to get a better look.

"Lucy loves Conor," he breathed as he rubbed himself, his breath hot on my boobs. "Lucy loves Conor."

Thinking quickly, I pretended to stretch in my sleep and swung my knee sharply in the direction of his groin. I was rewarded with a loud strangled cry as I connected with the *balls*-eye. I opened my eyes and feigned confusion.

"What? What happened? Oh God. Conor, did I fall asleep? I'm sorry." I yawned and stretched my arms, causing him to flinch. "That's so embarrassing."

"That's O-O-K," Conor stammered, and crouched awkwardly on the bed clutching his junk in his hands.

"Did you want to keep going?" I reached my hand to him, but he scooted farther away.

"No, it's grand. I'm pretty tired too."

"Are you sure?" I winked, moving closer and patting the bed next to me. This made the poor guy jerk back so swiftly, he fell off the bed. He nodded, his eyes, wide with pain, visible above the side of the bed.

"Okay well, I'll probably be off then," I said, pressing my lips together so I couldn't smile. Poor guy.

I dressed as fast as I'd ever done in my life and with a quick "Thanks Conor" I shut the door behind me, leaving him to imagine jerking off onto my wedding dress after we said our vows—in peace.

Instead of heading back to the hostel straight away, I wandered through the streets, filled with drunken revellers, and headed towards the sea. It probably wasn't the best idea to sit alone on the beach in the early hours of the morning, but I was oddly comforted by the chaos surrounding me and the sound of the waves and felt perfectly safe, like I wasn't actually all by myself.

As I sunk my toes into the cold sand I thought about my reaction to Conor's request. Yes, it was bizarre that he wanted me, almost a complete stranger, to tell him I loved him, but I knew I'd overreacted.

If I was honest, what had freaked me out the most was how much I could relate to his craving to be loved. I could see my desire for love—my clutching, grasping and needing—reflected back at me.

For so long, I'd desperately wanted someone to love me, to show me that I'd been mistaken about feeling so deeply unlovable. Someone to pick *me* out of all the women in the world, and tell me that I was worthy of love.

And, I thought I'd found that with Mike. And when he'd gotten down on one knee and proposed to me, it felt like everything had finally clicked into place. We'd been a couple for a few years and had bought an apartment together, so marriage was the next step. But to me it meant that he loved me enough.

For months, I'd floated in a squishy, cotton-candy shaped cloud while planning the big day when Mike would tell the whole world that he wanted to spend the rest of his life with me. Me—Lucy Agnes Hart, with my tubby arse and my bad posture. Until the day I walked into my manager's office to discuss an article with her and found my fiancé inside her. It had felt like I'd been kicked in my stomach by a large rugby player. But that was nothing compared to what had happened later that night when I'd sat across from him at our new oak dining room table with tears pouring down my face.

"Why?" I'd sobbed, as he'd fiddled with the screw on top of the pepper grinder. "Do you love her?"

Mike shook his head.

My body responded with shaking relief.

"So, we'll work this out. We'll go to counselling. We'll do whatever we need to do."

"Lucy, I only cheated on you with your boss because I knew you'd find out." Mike had stared at that fucking pepper grinder and I remembered wanting to rip it out of his hands. "I thought it would be easier than telling you I didn't love you anymore."

Picture my heart being slowly hand-cranked through a rusted old meat grinder, because that's what it felt like.

The conclusion I'd drawn from the whole experience? There *was* something wrong with me. There was something definitely wrong with me. Also, love was too hard. And it hurt too much.

I sat there for ages on the beach, just fiddling with the bracelets on my wrist like Mike had done with the pepper grinder, remembering the pain like it was a phantom limb.

When I looked up I was surprised to see the sun starting to rise in the sky.

I needed to shake it off. It was a new day and I wanted to put all that crap behind me. After a moment's reflection, feeling inspired I tipped the contents of my bag onto the sand and rummaged through it all until I found what I was looking for. The bottle of "love potion" I'd bought in La Paz. I'd carried it with me ever since the witch had handed it over all those weeks ago, pulling it out every now and then, wondering when it would start working.

But what had happened with Conor had reminded me of all the pain I'd experienced with my ex and I suddenly wanted to get rid of that little bottle.

Because love could suck it, right now.

I stood, dusted myself off and, clutching the love potion in my hands, walked towards the sea and threw it in to be swallowed by the waves.

I felt lighter walking back to our hostel. Throwing away that bottle made me feel good. I thought about Conor and wondered if, lying in his bed in the foetal position, he was coming to his own realisations, something along the lines of, "Stop asking crazy women to tell you they love you."

I stuck my key in the lock but it was already open. When I tiptoed into the room I expected to find Jack sleeping, but he wasn't. He was sitting on the bed, leaning against the wall, his legs extended. Maybe he hadn't slept all night either.

"Morning," I said sheepishly, my hand still on the doorknob.

"What the fuck, Lucy?" he said, glaring at me. I blinked and stepped backwards.

"Wha-at?"

"Where the hell have you been?"

"I've been out. Jesus. Why are you so angry?" I stuttered, letting my bag drop to the floor.

"Lucy," said Jack, his voice quiet and calm now. "I'm not angry.

I was worried about you," he said, rubbing his eyes and running a hand through his messy dark hair. He got up and walked over to me.

"Well it sounds like you're angry." I bent over and haphazardly pulled things out of my backpack, my face, red and hot, turned away from his.

"I'm not, Luce. Really. I just … where were you?" He seemed to struggle to keep his voice level.

"I went out. You know, you're not my dad," I mumbled into my chest.

"I know, but I *am* responsible for you. What am I supposed to do when you don't come home? I walked around for hours looking for you, thinking the worst. I was out of my mind."

I turned and stared at him. He looked like crap. Maybe I *had* misjudged the situation. When I'd left the room I'd just wanted to get away so I didn't have to hear him speaking to Nöel, but I hadn't thought to tell him where I was going. Bugger.

"I'm sorry, Jack. Really. I didn't even think."

"It's okay. And I'm sorry I shouted at you. I'm just glad you're alive." He stretched his neck from side to side and rubbed his face. God, now I felt awful that I'd worried him, and I was touched he cared that much. I took a step forward, feeling a strong urge to wrap my arms around him.

"So nothing happened to you. You're okay?" Jack looked me up and down, apparently searching for stab wounds.

"I'm fine. Really." I took another step closer. His face was so full of concern and something else I couldn't quite place that I just wanted to be near him. I pulled him into a hug and rested my head on his chest. After a moment he hugged me back and sighed. "I'm sorry," I whispered into his t-shirt.

"S'okay, Luce." Then, after a moment, "Where were you?"

"Do you remember that Irish guy, Conor, from La Paz?" Jack

pulled away enough to look down at me, his eyes narrowed. "I didn't tell you but I ran into him yesterday when you were looking for a place to stay. When you were talking to Nöel I went to his hostel. We had a few drinks and I kind of ended up hooking up with him."

He didn't need to hear all the gory details of what had actually happened. Jack dropped his arms like I'd told him I was radioactive.

"You had me worried the whole night and you were out sleeping with the biggest douchebag on the South American Continent? I can't fucking believe you! Do you have no self-respect? Seriously, Lucy. Come on!" He picked up his daypack and stormed to the door. "I can't even look at you right now," he said, before slamming the door behind him so hard the walls shook.

I don't know how long I stood there shocked, with my mouth hanging open, before my internal switch flipped to rage. I was furious at what Jack had just thrown at me before leaving. I picked up my hairbrush, the first thing I could find, and threw it across the room. I kicked off my flip-flops, picked them up and threw them, one by one, at the door. When that didn't make me feel any better, I kicked my backpack hard with my bare foot. Which didn't help in the slightest because my toe connected with the guidebook shoved in the side of my pack, making me even angrier. I swore and jumped around clutching my foot in my hand—until my hopping foot found itself tangled in my backpack strap and I fell over onto the cold hard cement floor.

"Dick! Balls! Whores!"

I was furious at Jack for what he'd said, but I was more furious that he'd left before I could defend myself. He thought he'd guaranteed having the last say by storming out like that. Well, I was going to show him, because I was going to just leave. Leaving was the ultimate last word. I quickly packed and left, slamming the door just as hard as Jack had.

Chapter 25

* * *

"Hi, Mum!" I waved at the computer screen while attempting to
stretch my face into a smile.

"Lucy, darling. So lovely to see you!" yelled my mother, her face up
against the camera. "But what's wrong with your face?" she screeched.

"Mum. You can talk normally. I can hear you fine. And maybe
just sit back. All I can see is an eyeball and the top of your cheek."

"Oh." She sat back in her chair. "Is that better?" she yelled.

I sighed. I loved my mother dearly but speaking to her on Skype
was still a bit of a process.

"Yes, Pat. I can hear you. Everyone in Colombia can hear you." I looked around the hostel common area, which thankfully was empty.

"Okay, just checking. How are you? You look a bit pale. Are you eating enough vegetables?" She pressed her face closer to her computer to get a better look at me.

"I'm fine, Mum. I'm not pale. It's just the fluorescent lighting in here. And yes, I'm eating vegetables. How are you? Are you eating *your* vegetables?"

She laughed, which made me smile for real this time. My mother's laugh was like medicine.

"Who're you talking to?" my dad shouted in the background. "Is that Lucy? Is that my girl?" he asked, his face—or least his nose—appearing on the screen.

"Hi, Dad. It's me. How're you?"

"We're miserable without you. When are you coming home?"

"Just a few more weeks."

"Are you on a bus? Every time I hear from you, you're either getting on a bus or getting off one."

I laughed. "It certainly feels that way."

My mother's face reappeared. "You know, we went to dinner the other night at that new Mexican place down the road, and your dad asked the waitress where she was from. When she said Ecuador, we told her that our daughter had just been in Ecuador."

"She was very impressed. So much so she even gave us a free side of chips," my dad said. "What are those chips called, Patricia?"

"Nacho chips," my mum replied patiently.

"Yes, nacho chips." He nodded. "Your last email said you were in Salento, so I looked it up on Google this morning so I could visualise where you were."

"Where's Salento?" interrupted my mum, frowning at the camera.

"Really, Pam. Keep up. Salento is in Colombia. Dur!"

"I didn't know you were going to Colombia. Isn't that the dangerous one? Don't they kidnap people in Colombia?"

"Apparently not any more, Mum. I'm sure I'm perfectly safe."

"Pat, did you know that Bogota was the capital of Colombia?" I saw him turn to my mother and look at her expectantly.

My mum bristled. "Yesss. I knew Bogota was the capital of Colombia."

"I bet you didn't. What's the capital of Ecuador?"

"Guys, please can we stay on track?"

"Now have you met back up with Jack yet?" asked my mother.

I'd emailed my parents to let them know Jack and I had fought, although I didn't say about what, and that we'd parted ways. "I really liked him."

"Mum, you met him once on Skype. How can you know whether you like him or not?"

"You just know. I'd feel much better about you in Colombia if I knew you weren't alone."

It had been four days since I'd seen him and I'd felt every single one of those days. He'd sent me a quick WhatsApp message to check I was okay when he'd come back to the room to find me gone but other than that there'd been radio silence. "Then you'll be happy to know that I'm meeting with Carol, my Canadian friend, in Bogota tomorrow." Carol and I had messaged each other and made a plan to meet.

"Good. At least you'll have someone to talk to," she said. I didn't tell her that I was constantly surrounded by people to talk to— whether I wanted to or not. "But I still think you should make up with Jack."

"I'm not making up with him. I don't need him. I'm completely fine without him," I lied.

My dad's face appeared again on the screen. "Lucy, the golf's on

TV so I'll leave you to talk to your mother."

"Okay, Dad. Nice to hear your voice. Love you," I said.

"Love you too." He waved then was gone.

"Lucy, how are you really? You can tell your mum."

Her face was the picture of concern, and I crumpled a bit in response.

"Oh sweetheart. What is it?" When I didn't respond she continued gently. "Why don't you call him and apologise for whatever you two were fighting about?"

I shook my head. "He was so angry with me, and then I stupidly left without even telling him so I'm worried I made him even angrier. He won't want to hear from me. I really screwed things up, Mum."

"Of course he'll want to hear from you. I'm sure he's sorry too."

I pictured him coming back to the empty room and flinched, thinking about how childish I'd been. How caught up I'd been in how angry Jack had made me when he'd stormed out without letting me explain myself, that I hadn't been able to engage my brain long enough to stop from behaving so stupidly. He'd been so good to me. He'd looked after me when I was sick and scared and I'd repaid him by making him worry that I'd been murdered and then running out on him.

"If I was him I wouldn't want to hear from me." I sniffed.

"Nonsense. I bet he misses you as much as you miss him." She gave me a knowing nod.

I frowned. "I never said I missed him."

"You didn't have to. It's obvious, sweetheart."

Suddenly I just wanted to get off Skype. I didn't want to talk or think about Jack anymore.

"Listen, Mum. I'm going on a hike soon and I need to get ready," I said, making a show of looking at the time on my phone.

"Okay, darling. Well, you know I'm here if you need to talk. And, at least give it some thought, about apologising to Jack and clearing everything up."

"I will do," I said, wanting to add "nothing of the sort", but refraining. "Thanks for the advice. Love you."

"Love you, Lucy. Stay safe, please."

* * *

Later that night, after my call with my mum, I was still thinking about what my mum had said while I was squished between a large Dutch backpacker named Joost and his friend, also confusingly, Joost. That afternoon, a group of randoms from the hostel had hiked together through the Valle de Cocoro and were celebrating with a massive meal.

The little restaurant, which was hidden down a poky alley, had been highly recommended by my guide book, which meant that every traveller within a five kilometre radius was currently dining there. It was like being stuck with forty-nine other people in a lift whose capacity was only seventeen, and everyone was talking at once. Lively conversations all around me covered everything from the right way to travel, to refusing to pay full-price for dorm rooms, to how riding in taxis while backpacking was a crime against humanity.

No one seemed to notice me as I picked at the arepa, a type of corn tortilla, on my plate and nursed my litre of warm Aguila beer. I nodded every now and then and laughed when everyone else seemed to laugh, even when someone switched to Dutch or German or Russian and I couldn't understand the joke.

I played with the bangles on my wrist. They were the ones the lovely Irish girls had gifted me with during my makeover, the ones Jack had jokingly called my cowbell. He'd remarked that he always knew when I was close on account of their jangling. I shook my wrist gently but the sound of them knocking together was drowned out by all the opinions in the restaurant. Jack, wherever he was, couldn't hear them. My mum was right. I missed Jack so much that it felt like someone had put a microwave on my chest. But I couldn't take it back and he hadn't emailed or called or texted or Instagrammed or Tweeted or Whatsapped since that single message so I could only assume he was more than happy to be rid of me. And I didn't blame him.

Now all I could do was drink more beer. I gestured to the waiter for another bottle, and by the time we left the restaurant I'd polished off two litres by myself. When we left the restaurant, instead of turning towards the hostel, the group headed towards town.

"Where're we going?" I asked a woman whose name I couldn't remember.

"To play tejo." She explained that Tejo was a Colombian pastime. It was played by throwing heavy discs, called tejos, at targets wedged into large rectangles of clay which was surrounded by a wooden frame. It was apparently like the French game, bocce, in that the aim was to hit the targets. However, in this game, the targets were loaded with gunpowder. And why not? Gunpowder and alcohol sounded like a marvellous combination.

"Sounds like the most fun," I replied, punctuating my response with a hiccup.

I realised how drunk I was when I arrived at the venue ten minutes later and tried to pay for my next beer, and the game, with a napkin I'd drawn a smiley face on.

Everyone else realised how drunk I was when I threw my first tejo.

"Lucy, that's not the target," said Joost.

"Watchu talking 'bout?" I slurred, stooping to pick up another tejo from the dirt, spilling half of my next litre bottle of beer in the process.

"You threw your tejo across two different games to that target over there," he tilted his head, "but you should be aiming in *front* of us." He pointed down the line to our target, about eight metres in front of me. We were on the far right side of the large hall. Several groups of locals occupied the remaining four lanes.

"I can do that," I said. I chugged my beer and squinted with one eye closed as I lined up the target. With a loud hiccup-burp hybrid, I pulled my arm back and threw the disc as hard as I could. But, instead of connecting with anything—clay, wood or gunpowder— my disc flew over the fence and disappeared into the night sky.

"Ha!" I said, spinning around to face the group and swaying slightly on my feet. "Who said I throw like a girl?"

Other Joost frowned. "No one said that."

"Why don't you just sit down and watch the game?" someone suggested.

"What? No way. I think I'll play a few more rounds. This is fun," I said, my voice echoing in the hall. I drained the rest of my beer and looked around for another disc. There weren't any spare and no one wanted to share theirs with me. But I remembered I'd thrown one off to the side and decided I was going to look for it, knocking over my empty bottle as I did.

While the others were engrossed in their game, I looked for my tejo.

"Don't worry. I found it," I said, more to myself than anyone else, spotting the lone puck several lanes over. It was quicker to just walk diagonally across the lanes than head along the back and down, so I weaved sideways across, only slightly unsteady on the uneven surface, until I heard a shout behind me. I spun around to locate the source of the shouting, but the spinning made me wobble, and I staggered slightly. Right in the path of a flying tejo. I dropped to my knees and yelped in pain. My arm was hot and stinging where the hard disc had connected.

"Disculpe," said the Joosts in tandem, before dragging me to my feet and out of harm's way.

They stuck me on a bench, and I rubbed my arm, sniffed, and tried to ignore the fist-shaking from the players of the game I'd just interrupted. One Joost offered to take me back to the hostel.

"I'll help too," said the other.

"Come on. Let's get you home before you get a tejo to the *hoofd*," said one of them.

Back at the hostel, they moved stealthily, trying to get me to my room in the dark so the rest of the dorm wouldn't see a grown woman being put to bed like a drunk child.

"Which one's yours?" whispered a Joost.

"There," I said, pointing randomly in the dark. They helped me to my bed and I flopped onto my side. And onto someone's warm body.

"Shit. That's not her bed." Joost said, as he lifted me off the bed. Whoops.

When I was safely deposited on my actual bed I grunted my thanks and quickly rolled over. Even though I was plastered I still managed to berate myself for getting into yet another mess. For a second there, I'd thought I wasn't actually a waste of space. But I'd been wrong. I was so fucking sick of myself. Jack was *lucky* that I'd run away. Jack. As I drifted drunkenly off to sleep I shook my wrist one last time, hoping he'd hear me over the sound of my disgust.

* * *

My eyes were bloodshot from the previous night's beer and embarrassment. I shielded them from the sun as I stood outside the bus I'd just taken from Salento to Bogota via Armenia. My guidebook was in my hand, but I had yet to open it, hoping the knowledge of how to get to my hostel would somehow enter my brain by osmosis. Passengers jostled around me and the big pack on the ground at my feet. My daypack was slung over my shoulders and I adjusted it so it wouldn't touch the bruise that had bloomed on my arm where the tejo had hit me the night before. I prodded the spot and winced. I was so busy feeling sorry for myself, I didn't notice the man in front of me until he started talking.

"Hola guapa." Hello pretty lady.

I stifled a yawn. "Hola."

"Esta el autobus de Salento?" Is this the bus from Salento?

"Si." The sign was clearly written on the bus.

"My sister was supposed to be on the bus, but I can't find her. She is only thirteen and is wearing a yellow shirt," he said, switching to English.

I hadn't noticed anyone who fit the description. But then, I'd spent the entire journey wallowing in misery, cursing the bus's broken DVD player which had left me alone with my thoughts for ten hours. This was too much time to be allowed to think about one's mistakes—Jack Dawson related or otherwise.

I was exhausted and just wanted to get to my hostel without incident so shook my head. "Lo siento." I'm sorry. Surely she had a phone. Everyone in Colombia had a phone.

He gave me a curt nod. "Gracias," he said before turning on his heels and walking off. I pulled my notebook out of my daypack, remembering I'd written down the hostel's address. Screw trying to get a bus or walk. I was going to get a taxi. I'd just show the driver the address and he could take me there. I sighed and bent down to haul my backpack onto my back.

But it wasn't there.

Chapter 26

I spun around in a circle, making myself dizzy, sliding further into panic.

What had I done with it?

I remembered standing near the hold as the conductor pulled out the bags. I'd handed him my bag stub, and he'd handed me my bag. I'd dragged it along the ground and out of the way as I tried to figure out how I was going to get to the hostel. I was sure it had been at my feet—until that man had come over to ask me about his sister. Shit! I was so stupid. Jack had warned me about scams like this. I ran into the bustling bus depot and looked around for any signs of the man. But I knew him and his accomplices would be long gone—along with my bag.

* * *

My taxi driver was surprised at how light I was travelling, taking in my small pack, when I slouched up to the taxi rank. He'd been even more surprised when I started to talk to myself in the back of his car.

My bag getting stolen was the last straw. I needed to speak to Rob, but I needed to rehearse my speech first. I thought back to the conversation I'd had with him when he'd first handed me the "opportunity" to take on this whole stupid assignment. He'd said that travel writing in South America would be good for me. But he'd been wrong. I was still a loser. Now I was just a loser with no clothes. I practised:

"Rob, it's Lucy Hart. Before you say anything, I want to tell you that my bag has been stolen. I don't feel safe and I want to come home," I said aloud. "Also, please don't fire me."

Coming out and asking him straight up was better than my first idea, which had been to change my flights and return home early, without telling him. I briefly thought about hiding at my folks' house and making up and/or plagiarising blog posts from the Internet. There was a lump in my gut—as if I'd eaten fourteen extra-thick arepas that had morphed into a giant cornball of anxiety. The last time I'd hidden out at my parent's house I'd been so determined to do everything I could never to end up there again. Desperate times. Why was it so impossible for me to get my shit together? Other people seemed to do it with no problem. What did people like Angel know that I didn't? And what about Carol? She walked through life so unafraid, so sure that she'd make it to the other side unscathed. And Bucket List Barbie? And even Nöel, who I'd never met but who I'm sure had never even considered hiding from the world?

* * *

In my empty hostel room later, I took a deep breath and dialled Rob's number.

"This is Rob." He answered straight away, and that threw me. What time was it at home?

"Uh, Rob. It's Lucy Hart," I stammered, my hand shaking so badly, I almost dropped the phone.

"Lucy, how are you? Is everything okay?" he asked.

I tried to launch into my speech, but the words wouldn't come.

"Hello?"

I started to cry, and clamped my hand over my mouth to hide the sound as I tried to pull myself together.

"Lucy? Are you still there? I think we may have been cut off. Lucy?"

I took a loud shuddering breath.

Rob must have heard it. "Oh Lucy, what's wrong? Are you okay?"

The concern in his voice just made me cry even more. "Rob," I said, between sobs, "I can't do this anymore. I've tried. But stuff keeps happening to meeee," I wailed into the phone. I pictured him moving the phone farther away from his ear.

"What happened? Are you hurt?"

"Technically I'm not hurt. But my backpack got stolen this morning and I don't have any clothes."

"What? Where was Jack when this happened?" he asked.

"Jack isn't with me."

"What? Where is he?"

I paused, unsure of how Rob would react to what I was going to say next. "I don't know. We had a fight." It had been a week since I'd last seen Jack.

"What the …" he began. "Okay, but physically you're all right? You're safe?"

"Yes." I looked up at the fan spinning lazily above my head. "But I still want to come home, Rob. I can't do this. I told you I couldn't. And I think I've proven my point. I'm sure I can make a plan for the rest of the posts."

"Lucy, that's just not going to happen. You need to stick it out. The blog is doing well."

"But I don't have any clothes or anything."

"Did they take your passport and wallet?"

"No. Those were in my daypack and I had that on me."

"Good. You're covered by insurance so you should get paid out in a week or so if you put the claim in now."

"But it's just two more weeks! Surely it won't make that much difference if I come home now." Damn. I'd think I'd just made his point for him.

"Exactly, Lucy. You only have two more weeks to go," said Rob, quietly.

I wished I'd written my speech down because none of this was going as planned.

"And, I want you to get in touch with Jack and get over whatever it is you were fighting about," Rob added.

"But—"

"Lucy," said Rob, his voice sharp. "I don't have time for this. You sort it out right now. Apologise. Do whatever you need to do to just sort it out and get back on schedule."

"Rob, please, I'll do anything but this. I'll clean toilets at the newspaper if you want me to. I just want to come home." I started crying again. I should have lied and told him I had mould growing on my fallopian tubes and had to have them removed. He couldn't have said no to that.

"Stop it, Lucy! You *can* do this and you *have* been doing it," he said, jerking me out of my thoughts. I'd only managed to make it because I'd had Jack by my side, but I didn't want to admit that to him.

"Please, Rob," I pleaded pitifully, one last time, throwing in a pathetic hiccup for good measure.

"No, Lucy. Talk to Jack. End of story," he said, before hanging up.

Shiiiiiiiit.

"Hello, Silly," came a familiar voice from the doorway as I stared down at the phone in my hands and contemplated throwing it across the room.

"Carol!" I ran to the door, throwing my arms around her in relief. "That is some kind of welcome," she laughed, until she heard me sniffling and realised I wasn't letting go of her anytime soon. "There, there," she said, rubbing my back. "I know."

"How do you know my bag was stolen?" I pulled away, looking at her in confusion.

"What? No! Lucy. I didn't know you'd had your bag stolen. What happened? Tell me everything."

"Okay, but I need a shower first, and I'll need to borrow your toiletries and some clothes please. And then beer. And then we can talk."

* * *

"Dos mas cervesas, por favor," I ordered, taking a quick break from my tale of woe to request that the beers keep coming.

"Dude, that really sucks. You haven't had the best luck have you? Like this whole trip," said Carol. She'd been listening patiently to my sob story for the last hour. In a weird twist she'd lent me the long colourful skirt I'd seen her wearing the day I'd clapped eyes on her on that street in BA and followed her back to the hostel.

"It's like I'm cursed."

"Have you told Jack about your bag? Are you guys talking yet?" she asked.

"Nope. I bet he's stoked he got rid of me." I let out a sharp, bitter laugh.

Carol leaned back in her chair. "You know, you don't know what he thinks until you actually speak to him?"

I shook my head and tried to change the subject. I didn't want to talk about Jack. "You said something earlier, when you first arrived. You said something like 'I know' and I thought you knew about my bag getting stolen. What did you mean?" I took a swig of my beer and started peeling the sticker off the bottle.

Carol shook her head, her blond hair swishing over her shoulders. "Never mind."

But I persisted. Anything to stop talking about Jack. "Come on, tell me."

Carol hesitated. "I just thought that you were upset, you know, because you'd … figured it out."

"That I'd figured what out?"

"That you're in love with Jack."

I laughed. "I'm NOT in love with Jack." Sure, I'd started to have sexual feelings about him, but I'd just put that down to spending so much time together.

Carol just looked at me. The silence unnerved me, and I babbled to fill it.

"He was a complete dick in the beginning. Yes, so, he redeemed himself somewhere in the middle there, but then he just went back to being a dick again. He's annoying and he thinks he's above everyone and—"

I stopped as an image of Jack, from the morning after I'd been so sick and he'd looked after me, popped into my head, his kind face so close to mine. Another image. The time Jack held my hand during the strike. Then, Jack laughing at me after the llama ate my hair, his eyes crinkled in mirth, before he'd licked my face. And Skyping with my parents. Falling asleep on his shoulder on the bus. Looking at him from across the bar the night of my makeover.

I thought about his dark brown eyes that were like a mood ring, changing colour depending on how he felt. I thought about the way he smelled after a shower and his messy hair that he insisted on combing with his fingers.

And then I thought about the way he made me feel safe, even as we lay in the dirt on the side of a road in the middle of nowhere, and it was then I realised that I was bloody in love with him.

I gaped at Carol, who just smiled knowingly.

"Holy shit. I *am* in love with Jack. I need to call him." And before Carol could stop me I pulled out my phone and jumped up.

Chapter 27

I marched outside the bar on to the street and hit the call button before I could chicken out. I knew if I didn't tell him now I never would.

"Lucy, I was just about to call you," said Jack, answering after one ring.

"You were?" I leaned against the wall behind me, my heart thudding so hard in my chest I could feel it in my throat. He'd come to the same realisation as me?

"Rob just called me."

"Oh. Right."

"Apparently we need to get over ourselves."

"He gave me a similar speech," I said, nodding even though he couldn't see me.

"Luce, I'm really sorry about how I spoke to you. I was … worried."

"No, *I'm* sorry."

Silence. I wanted to ask him where he was, what he was doing right before I called him, what he'd eaten for lunch. Instead I went with: "How've you been?"

"Fine. You?"

"Fine."

More silence. This was weird. Maybe he already knew what I wanted to tell him. I took a deep breath. It was now or never.

"Jack—"

"Lucy—"

We both laughed awkwardly.

"Just hold on, Lucy," he said, before I heard him talking to someone else on the other end of the phone. "Listen I have to go. Let's make a plan to meet up so we can get this show back on the road. I'll WhatsApp you later, yeah?"

"Okay, but …" I managed to splutter before he disconnected.

I slunk back inside, eleventy-thousand unsaid words banging around my brain.

"And?" asked Carol.

"I didn't tell him," I replied.

She nodded like she agreed with me. "So you remembered that he had a girlfriend, after all?"

CRAPBAGS. I'd conveniently forgotten that important fact.

I nodded, before downing the rest of my beer. "Sure. That's what happened. I remembered he had a girlfriend and decided it would be dumb to tell him that I loved him," I lied.

* * *

Jack would be arriving at any moment and I was still stuffing around, trying to figure out what to wear.

Ugh. I stared down at my bed, at the only clothes I currently possessed, and sighed at what I had to work with.

1 x pair of men's baggy rugby shorts (found stashed behind a set of drawers)

1 x button-down orange peasant blouse (purchased at a market)

1 x black and white striped tank top (donated to the "Cloth Lucy" cause by one Carol Hagen)

3 x cheap white pairs of underwear (of 4-pack)

1 x pair of shiny The Simpsons-themed tights (gifted to me by a guy in Bogota, who was 'hella into yoga')

On top of this assortment of crazy, I was wearing a bright purple bra, a pair of ridiculous Star-Spangled Banner leggings Carol had bought me as a joke, green flip-flops and a t-shirt that said "I'd Hit That" over a cartoon of a piñata. I'd really wanted to look at least presentable when Jack arrived, but after trying on different combinations for the last 10 minutes, I doubted that was going to be possible.

I stared at myself in the floor length mirror on the back of the door and laughed. Until my insurance money came through I was going to have to be content looking like a homeless meditation teacher. And, people had been so kind that I couldn't complain. Besides clothes, I'd been given shampoo, conditioner, toothpaste, a toothbrush (thankfully new), face wash, and even moisturiser.

I tugged off the t-shirt and pulled on the orange peasant top again and turned to the mirror. I sighed. All I needed was a top hat, a plastic parrot on my shoulder and a hula-hoop and I'd look like I was on my way to face paint fairies at Burning Man.

I yanked the peasant top off over my head. However, since I hadn't yet purchased another hairbrush, one of the blouse buttons seemed to get stuck in the tangled birds nest at the top of my head. Crapness Everdine! I tugged hard and winced in pain. The fabric covered my face and the more I yanked and nothing happened, the more I panicked.

"Aaaaaah!" I wailed as I flailed about, hyperventilating into the bright orange material. "I'm going to die in here!"

"Do you need some help with that?"

My heart flip-flopped when I immediately recognised the voice.

"Jack, is that you?" I yelped, sounding way more excited than I meant to. Be cool, Hart.

"Yes it's me, Lucy. Stop moving around so I can get you unstuck," he said, laughing.

"Don't laugh at me, Jackass!" I shouted through my top in mock-indignation.

"I'm sorry," he said, fussing with my top. "Wait, hold still." He put his hands on my bare arms to stop me from wriggling and I stopped moving—and breathing—immediately.

I waited for Jack to untangle my hair from the buttons. When he eventually pulled the blouse all the way off my head I blinked in the bright fluorescent light and sucked in a deep breath. When I registered Jack's cheeky, smiling face in front of me I threw my arms around his neck and he pulled me into a hug. I buried my nose into his hair and sniffed, feeling happy hormones flood my body as I took in his minty Jack scent. I wanted to stay like that forev—.

"Lucy, this is my girlfriend, Nöel," said Jack, pulling away from me way too soon to grab the hand of the beautiful, willowy blonde beside him. A blonde I hadn't noticed until then.

Fuck! I blushed thinking about how I'd just sniffed his hair and—double fuck—I wasn't even wearing a shirt! I dived for the piñata t-shirt crumpled on the bed and yanked it over my head.

"Nöel! Hey, nice to finally meet you. I've heard so much about you. Obviously. Jack is always 'Nöel this, Nöel that'." I stopped rambling and stuck out my hand, unsure of what else to say. "I've got a bit of a cold," I added, hoping to provide a legitimate reason for why she'd just seen me sniffing her boyfriend's hair in my purple bra. I sniffed noisily to make my point.

Nöel stared at me like I'd just crawled out of a soup can.

"Forgive me, but if you're contagious I really shouldn't be shaking your hand. I work with people with AIDS, and a cold could literally kill someone."

"Yes, of course. I don't want to kill anyone." I dropped my hand to my side.

"So, Jack didn't tell me you were going to be around. I mean, it's super exciting that you *are* here, though. Did you get some unexpected time off?" I babbled.

"Yes. We controlled the outbreak of cholera in Zimbabwe earlier than expected so we were allowed a break. I decided to come meet Jack in Colombia. I have beautiful memories of this country. I was here a few years ago, helping after the floods of 2011. The people are so wonderful and warm." Nöel, in her beautiful white sundress and her perfectly manicured nails, flashed me a Mona Lisa smile. How had she been living in a camp full of cholera and still managed to look like she'd just stepped out of a spa?

"Wow. Well done," I said, deciding that was the appropriate response for something as impressive as that. I swallowed hard, hoping to get rid of the taste of jealously in my mouth.

She smiled down at me. Yeah, on top of everything else, Nöel was tall. And skinny. And gorgeous.

"It's just what I do, Lucy. Helping people is my calling." She cocked her head and blinked at me as if to say: *What is your calling, you hair-sniffing dimwit? Being sarcastic? Drinking wine? Trying not to trip over your feet?*

I clicked my tongue and gave her a thumbs-up. "Good for you."

Jack cleared his throat. "Uh, we'll leave you to it, Luce. We've just arrived, but I wanted to say hi. We thought we'd shower and change and head out for an early dinner if you wanted to join us."

"It looks like Lucy is about to go to yoga. We don't want to keep you if you've got other plans," said Nöel, looking pointedly at my ridiculous outfit.

I let out an uncomfortable laugh. "Oh this?" I pointed at my leggings. "I got my backpack stolen in Bogota so I'm basically clothed by the kindness of strangers."

Jack stuck his hand on my shoulder and gave it a squeeze. "Shit, Lucy. I'm sorry to hear that. What happened?"

"One of the scams you warned me about. And this time you weren't there to save me. I've bought one or two things but I'm waiting for the insurance money to come through. And we've got like two weeks until the end of the trip anyway, right?" I asked, offering him a smile. He didn't return it.

"You poor thing," said Nöel. "I can definitely give you a few things to tide you over. I mean, you're much bigger than me but you might be able to squeeze into a few things that are on the large side. I'll have a look when I get back to the room." She smiled.

"Thanks, Nöel. That's very—" Condescending? Bitchy? "—kind of you."

Jack cleared his throat. "Why don't we meet in an hour for dinner?"

I nodded but avoided eye contact with him. I felt like my feelings for him were written all over my face, and if he looked in my eyes he'd see.

"Do you have any suggestions for dinner since you know the area so well, Nöel?" I asked.

"Vamos ir a el restaurante Heraldo's. Su comida es excelente."

She looked at Jack like she was a dog who'd done a trick, and I fought the urge to roll my eyes as hard as she'd rolled her R's. She'd recommended a restaurant called Heraldo's on account of their excellent food, but I was not in the mood to play along so I pretended to misunderstand her.

"Your grandfather's name is Heraldo and he has excellent hair?"

Nöel stared at me in confusion while Jack stifled a laugh.

"No, that's not what I said. I was talking about my suggestion for dinner. You know Lucy, you really should be able to speak Spanish if you've been travelling in South America this long."

I tried and failed to keep the sarcasm from my voice. "You're right Nöel. After six weeks in South America I *should* be fluent."

"We'll meet you outside at six, Lucy," said Jack, ushering Nöel out the door, knowing it was the right time to leave.

"I mean do you know any Spanish at all?" asked Nöel, turning at the door to look at me.

"Mi nombre es Pepe y este es mi llama," I recited like a school kid. Translation: My name is Pepe and this is my llama.

Nöel frowned and cocked her head. "Anything else?"

"No tocaras las bolas." Don't touch my testicles.

Jack threw his head back with laughter and pushed Nöel out the room before I could continue with my language lesson.

* * *

"Nöel, why don't you tell me how you and Jack met?" I asked, almost ripping the cardboard menu I held tightly in my hand. I would have rather choked on a tennis ball than hear the story, but we'd been seated at our table for a full five minutes without anyone talking, and I was dying to fill up the silence. Plus, I thought I might need to wave the olive branch and based on the interaction we'd had so far, I guessed that Nöel might be fond of talking about herself. I grabbed my beer and took a sip.

Nöel smiled and reached across the table for Jack's hand. "We met at a friend's wedding about three years ago. Jack asked me to dance and while we were dancing he told me he was going to marry me someday."

I choked on my beer and managed to splutter a single syllable between coughing into my hand. "Oh." My stomach clenched and I felt sick as I pictured him holding her, leaning down to whisper in her ear. Maybe he'd even pressed his mouth into her shoulder and— damn you imagination. I didn't want to think about them together.

Jack cleared his throat and got up suddenly. "I'm going to the bathroom," he mumbled before marching off.

"Three years is a long time," I said, after he'd left. "You guys are probably thinking about getting married soon." Say no.

Nöel sighed dramatically and took a sip of her white wine. "We're just waiting to be in the same place for long enough. To tell the truth I was hoping that Jack would be over this whole photography thing by now. It would be much easier if he was back in London where he'd been at the beginning of our relationship. I love what I do too much to quit."

"Jack really loves what he does too," I said, feeling like I was stating the obvious.

She wrinkled her lovely nose. "Photography just doesn't seem very … fulfilling."

And working in Banking was?

"It's just tough being so far apart all the time."

And that's the way I wanted it to stay. But I clucked sympathetically and felt like a right bitch. "I can imagine. When was the last time you saw each other?"

"Before this week, the last time we were together was two months ago in Morocco," she replied. "We usually manage to get a week together at least every three months."

The time Jack and I had spent travelling together in the last six or so weeks was more than the time they'd spent together in the last year and a half. That wasn't really fair on either of them, and as much as I tried not to I couldn't help but feel sorry for her.

When the waitress came over to take our order, Jack still wasn't back from the bathroom.

"Mi novio y yo comeremos ceviche," said Nöel, ordering Jack and herself the ceviche. Bad move.

I cleared my throat. "Nöel, Jack hates ceviche. It's literally his worst nightmare—along with a sharknado," I said gently, hoping a little humour would take the edge off the sting. It didn't surprise me that she didn't know this about her boyfriend, having just heard about how little time she'd spent with him.

Nöel thrust her pretty chin upwards. "I think I know what food my boyfriend eats."

I didn't argue.

"Y para mi el pollo, por favor," I said, ordering the chicken dish, knowing Jack would want it instead. I loved ceviche. The worst part of eating it was sitting through Jack's theatrics of pretending to vomit while he watched me eat. Hopefully Nöel enjoyed seeing her boyfriend behaving like a child.

When the waitress left with our orders, I continued with my previous line of questioning. Maybe hearing more about their life and their plans for the future would nip my inconvenient blossoming love for Jack in the bud.

"Has Jack actually asked you to marry him?" As far as I could see, Nöel wasn't wearing an engagement ring.

"No, but I know he will. Jack always does what he says he will," she replied.

"Testify. This one time Jack dared me to eat guinea pig but I said only if he ate a maggot. And he totally followed through."

Nöel wrinkled her nose.

"Oh well that's …" she said, bringing her wine glass to her lips so she didn't have to finish the sentence.

We sat in silence for several awkward minutes. Nöel would occasionally look at me, with an expression that said she was surprised I was still there. I could only imagine what she saw when she looked at me.

But it was her who eventually broke the silence. "You know, I have to be honest. Jack has talked about you a lot on Skype calls and emails and I got quite worried about him spending so much time with you, travelling around South America, something I just can't do because of my work—"

I interrupted her, my eyes wide in surprise. "Nöel, you have nothing to worry about." I knew what it was like to be cheated on and the last thing I wanted was for her to feel threatened by me. Sure, I was in love with her boyfriend, but that didn't mean I was going to do anything about it.

"I know. That's actually what I was going to say. Meeting you I realise I had nothing to worry about, and I feel so silly. You are *so* not his type," she said. Her smile was so wide you'd think she'd just paid me a compliment.

"Good," I replied through gritted teeth. I looked up and noticed Jack making his way back to us. As he took his seat, I raised a brow at him and looked pointedly at the imaginary watch on my wrist.

"What?" he said grumpily. "Do you want a play by play?"

"Gross. I'd like to keep my appetite, thank you."

"Well, we wouldn't want you to lose your appetite, now would we? Speaking of which isn't it past your dinnertime? I'm surprised you haven't punched me in the face," he teased.

"It *is* past my dinner time and the only reason I haven't punched you yet is because you've hardly been at the table."

Nöel looked back and forth between us like a spectator at a tennis match, then quickly grabbed Jack's arm to get his attention.

"Jack, what's a sharknado?" she asked.

Jack's face went white and his eyes popped. I couldn't help but smile.

"Sharknados are only the most terrifying phenomenon in the entire world. Why? What have you heard?"

Nöel looked at him like he'd lost it. "Nothing. I just—Lucy mentioned them and I didn't know what they were."

Jack let out a sigh of relief. "It's what happens when massive man-eating sharks get whipped up into a tornado and get dropped into places where there normally wouldn't be. Like swimming pools."

Nöel frowned. "But it's obviously something that could never happen?"

"But can you imagine if it did?" Jack sat back in his chair and looked into the distance. I could tell he was picturing being caught up in a real-life shark-infested weather system. He had a wonderful imagination. It was one of the reasons we got along so well. We'd spent hours making up back-stories about the people we saw on buses, in museums and on the street. One afternoon in Cuenca we'd sat on a bench eating ice-cream cones and Jack had entertained me for a solid hour making up a story about the two little old ladies who were sitting across from us in the little park in the centre of the city. I'd laughed as he'd described how they were rival mafia bosses with knitting needles and guns in their handbags. How they'd both fell in love with the same man when they were seventeen and how the love had torn their friendship apart. But, it turned out that their mutual love Lorenzo had eventually come out of the closet at the age of seventy and so they'd met that afternoon to reminisce and bury the hatchet.

Jack shuddered and shook his head. Nöel just blinked and seemed to look at him like she wasn't quite sure who he was.

"Food's here," I said, gesturing to the waitress bringing our food to the table. She placed the ceviche dishes in front of them and the chicken in front of me.

"I didn't order this. I hate ceviche," said Jack, puffing out his cheeks like he was nauseous. The waitress shrugged and walked away.

"Here you go," I said, switching my plate for Jack's.

"That's better," said Jack, reaching for the tomato sauce. "For a second there, Luce, I thought you'd ordered me ceviche. You know how much it terrifies me," he continued, squeezing a generous blob of sauce onto his plate.

Nöel looked down at her lap and waited for me to correct him.

"Please, let's eat our meal in peace and don't start with your usual crap," I said.

"I don't know what you're talking about," he said, holding his hands up in front of his eyes so that he wouldn't have to look at the plate of ceviche.

I rolled my eyes. "You are a child," I said, giving Nöel a conspiratorial wink.

* * *

The next day I sat sulking at a cafe near the hostel, as I waited for Jack and Nöel to arrive for breakfast. I'd been awakened that morning by the melodious snoring of my large South African dorm mate and hadn't been able to go back to sleep, even after I'd thrown my shoe at him and he'd rolled over. I'd wanted to text Jack and tell him I'd rather snorkel through an alligator-filled swamp than see him and his perfect girlfriend holding hands over bacon and eggs. But I'd decided against it. The more I saw them together the more it cemented the fact that they were a couple and I needed to find my own person.

Jack was so deep in thought as he walked through the restaurant, he didn't notice me until he walked into our table.

"Morning," I said, looking up at his adorable, surprised face.

He gave me a small, strained smile. "Morning."

"Where's Nöel?" I asked, looking past him.

"Shopping."

"Well, I'm starving," I said, grabbing a menu and perusing it. It was lovely being back with Jack, but there was definitely a tension that hadn't been there before. I couldn't be sure if I was imagining it because of my feelings for him, or if the tension was real.

I had been known to fabricate many an elaborate scenario in my head about anything and everything, and the end of the world, so I made a concerted effort to dial that shit right back. I was an Olympic-level daydreamer. I could live a lifetime of stories in my head in the space of minutes. Once a handsome stranger in the tinned vegetable aisle of a supermarket had said four words to me—That tin looks dented—and I was convinced in the three seconds it took me to respond that we were going to be together forever, even though I didn't know his name, his address or his stance on brunching. And now I was imagining Jack knew I was in love with him and he was about to tell me to take a long walk off a short pier.

I could feel Jack's eyes on me as I stared at the menu. Shit. What if he'd suddenly developed the ability to read minds? I couldn't bear it any longer. "What is it? Spit it out," I said, not looking up from the menu.

"Lucy, I want you to know that I didn't know Nöel was coming. She surprised me and …," he said.

"Jack, you don't have to explain yourself. Really. I think it's great Nöel was able to join you. It doesn't sound like you guys get much time together." It was true. Even though it hurt like hell to see them together, Jack deserved to be happy and Nöel obviously made him happy—or he wouldn't be with her, would he?

"I just didn't want you to think …" His voice trailed. He reached round to put his right hand on the back of his neck, his nervous tick. I'd read somewhere that if you found yourself being attacked by a grizzly bear the best thing to do was lie down and cover the back of your neck. I always imagined Jack covering his neck from a bear attack when I saw him do that. I thought back to my call to him a few days ago and realised she must have already been there with him and was the person he'd stopped to talk to before ending the conversation. Why hadn't he just told me? But the way he was looking at me, so miserable, made me stop.

"I'm glad I met Nöel," I said, trying to make him feel better.

Because in a sick, twisted way, I *was* glad. Now I could see she was a flesh and blood human. It made the relationship more real, and that made me less likely to confess my love for him, which would have just been stupid. A man wouldn't want a Hyundai when he could drive a Lexus. The same man wouldn't want polyester against his skin when he could wear cashmere. And he'd be mad to have to choose a toasted cheese sandwich over lobster.

Jack looked surprised. "Really?" he asked, cocking his head like a monkey.

"Yes, really. And she's lovely. I mean, it obviously takes an amazing person to dedicate her life to helping others. I couldn't do that. As I'm sure you can imagine." My admiration was genuine, if a little tinged with jealousy.

Jack's continued silence made me nervous, so I blabbered on. "So, I think I'm going to have the pancakes. What are you going to have? Okay, wait, let me guess. The huevos rancheros."

He gave me a funny look.

"Jack, seriously, what's with you this morning? You're being weird."

"Did Nöel order me the ceviche last night?"

"I can't remember," I said, returning my eyes to the menu in my hands. "I wonder if they have real cream?"

"Lucy?"

"No, you're right. It probably comes in a can."

"Lucy!"

"Fine. Yes, she did. But she didn't know you hated ceviche."

"Did you tell her?"

"Yes, but I thought it was easier if I just ordered what I knew you'd want so we could swap. It wasn't a big deal."

The strange undercurrent to his mood was freaking me out. My face was a mask of calm indifference, but I looked around the restaurant for a reflective surface just to check that my poker face was still intact. All I had was the fork in my hand.

"Should we wait for Nöel to order or do you think we're okay going ahead without her?" I asked, hoping for the latter. If Jack and I had our mouths full we couldn't talk.

"Whatever, it doesn't matter." Jack fumbled with his menu, then looked at me again. "Lucy, I have to tell you something."

"Okie dokie," I said, waving at one of the waiter's to get his attention. "Sorry. I'm just trying to get one of these guys to come and take our order."

"Buenos dias. Crepes y cafe con leche por favor?" I ordered when the waiter made it over to our table. When he turned to take Jack's order, Jack just shook his head.

"Look, there's Nöel." I pointed in her direction as she made her way through the restaurant, wishing for a moment that my finger was the barrel of a paintball gun. She was wearing a white, flowing maxi dress, and had a flower tucked behind her ear. She was photo-shoot ready and it was only nine in the morning. I, on the other hand, was wearing my Simpsons-themed tights, a striped tank top and a blob of toothpaste covered a zit on my chin.

"Lucy," Nöel said, greeting me with a wide smile that showcased all the straight white teeth in her mouth. She sat down on Jack's lap and put her arm around his neck. I flicked my eyes to the perfectly good chair next to him, but said nothing.

"Morning, Nöel. How are you?" I asked politely, my eyes fixed on a spot above her head so I didn't have to look at her sitting in the lap of the man I loved.

"I'm wonderful. Obviously." She smiled, looking very much like the cat who'd got the cream, that didn't come in a can.

"What do you mean, obviously?" I asked, looking out for the waiter and my pancakes, already deciding I was going to need extra syrup and a dump truck of ice cream.

"Didn't Jack tell you?" she asked, running her hands through Jack's hair.

I pressed my lips in a tight line and shook my head, resisting the urge to snap her fingers in half.

"We're engaged!" she exclaimed.

Chapter 28

Email:

To: l.hart@standard.com
From: j.henry@gbk.com.au

What happened with Jack? Did you tell him you were in love with him? x

Email:

To: j.henry@gbk.com.au
From: l.hart@standard.com

Well, I thought that might be a tad inappropriate since he just got engaged to his girlfriend after she happened to turn up in Colombia for a surprise visit.

Jules, seriously, I'm going to shave off all my hair and move to a yurt in Mongolia.

It hurts so much and I hate it. X

Email:

To: l.hart@standard.com
From: j.henry@gbk.com.au

Lucy, my darling, I'm so sorry. Are you sure he doesn't love you back? Don't you think you owe it to the both of you to at least find out? xx

Email:

To: j.henry@gbk.com.au
From: l.hart@standard.com

What was I going to say? He's made his choice, Jules. He loves Nöel. And what's not to love? She is so beautiful you can't actually look her in the face for too long or your eyes start to hurt. It's like looking at the sun. And she really has done some amazing things for the world. She's like Mother Theresa reincarnated in the body of a swimwear model. Granted, she isn't the type of woman I would have thought Jack would have gone for, but I've only known the man for like, seven weeks, so that is neither here nor there.

All I know is one minute we were having dinner and the next minute they were engaged. And in just over a week's time, Jack and I will be going our separate ways, and who he marries will be none of my business. They'll be together forever and I'll be sad and lonely with a garden of throw pillows. The shit thing is that soon we're going to head off on this romantic sailboat trip through the Caribbean, which was one of the only things I'd been looking forward to. And while we watch romantic sunsets together, I'll have to pretend I don't care that he's getting married and that I'll never see him again … x

Email:

To: l.hart@standard.com
From: j.henry@gbk.com.au

Lucifer Arnold Hart, now you listen to me. Jack is obviously a jizz straw if he doesn't love you back.

I know it sucks to feel like you're having your heart broken all over again. But you'll find someone lovely and kind and funny, with excellent table manners. I promise.

All the hugs. x

60 DAYS IN SOUTH AMERICA

Day 49-53: Lara Croft: Escape to the Lost City of Doom

I've just returned from a real life adventure, proper-trekking to La Ciudad Perdida, or the Lost City, and I feel like a slightly more out of breath and red-faced version of Lara Croft.

It all started when, after a bumpy journey from Taganga in the back of a pair of trucks, our group was dropped off at a little village for the start of the hike. It would take us three days to trek there and two days to trek back to the village, through the reddest mud I've ever seen. During the day we marched, stumbled and picked our way through the jungle, through rivers, over rocks and under tree branches. At night we bunked down in hammocks, counted our bug bites and listened to the nightlife roar just outside camp.

And yes, it's as epic as it sounds. So epic, that at one point I looked around—at the vegetation that was so overgrown I couldn't see the person behind me and the person in front of me—and felt like it could have been the year 1312 or 2016 or 2067. I could have been deposited on the coastline by a ship or a spacecraft and been tasked with finding gold or pineapples or pygmy hippos. I could have even been on another planet that resembled earth. At any minute I could have run into a triceratops. It all seemed timeless. The only thing that would have given me away was my backpack, my boots and my ability to recite whole scenes from the TV show Friends.

But as fantastic as it was, holy tits, was it hard as well. By the end of it all, I felt like I could punch through walls and swallow scorpions whole. And who doesn't want to feel like that at least once in their life? To be knee-deep in a roaring river, covered in sweat and insects, on a quest to a lost ancient city in the jungles of Colombia? By the end of the five day trek, I smelled like wet dog, and I was completely exhausted, but the sense of accomplishment of having stared danger in the eye, conquering pain while at it, and triumphing over everything nature could throw at me made it all worth it.

I may have gotten carried away though, when after arriving at the lost city, I stared down at the ruins, raised my hands above my head, and roared like Tarzan. I think my theatrics must have alarmed the members of the Colombian forces because, soon after hearing me, they sprung out from behind trees with their very large guns.

I have often wondered if I would have survived in a harsher time. I'd decided that if I'd been around in 1446, someone would surely have feasted on my brains before I reached middle age. But after those few days of epicness I now live in hope of actually surviving the impending zombie apocalypse.

And that's all I have to say about that.
Lucy

P.S. Plus if I was Lara Croft that would mean that I was a video game character, effectively unable to experience emotion of any kind. Emotions just make everything in life that much harder. Much better to be a badass, made from ones and zeroes, who is unable to tell the difference between heartache and a tin of tuna.

Next Destination: Cartagena to catch a boat!

Chapter 29

Jack and I stood on the deck of our sailboat hotel, The Ingrid, flanked on either side by Benny, Steve and Carol, who hadn't needed much convincing to join us on our last leg of the trip. For the perfect farewell to South America. With Captain Joe, who owned the boat, there were just the six of us, Jack having said goodbye to Nöel in Taganga a week ago, before our trek.

"Was it all worth it?" Jack asked, watching me lean over the railing and peer into the turquoise Caribbean sea. He was on his fourth piece of peanut butter toast and at the rate he was going he'd be eating Joe out of food with two more days still to go. I smiled at him and stared out at the small island, about 50 m from starboard, that I imagined looked like a donut from the sky.

I'd been a mess during the whole thirty-six hour crossing over from Cartagena, swinging wildly between nausea and being high on the dodgy Colombian seasickness pills I'd popped like M&M's. The open water was clearly not my friend. And while I'd been below deck, rolled into a sweaty ball, the rest of the gang had helped Joe navigate through the night, allowing him to get some shut-eye when he needed it.

I knew Jack wasn't just talking about the journey on the boat but about the whole goddamn thing.

I liked to think my sense of imagination was more developed than most, but even I couldn't have dreamed up all the shit we'd experienced—the good and the bad.

"Let me get back to you on that," I answered.

I thought back to how I'd been shaking in my hiking boots when I'd first gotten off that plane, and then looked at how far I'd come—metaphorically and physically. I hadn't 'changed' during my trip, thinking otherwise would be ridiculous. But I *had* realised that I was like a giant jigsaw puzzle and I'd spent the last two months collecting the puzzle pieces. I couldn't see the whole picture yet but I had enough pieces to give me hope that one day I might.

Benny slapped me on the back. "Oh come on! Your trip has been epic! Steve and I drove motorbikes—fucking motorbikes—up the continent of South America, and haven't ended up in half as much shit as you guys have!"

Carol broke off a piece of her lunch and dropped it into the water below. "Yeah. I don't think that's the aim of the game," she said, sounding unconvinced. Little fish crowded round the peanut butter toast and pecked at it frantically until it disappeared.

"But it makes for some epic stories," said Steve.

I shook my head ruefully. "True dat."

"What we need is an epic portrait to commemorate this epic trip!" said Benny.

Joe, the peach that he was, offered to position himself in the dinghy a few metres from port side, with Jack's camera in hand. When he gave us the thumbs up and shouted that he was ready, the five of us all joined hands and launched ourselves off the side in the obligatory 'jumping off a yacht' pose—holding hands, arms raised, smiles on our faces. The silly laughter and wet high fives that followed made my heart swell to the size of a pumpkin.

Jack, eager to resume his role as official photographer, swapped places with Joe and the four of us spent ages trying pose after pose, hitting the warm water below, scrambling back to the wooden platform, then clambering up the ladder to start all over again.

"I know what we can do for the next one," shouted Steve, as we all treaded water after the last jump. "But we're going to need a flame thrower and a bag of snakes!" I laughed and playfully splashed him with water.

"You're on your own!" said Carol, before swimming back to the boat. Instead of following her, I swam over to where Jack was sitting in the dinghy.

I folded my arms over the side and looked up at him. "Get any good ones?"

"Yeah, really good." Jack scooted over and shielded the viewfinder with his hand as he held the camera out for me to take a look. I smiled as he flipped through the photos, very aware of his face being so close to mine.

"Here we go. This is a great one of you," he said, showing me a hilarious photo of the troupe doing jumping karate kicks.

I laughed. "No way. I look ridiculous!"

"Watch this," yelled Benny, and I turned to see him standing on the outside of the railing, waiting for an audience. "Yew," he yelled before belly flopping hard into the water. Jack and I laughed as Benny rolled onto his back clutching his stomach as he surfaced.

"Watch this!" yelled Steve before doing a forward somersault off the boat.

Not wanting to be shown up by the boys, Carol scrambled to the back of the boat, obviously deciding to get back in on the action.

"Watch this," she shouted, mocking their tone as she did a double backflip from the top of the railing. I clapped and shouted loudly. After she surfaced she rolled on to her back and playfully flipped Benny and Steve the double-handed bird. They stared, mouths open.

Not to be outdone, the boys conferred for a moment before swimming back to the boat.

"Okay, so that was a good one Carol. But can you do this?" yelled Steve when they were back in position.

"Yeah!" shouted Ben.

And with that they yanked down their swim shorts, did the windmill with their willies and jumped off the side of the boat with their arms and legs outstretched like sea stars.

"Woohoo," I yelled. Jack rewarded them with a loud whistle.

"Why don't we call it even?" said Carol.

"I don't know if we'll be able to use that last one on the blog," laughed Jack, turning to show me the screen. I laughed and shook my head.

"Looks like they've called it a day," he said, glancing behind me, and I turned back to The Ingrid. The three of them were now sunning themselves on the front deck of the boat. I smiled when I thought about how Joe had told me off for calling it a boat and for remarking how much smaller the vessel was than I'd imagined it would be, when we'd boarded in Colombia three days ago. It was as if I'd insulted the size of his manhood.

Apparently she was a Ketch yacht, and at a whole fifty-two feet, should be shown the respect she deserved. He'd then patiently explained that the right side of the yacht, when you're facing the nose, was the starboard side and the left, the port side. The front was the bow, and the back, the stern. The yacht was sleek and white with two masts extending into the sky. She had a long nose, which was currently pointed towards the mainland of Panama in Central America, where we were headed, and a flat butt, off which a short wooden platform jutted.

The Ingrid's sleek lines were only marred slightly by the lump of diving paraphernalia that Joe stored at the stern—fins, masks, and small and large dive tanks. Equipment I'd adamantly told Jack I would not be making use of, because for the last two days of the trip I was determined to stay out of trouble.

Two more days with Jack. Three really, since we'd need to bus to Panama City to catch our flights out.

After we said our goodbyes in Central America, I doubted I'd ever see him again. He was going to end up married to Nöel and I was probably going to end up married to an extra-large bag of Doritos.

"I can't believe the trip is almost over," said Jack, echoing my thoughts.

I turned back to him and bit my wet lip. "I know, it's crazy. I feel like I've fit a whole lifetime into the last two months."

"We'll keep in touch afterwards?" he asked, staring down at me. I nodded and gave him a small smile, not wanting to think about what life without Jack would be like. If everything I learned during the trip were the puzzle pieces then Jack was definitely the corner bits. We watched each other, in silence, until I couldn't bear it any longer.

"I'll never let go, Jack," I croaked in my best Kate Winslet impersonation. Jack laughed and shook his head at me. I slipped my hands off the side of the boat, rigid as a board, and pretended to slowly sink below the sea, pantomiming that scene from *Titanic*, but with the roles reversed. "Jack, Jack, it's a boat. Jack," I whispered, pointing at The Ingrid and sinking further. "Promise you'll never let go," I said, before going under. I looked up through the water at Jack peering down at me.

But he wasn't smiling. And now, neither was I.

* * *

The sky had started to turn from pale blue to dusky pink when I grabbed my journal and pen from my cabin and headed back to the deck. With a sigh, I settled in on the raised section in the middle of the deck. Carol was downstairs napping and Joe and the boys had taken the dingy to an island a few kilometres away to buy more beer. Jack was lying near me under a makeshift fort he'd fashioned out of my sarong and one of his old t-shirts. His beautiful sleeping face peeked out from between gaps in the fabric.

I didn't want to say goodbye to him. He had quickly become such a large part of my life that the idea of leaving him felt like I was pulling out an internal organ—something vital like … my heart. I shifted closer to him and stretched my hand out to brush a tuft of hair from his forehead, stopping at the last second when I decided that would be too creepy. I ran my eyes along his face instead, committing every single centimetre to memory. His bare chest rose and fell and I had to sit on my hands to resist the urge to lie down next to him. There were also other things I wanted to do to him, like run my hands along the muscled V that led down below the waistband of his shorts. But I didn't want to think about that now, because if I did, I'd need a cold shower, and Captain Joe was rationing the fresh water on board. Anyway, soon we'd be on our respective flights out of Panama City, bound for destinations on opposite sides of the globe, and Jack would be out of my life.

Knowing how close we were to the end I suddenly had a strong urge. A need to tell him how I felt, before it was too late. And, while he was sleeping seemed like the best possible time for expressing sentiments that were probably better left unsaid.

"Jack," I whispered, lowering my face close to his. "I … I love you."

Jack stirred, and I held my breath, freaking out that he might have actually heard me. His eyes fluttered open and he looked up at me just as a noise that sounded like a gunshot rang out, before I heard a roaring of motors at the back of the boat. I stood and ran in the direction of the sound and saw a large speed boat pull up at the back of The Ingrid. The boat carried four men who were brandishing guns. They quickly tied up their boat, and three of them began boarding The Ingrid. Something told me they weren't coming aboard to borrow a cup of diesel.

Chapter 30

I scuttled back to a now wide-awake Jack.

"Jack," I hissed, crouching in front of him. "I think pirates have just tied up to our boat!"

"What? Are you serious?" he asked, sticking his head up to look towards the bow.

"They've got guns and they look like they mean business," I said, nodding like a bobble head toy. I peeped around the mast and saw two men climb onto the deck and the third head down below.

"Oh shit. Oh shit. Oh shit," I said, standing and backing away from them.

Jack got up and stood in front of me, shielding my body with his.

"Que quieren?" he asked. What do you want? "Por qué están en nuestro barco?" Why are you on our boat?

"We want your money, gringo," jeered one of the pirates. Well, technically they were pirates, having boarded us while on water, but they didn't really look like any kind of pirates I'd ever have imagined. The one who spoke first had an orange Oompa Loompa fake tan and wore his long hair in an oily ponytail so I nicknamed him Ponytail. It was almost difficult to take him seriously in his ripped jeans and t-shirt that looked like it had been attacked by a bedazzle gun.

His colleague was male runway model beautiful, his lips pouty and face all angles. In his sleeveless jean vest, he seemed to be flexing his muscled biceps, as though posing with his handgun in the air ~~like he just didn't care~~.

Jack kept his hands up in front of him. "We don't have much in the way of money on board, but we'll give you everything we have. Just don't hurt us." He was so goddamn calm, I couldn't believe it.

Below deck, Carol screamed. I flinched when we heard several thuds and then silence. The pirates laughed.

"We know you gringos always have lots of money. Our friend downstairs will make sure we get it all."

"Fine, but like I said, you don't need to hurt us, okay?" said Jack.

But the Backstreet Boys just laughed.

"We'll do what we want, gringo," snapped Ponytail.

"Our captain and our friends will be back soon," I ventured, my voice cracking with fear. But this just seemed to amuse them even more.

"Does your captain have guns, gringa? Because we do." Pretty Boy sneered as he shook his gun at us.

"Yes, and they're real," said Ponytail, aiming the gun in the air to shoot it.

I put my hands to my ears, but nothing happened. Ponytail spoke in rapid Spanish to Pretty Boy, who grabbed the gun and fiddled with it. Ponytail lunged to yank it back, stomping his foot like a petulant child. This was reassuring, since clearly we weren't dealing with professional pirates.

I glanced behind me, hoping Captain Joe and the boys had heard the first gunshot and were racing back to help us, but they weren't. I wheeled around just as Pretty Boy accidentally fired the gun into the deck during his struggle to remove the safety. Ponytail just grabbed his gun back from a sheepish looking Pretty Boy, when the third pirate stuck his head up from the door leading to the captain's bridge. On his shoulder was an unconscious-looking Carol.

"Jack, he's got Carol," I whispered.

This pirate gesticulated angrily, pointing at a small red hole in the leg of his trousers. The bullet must have travelled through the deck and hit him during the misfire. When he turned around, I sucked in my breath. Now *this* guy looked like a real-ass pirate, with a jagged scar etched on his face from cheek to forehead, gold grills glinting in his sneering mouth and short, slicked-back black hair. Well, he looked like a real-ass pirate until, with Carol still slumped over his shoulder, he started bitch slapping Ponytail and Pretty Boy, leaving angry red welts across their faces. Satisfied with his revenge for having been shot, he turned and climbed down the ladder backwards to the speedboat, where the fourth pirate I'd seen, when I watched them pull up, must have been waiting.

"Hey, wait," yelled Jack, taking a step towards them. "Take anything you want but just leave her alone. Please!"

The pirates shouted at each other in Spanish, conferring with the fourth still in the boat, until eventually they seemed to come to some sort of agreement.

Ponytail spun around and pointed the gun at us. "My friend checked, and you gringos don't have much money, so now we kidnap you and sell you for ransom to your rich gringo parents."

"No, please!" I wailed. "We're not rich. Please!" I sobbed into my hands as I watched Carol disappear from sight. My parents couldn't afford to pay a ransom. And I doubted whether the newspaper could afford to pay any kind of ransom for me. Either way we were all screwed, because unless Jack and Carol had been holding out on me I didn't think their family would be able to afford to pay up either— whatever kind of money the pirates were looking for.

Ponytail and Pretty Boy moved towards us, their faces grim.

"Lucy. Stay behind me!" said Jack.

My eyes darted around the boat, trying to find something to defend myself with, because if we got taken, Liam Neeson would *not* be coming to save us. Out of the corner of my eye I spied a mop leaning against the railing and I started inching towards it. This was obviously their first rodeo and I wondered if maybe we pushed back they might back down. At least until the cavalry arrived.

Pretty Boy must have decided I'd be a lot easier to take than Jack because he advanced towards me as I inched over to grab the mop. Ponytail kept his eyes on Jack. The men moved towards us so slowly, as if they were uncertain about what to do next. Surely Captain Joe and the boys had heard at least the second gunshot, even if they hadn't heard the first, and were already on their way back. When my hand brushed against the mop handle I grabbed it and yanked the mop in front of my body, ready to defend myself. Pretty Boy laughed at me crouched over in my ninja mop fighting stance and called over to Ponytail.

"Mira," he laughed, so unthreatened, he tucked his gun in the back of his tight leather pants.

"Your girlfriend wants to fight," said Ponytail to Jack.

I wanted to yell that I wasn't Jack's girlfriend but that I wanted to be. But I didn't and Jack didn't try to correct him.

Soon, Pretty Boy became bored with my dancing around and rolling his eyes, took a step towards me. But I was ready, and I rammed the end of the mop as hard as I could into his crotch. Pretty Boy roared in pain and grabbed his bits. Over his doubled-over body I could see the astonished faces of both Jack and Ponytail.

"Lucy—" started Jack, before he was cut short as Ponytail pistol-whipped him hard across the jaw. I winced as Jack hit the deck hard and cried out when Ponytail kicked him in the face. A swift kick to the head left Jack limp. Shit.

I needed to help him, and Pretty Boy was still doubled over in front of me whimpering like a kitten, so I moved round behind him and jammed the end of the mop hard into a butt cheek, sending him over the railing. Then I spun back around and walked straight into Ponytail's rock-hard fist. My head snapped back and I dropped to my knees, the mop falling from my hands and clattering onto the deck.

Ponytail dropped to his knees so he could get up in my grill. "You think you're a big deal because you got rid of that pretty motherfucker?" he shouted into my ear while I winced in pain, clutching my cheek. The pain was excruciating, and I could hardly focus on what he was saying. When I didn't respond, he punched me in the gut so hard it felt like he'd reached right through me to the other side. I held my stomach, bringing my head to rest on the deck, as if in prayer, and collapsed over onto my side.

Ponytail spat on the deck near my face, and satisfied I wasn't going anywhere, headed back to where Jack was lying on the deck. I lay on my side in agony, watching him haul Jack over his shoulder and head to the bow.

So much for pushing back.

They had Jack and Carol and I was going to be next.

Tears welled in my eyes as I squeezed them shut. It was a sick joke, being so close to the end of the trip that I could almost taste the airplane food, then having this happen. Earlier, I'd been basking in the magic of the day, and now I didn't know what was going to happen.

I curled into a ball and sobbed. I didn't want to die. I had lived so much during the trip that now, I had a taste for living. This realisation just made me cry harder.

I raised my head to wipe my nose, and heard a flapping, fluttering sound above me. I turned my head and saw my journal lying open, its pages blowing in the breeze. I grabbed it and brought it to my chest, hoping it would provide comfort as I waited to be taken. I read the final words of my last entry: "I smell bacon".

It was in no way reassuring that when I died my parents would be able to tell people that those had been my last words. I slammed the book shut, and as I did, something fell from its pages. It was the photo Jules had given me before I'd been forced to take this assignment. It was the picture of me standing like the Queen of the Castle on the top of the climbing gym at the playground, my arms outstretched, my head raised to the sky. My mouth open in a shout that I could practically hear through the image. How had I been so brave when I'd been so little? To a child, everything must seem so frightening, because everything is so much bigger than you are. And yet I'd still managed to eyeball the world and refuse to shrink away from it. I turned the photo over and saw that Jules had written something on the back that I hadn't noticed before.

I am Lucy. Hear me roar!

A strangled sob escaped from somewhere deep inside me.

I am Lucy. Hear me roar!

My God, I couldn't lie there and wait to be taken. I couldn't just let myself be kidnapped. That little person would have fought like a wild animal to survive this. She was brave. That Lucy had a roar that could drown out the entire world. Knowing that I'd been brave once before made me think I could be brave again.

I thought about everything I'd been through in South America and it dawned on me that even though I had been shit-scared ninety-nine percent of the time, I'd still made it through to the other side. Images flashed through my mind of all that I'd seen and done. I'd been to a crazy soccer match, ridden a runaway horse, swam in a river filled with caiman and anaconda, survived a mining strike, slept on the side of the road, been in a car accident and crashed a tuk-tuk while high on drugs. I hadn't thought I was going to make it and yet here I was. I'd made it. So much of the trip had been a mess, but I'd clawed my way through. Bravery wasn't the absence of fear. It was being terrified and doing what needed to be done anyway.

And I had to do that now, or at the very least I had to try. Carol was out and so was Jack. He'd carried me this whole way and now it was time to return the favour.

"I am Lucy. Hear me roar," I whispered as I pushed myself to my knees. I could hear the pirates shouting at each other. Someone would be coming for me soon. I had to be quick. The photo had given me an idea. I looked up at the mast in front of me and back down at the photo in my hand. I was going to climb it and wait for whichever pirate came, before launching myself at him as hard as possible. I'd managed to deal with one pirate already and I'd see if I could make it two. Height would be my advantage.

I tucked the photo into my pocket and wedged my foot on one of the short metal rungs that led all the way up the mast. I pulled myself up, put a foot up to the next rung and heaved myself up. Shaking the whole time, I climbed as quickly as I could, hoping to get as high as possible.

From my vantage point about a third of the way up the mast, I could see the pirates in the speedboat, who still seemed to be fighting about something. From what I could tell, the fourth pirate, a small bald man who I nicknamed Shortstack, with a very large gold chain around his neck, was calling the shots. He stood with his hand on the wheel of the boat and was angrily shouting and waving his hands.

Pretty Boy, who'd obviously made it back from when I'd shoved him overboard, wasn't taking part in the exchange, choosing instead to crawl into the enclosed space at the front of their large boat, which looked like one rappers would have used in music videos. I could just see Jack and Carol lying motionless on the floor, bound by their hands and feet.

Ponytail climbed back onto The Ingrid. When he got to the place he'd left me whimpering in pain, he spun around as he searched for me. He peered over the railing and even looked under the sarong fort Jack had constructed. I had to act now before my element of surprise vanished.

I said a little prayer and, with a loud roar, launched myself off the mast, knees first, aiming for his oily head. Ponytail looked up just as my knees smashed into his face, sending him reeling backwards so that I landed on top of him on the deck. The gun clattered from his hands and the force of me hitting him knocked him out cold. I flopped off of him, onto my back wheezing, winded from the fall.

I pulled my knees up to my chest and took a few deep breaths before crawling round the back of the mast to where the diving stuff was stored. I untied the rope holding the four dive tanks together, got into position with my back against the railing and my feet against two of the tanks, then waited to heave them at the next pirate who would come when Ponytail didn't return.

Eventually I heard Scarface shout up to his pony-tailed colleague. When he got no response, he inched up the ladder in front of me. I took a breath and waited until he was on board, before using my legs to push the tanks with all my might.

"Puta!" he swore, as the rolling tanks sent him, and his gun, tumbling onto the deck.

He scrambled to his feet and fumbled to find his weapon. Before he could grab it, I picked up a fin from the box of diving equipment and launched it at his head. I missed, but as soon as it was out of my hand, I was ready with the next. That fin smacked him right in the face. He took a step back and tripped over a tank, landing hard on his butt. As he struggled to get to his feet, a shot rang out and I ducked my head. The bald guy was shooting at me!

I needed to finish Scarface off or I was going to get a bullet to the side of my face. Scarface reached for the gun near his outstretched fingers. With a big backswing, I launched a portable breathing tank at his face. It connected dead-on, whacking Scarface right in the teeth, splitting his lip, and sending blood pouring out of his mouth. He dropped to his knees and shook his head like a confused water buffalo. I ran towards him, and with an extra-large fin, smashed him hard in the scar-free side of the face, knocking him out cold.

Someone, it must have been Shortstack, fired another shot at me, and that one felt much closer than the last. "Motherfuck!" came a shout from the speedboat below. I looked over the back and saw the short, bald pirate untying the speedboat. He gunned the engines and turned to take another shot at my head. I hit the deck to get out of the way. When I heard the engine roar, I lifted my head and saw that Shortstack was headed to the right of the small island in front of us.

I couldn't let him get away with Jack and Carol on board. I dived for the gun Scarface had dropped earlier, and holding the weapon with both hands like they did in the movies, I aimed it towards the boat and fired. I fired again, aiming at his bald head, which was slowly getting smaller and smaller. At the sound of gunfire, Shortstack spun around and ducked, jerking the boat's steering wheel and shifting the trajectory towards the island. I shot again, and he ducked again, oblivious to the fact that he was headed straight for the beach. I needed to keep firing so he didn't change course, and quickly shot again and again—until I ran out of bullets.

When he realised I was out of ammunition, Shortstack stood and turned to look at the sea ahead of him, just in time for the speedboat to bank violently onto the sand and send him flying over the left side of the boat. He hit the sand hard and when he didn't get up straight away, I tore my shorts and top off, yanked on a pair of fins, then jumped into the water, and swam as fast as I've ever swam in my life. In the shallows, I ripped off my fins, my eyes on Shortstock's still body the whole time. He'd landed about five metres from the boat and it looked like he was out cold.

I hoisted myself over the side, into the boat, careful to steer clear of the still-spinning motor. Pretty Boy was crouched up in the nose of the boat. I lunged for a gun that was lying wedged under Jack, probably dropped by Shortstack when he beached the boat. I pointed it at Pretty Boy with one hand and focused on untying Jack and Carol, who both thankfully were groggily coming to. I slowly untied the rope around Jack's hands and feet, then Carol's.

Behind me I heard a shout. Over my shoulder, I saw Shortstock on his knees shaking his head. He staggered to his feet and lurched towards me. I dropped off the side of the boat onto the sand and planted by feet, taking aim at him, but the gun just clicked when I pressed the trigger. I threw the gun at Shortstack and connected with his stomach but this didn't slow him down. It just made him mad. I frantically looked around for another weapon, but there was nothing but sand—no fins, no breathing tanks, no more guns.

"You fucking gringa bitch! You've ruined it! I'm going to feed your face to the fishes!"

I stood my ground, not wanting to end up with my back up against the boat, but also unsure of whether I would be able to move my feet anyway.

Shortstack shouted at me in Spanish, spitting the words out in fury, his face a dark, angry purple.

"Puta!" he screamed, the veins in his bald head rippling under the shiny skin. He was a metre away from me now, and still I stood there, unable to move. "Fuck your mother!" he screamed as he moved closer. He was going to tear me to shreds. After all that fighting back, I was still going to die. "Youuuuuuu! You ruin my life!" he screamed.

Holy shit he was mad. He looked ready to scratch my eyes out, his hands rigid, shaking claws at his side. Why was he so angry? I was the one who should be angry! He'd ruined *my* life. As always I was just trying to get through, endlessly minding my own business, never trying to take up more than my allotted space on the planet, like I might offend someone with my presence if I did. And I was tired of it. Fuck that! Fuck that very much. Shortstack could go to pirate hell. All of these thoughts unleashed an anger like I'd never experienced before. He couldn't be furious with me, because I was furious with him first!

"You puta!" I screeched, giving his chest a hard shove. He stumbled back in surprise. "Fuck *your* mother!" I yelled, completely letting it all out.

He just stood there, his eyes wide.

I'd had enough. This is over, I thought, as I jerked my right elbow back, and channelling all the rage I'd ever felt, punched him as hard as I could right in his bald pirate face, knocking him to the ground.

* * *

Email:

To: l.hart@standard.com
From: r.williams@standard.com

Lucy,

I got your voice messages. Tried to call you back but struggling to get through. I'm truly sorry to hear about your ordeal. I never would have sent you if I thought you were in real danger.

I have advised Jack's parents of the situation. They were listed as his emergency contacts on his contract.

We decided to put an announcement on the blog about what has happened.

Please take as much time as you need and forget about posting anything for the time being.

If you need anything else let me know.

Regards

Rob

* * *

"Mum, I'm fine. I promise," I repeated for the twelfth time as my mother sobbed on the line.

"But you almost got kidnapped by pirates!" she wailed.

We were all safe on dry land and I was trying to finish explaining to my parents, who were on speaker phone, what had happened the previous day after Captain Joe and the boys had returned to the boat.

The guys *had* heard the gunshots and had used a radio to contact Panama's National Air and Naval Service since we were closer to Panama, before rushing to our aid. Captain Joe, Benny and Steve had done a great job of tying up the pirates. Two boats had arrived an hour later, one of them whisking the pirates to jail, the other taking Carol, Jack and myself to Portobelo, a port town in Panama, for medical attention. Joe, Benny and Steve had followed behind in The Ingrid and had arrived several hours later. I'd left a voice message for my parents to call me and had promptly passed out—waking up the next day to a hundred panicked messages.

"I know. But we survived," I said, wincing as I touched my cheek where Ponytail had punched me.

"Are you *sure* you don't want us to come get you and bring you home?" said my mother.

"Thank you, Mum, but I'm fine. I'm better off than Jack and Carol," I said, trying to get her off the subject of me and on to something else. A knot formed in my stomach when I mentioned

Jack. I hadn't had a chance to speak to him alone since he'd regained consciousness. After the whole almost getting kidnapped thing, it was ridiculous to be wondering if he'd heard me telling him I loved him, but that was all I could think about.

"How are they doing?" asked my dad.

"The doctor says they're fine. They both have mild concussions from getting knocked around. Carol has broken ribs, and Jack needed a few stitches. But they'll live. They're staying at the clinic for observation. But I think they should be discharged tomorrow or the next day."

"I mean, pirates? Who would have thought?" clucked my mum.

"I know," I said, holding the phone farther away from my ear and sighing. I was standing outside the clinic, having just arrived when they'd called.

"They're obviously not very good pirates," she remarked.

"Apparently, this was their debut. One of the federal police told me that they are wannabe pop stars and they were trying to raise money to fund a music video for their boy band." I could scarcely believe it myself. "The ringleader confessed to borrowing his cousin's boat and guns. The cousin is supposed to be the leader of some drug cartel here in Panama. And they were so scared about doing serious time in prison that they squealed on the cousin's operations to get their sentences reduced. With all the evidence, the police had grounds to arrest this guy and they think he's going to be put away for a long time." This explained why Shortstack had been so furious and adamant that I'd ruined his life.

"That's crazy! Why didn't they just look into running a Kickstarter campaign?" said my Mum.

"Mum, how do you know about Kickstarter?" I asked.

"Cheryl's son, Sean, launched a campaign to release a comic book," said my mum. I smiled.

"If they had Kickstarter they could have hashtagged it," offered my dad, which made me laugh.

"I don't think they will be hashtagging much from prison. Anyway, Mum, Dad, I have to go. I'm at the clinic. I'll be in touch soon. I love you."

Chapter 31

"Hola." I waved at the policeman stationed just inside the front door of the clinic. He nodded as I walked past. Apparently, their presence was just a precaution, since we'd inadvertently helped put this drug lord behind bars. But, I didn't have space in my brain to think about what that all meant. All I could think about was Jack.

As I neared his room I slowed and took a few deep breaths. If I could defeat a band (literally) of wannabe pop-star pirates, I could ask the man I loved if he loved me back. I peeked my head round the open door into his room.

And my heart sank.

Nöel was standing over Jack's bed, dressed in a pair of dark blue jeans and a crisp white shirt. Soft light seeped through the curtains, framing her face and highlighting the concern etched across her features. To Jack, she must have looked like an angel leaning over him. Before she could see me, I stepped back into the corridor. I'd forgotten about Jack's *fiancé*. I peeped back round the open door into the room. Nöel was looking down at Jack, holding his hand. Even though she was crying, she still looked fantastic. Jack's face, on the other hand, was a mess. His swollen lip appeared to be curled in a half-smile. One of his eyes was almost completely closed, so I couldn't read his expression. But I didn't have to when Jack lifted

Nöel's hand to his mouth and kissed it. His gesture said a thousand words. I slid down the wall to the floor and leaned my head back.

Jack loved Nöel.

Of course he did. She was beautiful and accomplished and graceful. And he was going to marry her. And I was going to go back home—alone. And that's just the way it was going to be. I wanted to be grateful that I'd met him in the first place, but all I had space for in my heart was sadness.

After a few minutes on the hard floor I pushed myself up and walked to Carol's room. She was sitting up in bed, looking like she'd lost a fight with a truck.

She smiled when she saw me. "My hero."

I rolled my eyes. "What does the other guy look like?" I asked, trying to deflect the praise.

She laughed and grimaced. "Don't make me laugh. It hurts too much."

"When are they letting you out?"

Carol shrugged. "I don't know. The doctor is being ridiculous. All I have is a mild concussion and bruises and a few cracked ribs."

"Oh right, that's all." I laughed.

She grunted and looked out the window covered in thick bars. "Whatever. I just want to leave and they won't let me."

"Don't they say nurses make the worst patients?"

Carol turned to me. "No, they say doctors make the worst patients. Nurses are actually wonderful patients."

"I'm not so sure about that. Anyway, you know they're just being super careful because you were nearly kidnapped in their country and they're probably under strict instructions to look after you?"

"Whatever. I'm discharging myself this afternoon whether they like it or not." She smoothed down the sheets before looking up at me. "Have you seen Jack?"

"I stuck my head in his room, but he was sleeping," I lied.

She frowned. "That's weird. I thought his girlfriend was with him and he was awake. She stuck her head in to see how I was doing. She jumped on the first plane out of Haiti when Jack's parents told her the news."

"Oh really? I didn't see her. Maybe she went to get something to eat. That's nice she was able to fly in at such short notice."

Carol gave me a funny look, but didn't say anything.

"Did that policeman tell you all about the pirates and their whole back story?" I asked.

Carol nodded. "Isn't it crazy?"

"I know," I said. "I keep thinking about what their music video would look like. I'm picturing them posing on their speedboat flying across the water singing moodily into the camera. They'd all be so busy singing to the camera no one would be watching where they were going, and they'd hit a sandbank and all fly out. The final scene of their music video would be them dragging themselves ashore, wet and bedraggled, still singing to the camera while spitting up sand and sea water."

Carol laughed and held her ribs.

"I'd prefer to imagine them singing mournfully through jailhouse bars," said Carol, before yawning.

"I'm gonna let you sleep. Your body obviously needs the rest to repair this damage," I said, sweeping my hand in a circle near her face to make my point.

"Thanks for reminding me, Lucy," she said rolling her eyes. I patted her arm and turned to leave, but she grabbed my hand.

"Lucy," she said, taking a deep breath. "I wanted to tell you I remembered where I recognised you from."

I opened my mouth to speak, but she squeezed my hand to stop me.

"I realised when we were still in Bolivia, and I knew that you knew but you obviously didn't want to tell me."

I made a face. "I was so embarrassed. Jack left me asleep on a bus—trying some kind of shitty tough love—and when I woke up I was all alone and I didn't know how to get back to the hostel. I recognised you and figured if I followed you you'd lead back to the hostel. I wanted to tell you but ..."

Carol nodded and bit her lip. "Knowing you now I thought as much. But you know you're amazing and brave and cool regardless, right?"

When I didn't respond she continued.

"You saved me, Lucy. You saved Jack. God knows what could have happened to us." She was getting choked up, and my lip started wobbling in sympathy.

"Shut up. You're going to make me cry," I said.

"I have to say this. Lucy, we're all just doing the best we can. Sometimes that looks like stalking a stranger and sometimes it looks like fucking up a bunch of pirates. You're a badass no matter what you do."

"Thank you," I whispered.

"Thank *you*, Lucy."

I gave her a watery smile. "I'm glad it all worked out." Although I didn't feel like it did work out. If it had, I'd be the one in Jack's room holding his hand.

"When are you leaving town?" she asked.

"This afternoon. I fly home from Panama City tomorrow."

"And you weren't going to say goodbye?"

I shook my head. "No, I don't like you very much."

Carol pinched me and I squeaked.

"Okay, fine, I like you so much I couldn't face saying goodbye. Happy?"

"We'll see each other again, honey," she said, pulling me into a gentle hug. I cleared my throat and wiped the tears from my eyes.

"I'm supposed to be catching my bus in an hour and I don't have it in me to tell Jack goodbye. And not with Nöel around. Tell him for me?" Then I turned on my heel and fled before Carol could protest.

* * *

"I wish you'd at least said goodbye to him, Luce, so you could have known for sure," said Jules a few days later, pushing her knife and fork onto her empty plate.

"I couldn't, Jules. It was too hard."

The wine glass suddenly seemed a lot more interesting than it should have been. When Jules didn't say anything else, I huffed. "Seriously if you'd seen them together … it was clear how he felt about her."

"And you haven't heard from him?"

I shook my head.

"After you saved his life?"

I sighed.

"Well he's obviously a massive knob," Jules said.

I smiled at my best friend. She'd listened to me ramble on for hours, over dinner at our favourite little Italian restaurant, about the trip, my feelings for Jack and not wanting to start back at work the next day. All that talking had taken it out of me and I yawned loudly.

"Why don't I get you back to your folks?" said Jules. I was staying with them until I figured out what I was going to do with my life. I'd have to talk to Rob in the morning to figure out if he still had a job for me.

"That's probably a good idea. Even though I'm back safe in the country, my folks text me every half an hour to check up on me."

Jules used the universal sign for the bill to gesture to the waitress, when suddenly her face dropped. "Don't look now but your old flat mate Charlotte is walking over here," she hissed.

I glanced over to where she was looking and saw Charlotte, and her trademark smirk, sauntering over. She stopped at our table, popped a hip and flicked her long hair, all in one movement. "Hi Lucy. I haven't seen you for a while."

I crossed my arms. "Hello Charlotte."

Her eyes narrowed as she stared at me, hesitating briefly before she spoke again.

"How've you been?" she asked.

I don't think Charlotte had ever asked me that before. "Well, I've actually just returned from South America where I was almost murdered by pirates, which is where I got this black eye," I replied, pointing to the bruise on my cheek.

"Oh, that's nice," said Charlotte, knowing that to be the polite response even if she hadn't listened to a word I'd said. Typical.

"Did you hear what I said?"

"Do you know, it's actually amazing I ran into you because I've been meaning to get in touch?"

"Really?" I exchanged a look with Jules, who looked like she wanted to glass Charlotte.

"I hate to bring this up because it's kind of embarrassing for you, but remember I lent you my favourite leather jacket?"

I couldn't wait to see where she was going with this. "No, I don't remember."

"The black biker one? The one that was in your room when we were robbed."

I took a deep breath before replying calmly. "Charlotte, I never borrowed your jacket. You probably left it in my room while you were trying on my clothes."

"Either way, it was in your room when it was stolen, so I'm going to need you to pay me for it because it was really expensive," she said, pouting.

"How expensive?"

"Three hundred dollars," she replied.

Jules snorted and I gave her a quick shake of the head to let her know I had this.

"So you want me to give you three hundred dollars for a jacket you left in *my* room which was stolen by a guy *you* let into our flat?" I clarified.

"Yes," said Charlotte, not hearing how ridiculous the words sounded coming out of my mouth.

I threw my head back and laughed. "Charlotte?" I said, grabbing my bag and standing up, indicating to Jules that she should do the same.

"Yes?" she said, holding her hand out in anticipation.

"Get fucked!"

60 DAYS IN SOUTH AMERICA

And that's all I have to say about that

I can't remember the first time I decided that there was something wrong with me.

It wasn't an epiphany I remember having. I don't think someone said or did anything in particular to make me think this about myself. It was probably just the whispers of the world that I'd interpreted in a certain way, so that one day I woke up and it was just there. Like a cold sore only I could see.

Sometimes the feeling was a flashing neon sign. Often it was faint, like when you wake up in the morning and you sense that you've forgotten something but you can't remember what. Most of the time, though, it was just a buzz in the background, the screensaver in my mind: There is something wrong with me.

And it was like that until one day a man, for reasons unknown, picked me to be with. He picked messy, awkward, insecure me and we made a life together, the two of us. We wound our selves around each other like strands of cold spaghetti, until I couldn't tell where I started and he stopped. But that was okay, because nothing mattered more to me than the fact that someone loved me enough. Because that meant that (a) there was a possibility there wasn't something wrong with me and (b) I didn't have to bother trying to love myself at all.

Well, that was until he cheated because he didn't love me after all; until he decided that actually forever was too long to spend with me.

And I realised I'd held my breath ever since the first moment he'd held my heart in his hands and told me that I was it for him.

Then I was right back where I started. Except now my heart looked like it had been attacked with a staple gun.

And for a while, my life felt suspiciously like the flat green line on a dead person's heart monitor. Until I was handed an "opportunity" that I didn't want anything to do with: writing this blog. I didn't want it, because frankly, I was terrified by the whole idea of it.

So I fought it. But it fought back.

And I was right to worry, because travelling was a bag of dicks.

It was uncomfortable and awful and stupid and hard. It was a hand mirror held up, reminding me of everything I sucked at. If you could only peer through my ears into my brain, reader, you'd know how I questioned everything I said, how I wondered constantly what people thought of me and just how much I thought I was fucking up at being me.

Travel took all that and raised it to complete and utter chaos.

But in that chaos, somewhere along the way, because I couldn't tell which way was up, I stopped holding on so tightly to the idea of myself and what a bad job I was doing at being a person.

The time I spent in Latin America was like a giant ice pick chipping away at bits of me that I didn't need anymore—which, yes, is as uncomfortable, and painful, as it sounds.

The thing is, it's more difficult to think about what you're doing wrong when it's a real possibility that you're going to die, when you're balls deep into a car chase, when you think you're going to get blown to bits, when death by hot dog is a very real threat.

So I let go a little. I surrendered just a fraction. And I waited for my world to fill with toilet water.

But it didn't. It filled with kind people and forgiveness instead.

Because you see, it wasn't all small vehicle theft and hair-chomping llamas. It was playing Marco Polo in the dark on the side of the road after nearly shitting myself. It was stalking women with long blonde hair to find my way home. It was movie montage makeovers in Bolivia and the gifting of portable defibrillators in Buenos Aires.

This whole experience—the good times, the shitty times, the mistakes and the joys along the way—made me see that there's nothing wrong with me. That there never was. I'm doing the best I can with what I have. You, too, are probably just doing you the best way you know how. And that's excellent, because what the hell else can you do?

Yes, we're fragile and lame and sometimes we smell like bad choices and cheese. But we're also strong and wonderful and we can be brave and we can be kind and we can have awesome hair.

Our job isn't to be perfect. We're here to be humans, not robots.

It only took me thirty-two years and 60 Days to realise that.

You know the drill.
Lucy Hart

Chapter 32

Riding the elevator up to my level for my first day back at work, I was high on the heady mix of bravado from my take down of Charlotte the night before and the sugar from the muffin I'd eaten for breakfast. In some ways, the whole pirate thing had seemed like a fluke—a mess of fumbled guns and ridiculous hair—and I didn't feel like I actually deserved the attention for "saving" anyone. I knew that if those men had known what they were actually doing we'd be chained up in a basement somewhere. But last night I'd stood up for myself for the first time in the longest time. I'd shut Charlotte down abruptly in a way I'd never done before.

I glanced at the elevator's mirrored walls and saw the yellow-blue bruise on my cheek that I'd failed to cover properly with makeup. I had to admit it that it made me feel kind of awesome. I was Don Johnson after busting a perp—even with a plastic bag in my hand that held the sandwiches my mum had made me for lunch. When the doors opened I took a deep breath, and with the plastic bag slung over my shoulder like a sports jacket, I adjusted my sunglasses and stepped out.

As I walked towards my cubicle, people seemed to stop in their tracks when they saw me.

Linda, who used to be Lionel, was by the printer and I winked and aimed a friendly finger gun at her.

I eased my sunglasses off my face, one side at a time, and pointed them in greeting at some guy I didn't even recognise before sticking them on top of my head. Sam, from Sport, received a drive-by gangsta chin pop. Donald was coming out of the kitchen holding a steaming hot beverage and I aimed two fingers at my eyes and then jabbed them back in his direction. *I'm watching you, buddy.* His piggy eyes widened in alarm and he fumbled with his cup, sloshing hot brown liquid onto his stumpy fingers. I allowed myself a triumphant smile.

In my cubicle I plonked my feet on the desk and leaned back in my chair with my hands behind my head.

"Lucy."

Busted.

I swung around to see Rob standing behind me, giving me an amused look. He'd probably witnessed my whole dorky swaggering entrance.

"Glad to see you back in one piece."

"Thanks, Rob." I noticed a thick envelope in his hands. He handed it to me.

"What's thi—" It was Jack's writing. I stared at the envelope for ages and when I looked back up, Rob was gone. I peered inside the thick envelope to find a stack of photographs. Maybe this was Jack's way of saying goodbye, I grumbled as I pulled the pictures out. I didn't need any reminders that he was now out of my life.

The first picture was a black and white photo of me. One that I couldn't remember Jack taking. It was the day on the bus in Buenos Aires before Jack left me. I had my head against the window and was staring out at the street, my hand pressed against the glass.

The next was a colour photo of me riding my bicycle through the vineyards in Mendoza, the wind in my hair, an intense look of concentration on my face. There was one of me frowning, on my horse in Salta. It looked like it had been taken while I was trying to give Rambo a pep talk. There were other photos. Me lying on the bonnet of our 4x4 vehicle on our tour of the salt flats, my hands behind my head as it rested on the windscreen. Me with the little old lady in the witches' market in La Paz before she handed me that love potion.

I flipped through them all and found that they were all of me. All photos I couldn't remember Jack taking.

Each photo, a little closer, a bit more cropped to cut out the rest of the world, to focus on just me. Me—smiling, frowning, laughing, staring. They were candid shots, as if Jack had been studying me, trying to understand me through his lens.

The last photo was of me with my arms folded over the side of that dinghy, the afternoon before the pirates invaded our boat. I had a huge, wet smile on my face. I looked so happy—half-squinting into the sun, with a few strands of hair plastered against my pink cheek. I sucked in my breath and my heart sped up.

The photos were so intimate that … it couldn't be. Could it?

I flicked through the pack again, desperate to be right. I spied the same corners of Lima, Cartagena, Arequipa in the background, the little clues from all the museums and streets and galleries we visited together, on buses, in common rooms and at street side cafes.

Jack was sneaking photos of me the whole time, and I'd been completely oblivious to what was happening. While I was falling in love, could he have been doing the exact same thing?

But he was going to marry Nöel. He loved *her*, not me.

I had another look at the envelope. No stamp or address. Just my name. Maybe Jack had hand-delivered the photos to Rob. But why hadn't he given them to me himself?

At the door of Rob's office, I knocked and peered in, half hoping to see Jack sitting there, looking up at me with his beautiful grin.

"Rob, these photos," I waved them at him. "Did Jack post these to you?"

"Nope. He handed them to me when he came in this morning." Rob's face was unreadable. My stomach lurched like I was on a rollercoaster.

"Jack's here?" I squeaked. I turned back to the office and scanned the floor.

"Yes. He came in to sign some documents."

"Here? Where is he? Did he ask about me? What did he say?" The words spilled out before I could shove them back in. Rob arched an eyebrow.

"If I'm not mistaken, he's in meeting room two signing the last of the release forms."

"Meeting room two? Our meeting room two?" The room was across the floor, its door closed. I gripped the doorframe and took a deep breath.

Rob nodded. "I did tell him he could just email us the forms but he was keen to come to the office for some reason," he said with a shrug.

I nodded and scuttled across the floor, feeling like I was floating, but also like I wanted to be sick.

When I reached for the door handle my hand felt like it was stuck. It was one thing to whisper that I loved him when he was sleeping, but what would I say when he was wide awake and standing right in front of me? Was I brave enough to tell him, to face him, to face having my heart broken again? I opened the door and found Jack facing the window, leaning back against the large rectangular table in the middle of the room.

"Jack?" I said, my knees wobbling.

He turned to me and flashed his gorgeous smile. "Hi, Lucy."

How could I *not* have fallen in love with his man? He made my heart beat like an African drum.

I closed the door and leaned against it. "Thank you for the photos."

"You didn't say goodbye," he said, slowly coming round the table towards me.

I shook my head. "I couldn't. It was too hard." Now it was Jack's turn to stay silent. "Don't tell me you came all this way to give me those photos and say goodbye?"

Jack looked at the photos in my hand. "So, you actually looked at them?"

I swallowed hard and nodded.

"And what do you think?"

"Honestly? The composition was a bit off, they lacked depth and I'm not really sure what the artist was trying to tell me."

Jack snorted and stepped closer, so close I could see that his eyes were soft and warm like hot chocolate.

"You really don't know what I was trying to tell you?"

"Jack, I don't know. I saw you in the clinic and—" I stopped when I remembered him lying there, kissing Nöel's hand. I frowned and looked down at my feet. But Jack put his hand under my chin and tilted my face towards his.

"Lucy, I heard what you said to me on the boat—before the pirates."

He grazed his hand across my cheek. It felt like he was tracing the outline of my bruise with his fingers. "I love you, Lucy."

I sucked air into my lungs, but because I was on the brink of both crying and laughing I let out a strangled choking noise, like a psychotic parrot. Embarrassed, I slapped my hand over my mouth. Jack laughed and pulled me closer. I moved my hand from my mouth and placed it on his warm chest. I could feel his heart thunder beneath my touch, just like mine was doing.

"Are you sure, Jack? If it's Nöel ... it just looked like you still loved her and I don't want to break you up if she's the one you want. I mean. You were going to marry her."

"That was a mistake, Lucy. The night we got engaged she was adamant I needed to commit to her. And I'd been feeling so guilty about my feelings for you that I felt it was the right thing to do. I did love her and at one point I would have even married her. But my heart hadn't been in it for a while. We were different people. You saw that. And then I met you." He gazed down at me—and wow. Those eyes. I wanted to swim laps in those eyes forever. He let out a little snort. "Why do you think I lost it when you told me about you and Conor?"

My eyes widened at his admission. I thought back to that day and realised he didn't know the whole truth. "Actually, just so you know, I didn't sleep with Conor. I think you might have been right about him. But that's a whole other story." I coughed. "Anyway, please continue," I said primly.

"You're the one I want, Lucy."

"But you kissed her hand."

"I think what you saw was me breaking up with Nöel, not me telling her I loved her. She's a good person and she took it well. I told her that almost dying made me realise I can't always do the right thing by everyone else. I have to do the right thing by me. And that means being with you."

I frowned, remembering meeting Jack for the first time at the airport, a memory that made me drop my hands to my sides. "But you hated me in the beginning."

Jack chuckled, not put off in the slightest. If anything my questioning just seemed to encourage him more and he snaked his hand further around my back and pulled me closer, the other hand tugging gently at my hair. "I knew you were going to fight this, Hart. That's why I asked Rob to give you the photos first."

"What do you mean?"

"I know you, Lucy. I know you're scared to get hurt and for some reason, you don't see yourself how the rest of the world sees you— how I see you. I wanted you to look at the photos first so you'd know what I saw when I looked at you."

"I'm sorry but you're going to have to actually spell out why you love me." I wasn't taking any chances. I knew now that I could be brave, that I was brave enough to love. But still, this felt scarier than a hundred pirate attacks.

Jack sighed and leaned his forehead against mine. "When I look at you I see this funny, gorgeous, kind, brave, extremely weird woman."

My lips curled into a tentative smile. "You dig that I'm weird?"

Jack smiled and nodded against my forehead.

"And when you first met me? In the airport when I looked like a clown? What, you wanted to rip my clothes off and have me on the floor, right there and then?"

Jack rolled his eyes and snorted.

"Was it the snow gaiters? It was the snow gaiters, wasn't it?"

At this he threw his head back and laughed, before pulling away from me. "You're not going to believe this, but—" He walked over to his backpack on the table.

My mouth dropped open. "You're kidding me?"

Jack pulled them out, those fucking charcoal snow gaiters. "I just couldn't bring myself to throw them out. I kept them the whole trip. I think a part of me knew even then."

I squealed, dropped the photos on the table, and scuttled over to him, reaching for his shoulders and jumping on him, swinging my legs around his waist. "You really *do* love me!" Now that I was sure, there was no stopping me. My fingers were on his neck and in his beautiful hair and I pulled him close so I could inhale him. I stuck my nose behind his ear and sniffed him so aggressively that he laughed and shook his head.

"God, you're weird."

I waggled my feet, happily currently clasped around his waist, and smiled.

"I can't believe it was the gaiters that sealed the deal," he mused.

I smiled at the man I loved, feeling so freaking happy I thought I was going to explode. "I love you back, Jack."

And then he inched his mouth down to mine slowly and kissed me, and it was—holy shit. He kissed me with such urgency it was like he'd been waiting forever to feel his lips on mine, like if he'd waited another second he might have exploded. Jack pulled me in tightly, possessively and my stomach did that thing—like I was in an airplane falling out of the sky—and it felt wonderful and scary, and I knew I couldn't go back.

And I realised how far I'd come because I also knew I didn't want to.

THE END

Epilogue

"I can't believe you talked me into this." Jack was leaning back in his seat, a smile on his lips as he shook his head.

"Oh come on, it'll be fun."

I smiled, looking to see if they'd switched off the seatbelt signs so I could retrieve my guidebook from the overhead baggage compartment.

"The look on Rob's face when we pitched him '60 Days in Central America' was priceless." Jack laughed and I smiled, thinking back to our meeting with my boss just a few days earlier.

"He thought I was messing with him for at least the first ten minutes," I said.

Jack took my hand in his and gave it a squeeze.

"You do realise we're going back to the place where we almost got kidnapped and murdered?" He raised his eyebrows.

I'd thought about that, but I'd come to the conclusion that this next trip was going to be different, because I felt different. And so I was as calm as a Hindu cow about flying back there to start our next trip.

"But that's exactly it. We *did* almost get kidnapped and murdered. And we got caught in a strike and we slept on the side of a road and I almost died from food poisoning and I had my bag stolen. The bad things have already happened, so from here on out everything is going to be tacos and rainbows. You'll see. We're going to be fine, Sugar Tits." I patted Jack's knee and gave him a wink, before leaning back in my seat. "Trust me."

* * *

Did you enjoy **60 Ways to Die in South America?**

I would be so grateful if you'd consider leaving a short review on the page where you bought the book. This helps other fine readers such as yourself find the book. Thanks. I really appreciate it.

And if you want to know the very second **60 Ways to Die in Central America** is released later in the year then sign up to my mailing list at my website: www.tracyashworth.com

Acknowledgments

If I really put my mind to it I'm sure I could write an Acknowledgements section that was as long as this book since this is my first novel and I have *that* many people to thank.

To my parents, who are just like Pat and Dale Hart, the most wonderful people who for some reason are always disgustingly proud of me, no matter what I do. I love you.

To Rick and the rest of my lovely family who have been so kind and supportive: thank you. But to my cousins Jo and Sarah in particular, you two are seriously the bomb diggity bomb, because you make me feel like I'm already a success. When I wrote this story it was with you guys in mind.

To all my friends, acquaintances, ex-work colleagues, Facebook friends, virtual friends, my parents' friends, my friends' parents and friends of friends who have been so freaking awesome during the ride to get this done. No one rolled their eyes once, even when I mentioned writing this stupid book for the eleventy millionth time. Thank you.

To everyone who read different versions of the book and gave feedback, thank you so much: Sarah, Little Sarah, Jewel of the Ocean, Jo, Sarah, Caroline, Sally, Shauna, Geri, Nicky, Christine Mary,

Rachel, Tree, Janna, Lou, Sandy, Angie, Sarah B, Greyson, Silvie, Donna, Pernille, Lesley and even my dad (who has already found an actor to play Jack in the movie).

To Sarah Rail. You are such an amazing friend. You kept me going even when I thought everything I wrote was a hot cup of garbage juice. Thank you as well for all your generous design and website work. And thank you also to Sarah's designer, confusingly also Sarah, who designed the insane-in-the-membrane cover that I adore.

To Little Sarah. Thanks for always reminding me to be kind to myself and for all our writing dates.

To my Chunkies (Sarah, Leigh, Nix and Lis). You guys rock my world every day and twice on Tuesdays.

Thanks to my Bali ladies especially my Podsters and "Pat's Group". I struck gold with you guys and I will forever be grateful that you are now in my lives.

Thanks to my developmental editor, Pat who got me on the right track and always answers all my questions with so much patience, grace and love.

Thanks to Grace, my copy editor, who not only made the book sound super profesh, but made it better in terms of story as well.

Thanks to speedy Steve who did the proof read and said nice things about the book when I needed it the most.

Thanks to Señor Chuecos for helping with the Spanish translations. I'm sorry I made you translate 'I want to spread you on a cracker'.

To my virtual cheerleaders, Hayley and Leanne, who coached me through the rollercoaster that is my life, especially when I was balls deep into writing the meat of this book and I needed all the support I could get. Thank you.

Okay, enough now. What is this an Oscar speech?

About the Author

Tracy Ashworth is a Zimbabwean-born Australian citizen who has recently run away from home for the second time. A travel evangelist from way back, Tracy is a fan of finger guns and man buns (and rhyming apparently). She is STOKED that you read this book.

60 Ways to Die in South America is her first novel, which is inspired by her own travels in Latin America. She would like the record to show that she is actually a massive fan of both South and Central America and at no point during her travels did she think she was going to die (except for that time in Peru when it was snowing so hard she thought she was going to have wait out the storm inside a llama Bear Grylls-style.) Unfortunately she didn't end up meeting a Jack during her travels but she may or may not have had the pleasure of meeting some version of a Conor and her Spanish teacher in Buenos Aires really *was* the hottest piece of ass.

She'd love it if you connected with her on social media, or checked out her website where she writes about the science experiment that is her life.